GALVESTON: 1900

INDIGNITIES

Book 2
The Aftermath

N.E. BROWN
S.L. JENKINS

MINDSTIR MEDIA

Galveston: 1900 – Indignities
Book 2: The Aftermath
Copyright © 2013 by N.E. Brown and S.L. Jenkins. All rights reserved.

Published by Mindstir Media
1931 Woodbury Ave. #182 | Portsmouth, NH 03801 | USA
1.800.767.0531 | www.mindstirmedia.com

Printed in the United States of America

ISBN-13: 978-0-9897168-6-4

Library of Congress Control Number: 2013948782

The Aftermath

CHAPTER 1

The tornado that hit the Sugar Land plantation on September 8, 1900, was an offspring of the tropical storm that was beginning to grow in Galveston, Texas. Three miles due west of the plantation was a prison farm that housed about sixty convicts who had been leased by the Texas Prison System to the plantation owner, Peter Esquire. Two of the convicts who worked the sugar cane fields were taken to the plantation early that morning to work the gardens and make repairs to the main house. David Brooks was one of the convicts who had been given this special assignment.

Brooks was a prisoner because he had kidnapped a young woman named Catherine Merit from Galveston, Texas, and violently assaulted her. She was married, attending medical school and working at St. Mary's Hospital in Galveston, Texas. David had stalked Catherine Merit for months in Galveston and had made the mistake of getting caught after Catherine's escape. Now, he was paying for it with his own life. Conditions at the prison farms were less than habitable. What food they had to eat was unappetizing and was handed out in small portions. The convicts were expected to work in the hot fields from dawn to dust, and if the labor did not kill them, the Texas heat would.

The day began as it usually did. One guard on a horse, David Brooks, and one other convict made the three mile trek to the plantation. Their day started at 5:00 in the morning with a quick breakfast of hard rolls, water, and once in a while, a piece of dried beef. The humidity was high, and you could hear the labored breathing from the convicts. It usually took an hour to walk the three miles, and by the time they arrived at the plantation, beads of smelly sweat began pouring off their brows. Once they arrived, there was a welcomed small gust of wind that seemed to be strengthening as they got closer to the plantation. It was unusual for Sugar Land to have any kind of breeze during this time of year, and the sun was already buried behind thick rain clouds allowing a brief intermission from the Texas heat.

Brooks had been at the prison farm less than a year, and he was facing four more years, if he was lucky. Most of the convicts did not live out their sentence. They were either shot, or died of heat stroke or malnutrition. David was well liked by the foreman and he, along with two other convicts, was given special treatment. Working on the plantation meant you would eat the previous day's leftovers that the owners or help did not eat. It was far better than the food at the prison farm and often served as slop. The convicts never complained. It was far better than working the sugar cane fields and being tortured by the rays of the deadly Texas sun.

By 10:00 a.m.it was clear that a storm had begun overpowering the convicts, making their labors difficult. The escalating winds began pulling the tiles off the roof and the shutters were flapping. The two men had begun putting up the storm covers in the pounding rain and they were fighting debris that was flying in their faces. The guard told them to keep working and he cracked a whip. It was a slow process and finally, the guard blew his whistle for the men to stop for lunch.

They walked over to a small porch beneath the old slave quarters and welcomed the food that Jasper Cummings, another prisoner, brought from the main house. They were hungry, and it didn't take long for them to devour the food. They were taking turns waiting to use the outhouse, but David decided to skip his turn, for fear the wind might blow the shack down on top of him. The guard was watching closely when they heard the clanking of the dinner bell. Several people were yelling "tornado," and David looked in the direction someone pointed. A large black funnel cloud that seemed to engulf the sky was approaching at a magnificent force. The guard blew his whistle and motioned for the men to follow him to the slave quarters.

The guard dismounted his horse and had two pairs of handcuffs in his hand. Was he crazy? David thought. The guard was going to handcuff the prisoners to the railing and motioned for David to come forward. David had no intention of letting the guard cuff him to the post. He knocked the gun and the cuffs from his hand and was joined by the other prisoner. Together, they ended his life.

David looked towards the main house and saw Jasper motioning for him to join them in the storm shelter. David knew this would be his one and only chance to escape, so he gave a salute to Jasper and headed in the opposite direction. The other slave had already begun running toward the main road.

The old creek bed was located just south of the main house and the deepest part of the creek was downhill from there, so David ran and dove under a small footbridge. David perched up under the wooden slats that were attached to old railroad ties. He locked his arms around the smaller beam, and he held on for dear life, closing his eyes. The howling wind and torrential rains generated volumes of noise and at one point the suction of the tornado pulled David so hard, his hands bloodied from the splinters in the posts. The tornado's vicious strength was biting away at David's body like an alligator and he almost gave up. Just as quickly as the tornado struck, the eye brought false hope. David's body went limp and his face was buried in the mud. He managed to clear his eyes and reach for the posts again, just as the next force slammed pieces of siding and debris all around him. A few seconds later, David's body went limp again. Just as quickly as the tornado struck, it disappeared. He cleaned away the gum of filth from his eyes with his bloody fingers and then crawled down to the water's edge to rinse his hands. The rain had let up, but was falling hard enough so that when David turned over and looked up, it washed his face clean.

David didn't know how much time he had before the prison guards would come looking for him, so he quickly made his way in the direction of the tracks and followed the creek south. He knew the train tracks were about a quarter mile away. Previously, he had counted the time between the whistles when it arrived in Sugar Land and then again when it prepared to leave. Most of the time, the train would stay at the depot for about fifteen minutes. He had not heard the whistles that day, and figured it was late due to the devastating tornado. David continued to half run and half crawl along the creek bed. If he was going to make his escape it was imperative that he catch a ride on the next train.

The rain was continuing to pour down on David and he was pleased by that, as it would wash away his scent from the hound dogs and also his foot prints. It made his travels slower, but he did not stop. David had to cross a clearing in one of the fields and he was cautious, checking all sides of the clearing. He saw no one, so he took off running as fast as he could. He pushed himself through an overgrown corn field and when he came out; he saw what used to be an old farmhouse. The house was half-gone and the barn was merely a pile of lumber. The tornado had rummaged through the farm and taken its toll. He approached it cautiously, not wanting to be seen. He was still in his striped prison clothing, at least what was left of it. The tornado and wind had chewed up parts of it and it was barely covering his body.

As David got closer to the house, he heard a moan, so he picked up a plank he found on the ground and approached the area it had come from. Lying over a wood pile was a bulky older man with a large piece of pipe stuck through his neck. David watched and waited while the man bled out. The man was lying across a woodpile in an arched position so that the blood was running back towards his head. David walked over and watched as death claimed the old man's life. He began slowly undressing the old man, careful not to get blood on the man's clothing. The man was just about David's height, but probably outweighed David by twenty-five pounds. After David dressed, he checked the pockets and found an old railroad watch and a wallet with about eighteen dollars in it. Stupid farmers never used banks, he thought. David looked around to see what else he could find and saw some curtains hanging out a broken window. He pulled on the rope that was hanging by the window and it came loose. David used it as a belt to keep his pants from falling down. The shoes were a size too big but David put on the shoes and socks anyway. He rolled up what was left of his old clothing and put it under his arms. He scavenged around the remnants of the house, and came upon what was once the kitchen. He found some canning jars filled with corn, beans, and pickles that had not been broken. Just as he picked up a jar of corn and a jar of beans he heard the train whistle coming from the Sugar Land depot. He figured he had just enough time to get to the tracks and ready his jump onto the train.

David made his way to the tracks and positioned himself behind the trees, just in time to roll his two jars of food in his old clothing, and when an open rail car approached he began his run. The train had not yet picked up its momentum and was still gaining speed. David threw the two jars of food into the open door and then grabbed the handle. He continued running to adjust his footing and then made a leap, pulling himself into the rail car. He rolled over the jars of food before he came to a stop. David looked around and he was relieved that no one else was in the car. He figured that the tornado had run off any hobos or vagabonds who might have been on it.

David pulled the door closed, leaving about a ten-inch opening and then moved to a dark corner of the empty stock car. He was panting and laughing to himself at the same time. He was free. For the first time in almost a year, he was at last free. It was close to an hour when David heard the whistle again. He had no idea where he was but he knew the cars would be checked out once the train stopped at the depot. David had rolled up his empty jars in his old clothes and opened the door slowly. When he saw a cluster of trees coming up he made his jump and rolled down an embankment about six feet before coming to a stop. He was shaken up by the fall but the rain had softened his landing and prevented any serious breaks. When he hit the ground he heard the jars break so he emptied the glass behind some trees. David rolled up his prison clothes and put them under his arm. It had been dark inside the rail car so he took out the old man's wallet to see what else was in it. There was a card inside with a note that said: If this wallet is found return it to David Billings, Sugar Land, Texas. It was certainly his lucky day. He now had a new name. David didn't want to chance someone finding his old prison clothes, so he found a stick and dug a hole in the wet, muddy ground. David stuffed the roll of clothes in the ground and covered them with the mud he had dug out and topped it with a few large rocks.

David wasn't sure where he was, but figured he was outside Houston somewhere. It was still raining and the wind had picked up, so he followed the tracks for a while. He came to an intersection and the crossing sign said: Houston five miles. David turned and headed into Houston. It was getting dark, so he was hoping he could hitchhike the five miles into town. He held his thumb up every time an automobile or a horse drawn carriage or wagon came by.

David was about to give up when a man driving a wagon load of hay stopped and said, "If you can find a place on the hay to ride, jump on."

David grabbed a rope and hoisted himself up and crawled under a tarp that was protecting the bales of hay from the rain. It was a small load so he found a place and positioned himself with his head looking out the back. He rode for about forty-five minutes when the wagon stopped and the man waived for him to get off. David jumped off and saluted the driver. "Thanks," David said.

The wagon turned down a road and David tried to get his bearings. It was dark now and David saw some lights about a quarter mile up the road, so he followed the light to a small cluster of houses with a sign out front that read Diner and below that, Rooms-Vacancy. David was soaked, and went inside. He sat at the counter and ordered coffee. The waitress was a tall, attractive brunet who looked to be in her late twenties.

"You been out in that storm?" she asked.

David shook his head yes. "My house blew down in a tornado and I lost everything."

"Oh, I'm so sorry," she said. "I head there was a big one around Sugar Land."

"That's right," he said. "I almost got killed."

"You're lucky," she said. "I heard several people got killed. Coffee is on the house. You got somewhere to stay?" she asked.

"Nope," replied David.

"There's a cottage out back that's under renovation. It's not that nice, but it's a roof over your head and I can give you a bedroll," she told David.

"I'll take it," said David.

"By the way, I'm Louise."

"David, David Billings," he said, and smiled at her.

The waitress went over to the stove and took the lids off the pots. She grabbed a plate and piled it with roast beef, red potatoes and greens. She put a roll on another small plate and then took both plates over to David.

"We ain't gonna have much business tonight and I don't want it to go to waste," said Louise.

David thanked her and smiled at her again. He knew she took a liking to him and he wanted her to feel sorry for him, too. As dirty as he was, his rugged look always appealed to the ladies. David was only thirty-two years old, with a gambler's good looks, and he knew how to charm the ladies. His mother had performed in a striptease act with a travelling circus and she allowed David to be abused when he was younger. When he turned thirteen, he left, and drifted from place to place. He travelled from New York to Denver, and by the time he ended up in Galveston, Texas, he had already killed two men and a woman.

"There are some coveralls that the owner leaves in the back," Louise said. "You can put them on and I'll try and wash some of the dirt out of your clothes. If I hang them in the kitchen they should dry by morning."

"Thanks," said David. "I would appreciate that."

"You live here?" he asked.

"No, but I stay overnight two nights a week to give the owner some relief. Tonight's one of those nights," answered Louise.

David looked around the small diner and it was empty.

As if Louise read his mind, she said, "My last customers left right before you came in. I don't expect I'll get any more with this storm."

David finished eating and Louise put a slice of peach pie on the counter in front of him.

"You sure know how to spoil a guy," David teased.

"You have no idea," Louise smiled back.

When David finished, Louise took him to the back and gave him the overalls and pointed to a small bathroom. David changed and gave her his pants, shirt and socks.

"Is this all?" Louise asked.

"If you are referring to the underwear, I don't like to wear any," David grinned.

"Neither do I," she teased.

David watched her washing out his clothes and then she hung them by the stove over a chair. It had been nine months since David had been with a woman and he was trying to be patient. He watched her closely as she moved around behind the counter. He sat back down and asked for some more coffee. Louise grabbed the coffee pot and walked around the counter, putting her arm around his shoulder and pouring the coffee with her right hand. David looked up at her and their faces were just inches away from each other.

Louise put the pot on the counter and put her hand on his leg. David sucked in his breath and he had to stop himself from grabbing her.

"Would you rather stay at my place?" she asked.

"Thought you'd never ask," David answered.

"Let me just finish cleaning up first, won't take long," Louise answered.

David drank his coffee and watched Louise wash up the last of the dishes and put the pots of food in the icebox. She took off her apron and motioned for David to follow her. Louise's cottage was just outside the back door and it had an awning between the two buildings. It was just one room with a bed and small water closet.

They were barely through the door when they began tearing at each other's clothes. They were hungry for each other and absorbed in the passion of two lost souls looking for a cure for their misery. They were satisfied quickly.

They lay in bed talking for a while, passing some time, and then she began teasing David again.

"I don't want you to think that I jump in bed with every man who comes through here," Louise said. "There was something about you that caught my eye."

David answered her with a kiss. He didn't feel like talking much and since she made it easy for him, he didn't feel it necessary to give her any compliments. It had been a long time since his last kill and he wanted to do so badly, but something inside him stopped his hands from moving to her neck and ending her life. He would find the right time and the right prostitute to fulfill his fantasies. Louise had been nice to him. He wouldn't kill her, he owed her that.

David looked up at the ceiling with a smile on his face. Freedom, he thought, I'll never let anyone take that away from me again. He really had not thought about what he was going to do now. Everything had happened so fast.

The next morning Louise was up early and already gone. David saw his clothes lying over a chair. He washed up and dressed and walked into the diner. Louise poured him some coffee and put the Houston newspaper down in front of him.

"That storm really hit Galveston hard. All the phone lines and telegraph lines are down. Look on page two," Louise said. "There's something about that tornado in Sugar Land."

David read about the tornado hitting a plantation and killing several convicts and a guard. His name, David Brooks, was among those assumed dead. Louise put some scrambled eggs and bacon down for David to eat. He remained quiet and decided the less he said about the tornado and the plantation, the better.

"Where you headed after this?" asked Louise.

"Not sure," said David. "I have some friends in Houston."

The door to the diner swung open and a man and woman came in and sat in a booth. Louise went over and poured them some coffee and took their order. Shortly after that two deputy sheriffs came in, and David tried not to act nervous. He did not want to make eye contact, but they walked over to the counter and sat two seats over from where he was. David finished eating and put down some change and walked out. Louise followed him out the door.

"Will you be back?" she asked with a sad face.

"Sure baby, soon," he lied.

David caught another ride to the outskirts of Houston, Texas. He still hadn't made up his mind where he could lie low for awhile. He considered Rosie's place down in the red light district in the Fourth Ward, but decided too many people knew him there. He was about a mile from the train station so he took off walking. When David arrived at the station he went into a diner across the street and ordered coffee. He needed to collect his thoughts. Everything had happened so fast, he hadn't had time to think about his future. It felt good to be free of the chains and whips and he would die before he ever went back there.

David picked up an old newspaper called the Beaumont Enterprise and looked at the local news. There was an article about the Beaumont Rice Mill and how Beaumont had been steadily growing over the last ten years and had a population of around ten thousand people. It was also served by all the major railroads. He put the paper under his arm and walked back to the depot and up to the ticket window.

"How far is Beaumont from Houston?" David asked.

"'Bout eighty miles, two hours by train," the agent said.

Perfect, David thought to himself. He bought a ticket and waited for the 3:00p.m. train. David kept the newspaper so he could read it more carefully on the train. While he was waiting, he walked over to a wall that had a map illustration of the lower part of Texas and also showed which railroads serviced the area. It was interesting, he thought. Beaumont is due east and it looked like the road from Houston and Beaumont was a major one. He also noticed that Beaumont was bordered by the Naches River which flowed into the gulf. The climate wouldn't be much different than Galveston or Houston. It was worth checking out, he thought. He wanted to relocate to a nice town that was less than a day's train ride from Galveston. He still had business to take care of there, and Catherine Merit was at the top of his list.

Even though David slept most of the way to Beaumont, he did find some time to read the newspaper. There was an article on the back page that mentioned an oil company by the name of the Glacier Oil, Gas, and Manufacturing Co., that was exploring gas and oil in the area around Beaumont. David did not know much about drilling for oil or gas, but it would be important to his future business. More people meant more deaths. He had new skills now and wanted to pursue a more appropriate profession. David wanted something that would associate him with some of the more prominent people of

Beaumont. He was going to be Beaumont's new undertaker. He had learned the trade before he left Galveston and it seem to fit his personality.

David's stay at the prison farm had given him a lot of time to think. He knew he had to keep his nose clean and not draw attention to himself. He never made any friends so he figured his identity would be safe in Beaumont. It was a perfect hiding place for him and he would be able to fade into the crowd.

CHAPTER 2

David got off the train and found himself right in the middle of the business district. There was a saloon at the end of the street called the Log Cabin Saloon, so David walked towards it. He knew he must have looked a bit rough. His hair had grown below his ears and he had a two-day-old beard. He was still wearing the old clothes he had taken off the dead man and he wasn't surprised that everyone stopped and looked at him. David hadn't had a drink in nine months, so he decided he would start with a beer. He noticed an attractive woman eyeing him and pretended not to notice.

"You new in town?" he heard her ask.

"As a matter of fact, I am," David said.

"Where you from?" she asked.

"Houston."

"What brings you to Beaumont?"

"Opportunity."

She didn't know what he meant by that so she ignored his answer.

"Do you have a place to stay?" she asked.

"Not yet," he answered.

"Well, I got a boarding house up the street and I can give you a room for fifty cents a night."

"Just for the room?" David asked.

The girl pretended to blush and said, "Well, I might be able to get you a lady for the night, if you are interested." She grinned.

"And what would that cost me?"

"One dollar," she answered.

David paid for the beer and said, "Let's go."

David followed the woman outside and around to the back. They went through a side door and up some stairs, coming out on a landing that had six doors. She unlocked one and told David it would be about fifteen minutes. David took his shirt off and went into the water closet to wash up. Fifteen minutes later the woman came back and asked David for the money. He could see a young Mexican girl, about sixteen, standing behind her. He gave the woman the dollar and she pushed the girl into his room.

"She doesn't speak much English, but she knows why she is here. Just be easy with her. She's kind of new to the business," the woman explained.

She left and closed the door. David had already taken off his shirt and so he removed his pants. He motioned for the girl to come over to him and she obeyed. He looked into her frail, scared eyes and almost felt sorry for her. He figured she had been sold to the madam by the family for a few bucks and she was told not to humiliate the family. David unbuttoned her top and then pulled her skirt over her head. She had nothing on underneath. Her light brown skin was flawless, and while he sat on the bed he reached forward and started kissing her small, curved breasts. She crawled up into his lap as though someone had told her to. David lifted her onto the bed and joined her. He reached down and kissed her and she helped him remove his clothing. She obediently did as she was told and David liked that she was young and inexperienced. When he was finished with the girl, she got up, dressed and quietly left the room.

David hadn't had a cigarette in a while and he was really craving one. Occasionally, one of the guards would slip him one at the prison farm, but it was rare. Right now, he was too tired to get dressed, so he decided to wait until the next day to buy some and he rolled over and fell asleep.

David woke up at daybreak and dressed. He knew his funds were limited, so he decided to pass on the cigarettes he'd thought about buying. He found a café and ordered eggs, toast and coffee, which were the special for twenty-five cents. There was a Negro man behind the counter doing the cooking and the waitress was the Mexican girl he had slept with the night before. She poured David some coffee, but didn't make eye contact. After David finished, he walked outside and found the small town of Beaumont to be anything but interesting. At the end of the street he saw a sign that read Undertaker and it pointed to a back alley. David followed the sign and saw a small frame building with a horse tied up to a post. The sign said Robert Bailey, Undertaker. There was a bell at the front door and David pulled on it. A few minutes later a small, bald-headed man wearing glasses and about fifty years old, came to the door in a suit.

"How may I help you?" he asked David.

David introduced himself and told him that he was also an undertaker and had left Houston after his family had died in a tragic accident. The man introduced himself as Robert Bailey. He had opened the funeral home about ten years earlier and his was the only funeral home within fifty miles. He said that the livery stables sold coffins and shrouds but his was the only place that did embalming.

"You know, when I first opened, I only had five or six bodies a month. Now I'm up to about fifteen. I don't embalm all of them. Most people don't want to pay for that, unless they are shipping the body across the country," Bailey said.

"I was curious if you could use some help?" David asked.

"Well I've thought about hiring somebody, 'cause I'm getting on in years and it's hard for me to lift the bodies. Why don't you help me out for a week or so and see how it goes?" Bailey said.

"I used up all my money burying my family and I need a few bucks to get by," David told him.

"I guess I could pay you ten bucks a week, but you'll have to earn it."

"Sounds good to me," David said.

"I might even have some clothes you could wear unless you have some of your own," Bailey said.

"The fire that burned up my family took everything. All I have is what I'm wearing," David said, proud that he could be so creative.

"Follow me," Bailey said.

The office was at the front of the building and Bailey opened another door into a hallway that led to a back room with a large, slanted table in it. It smelled of formaldehyde and human decomposition, and there was a rubber tube coming from a faucet that David figured Bailey used to wash down the bodies. It was crude at best. Bailey opened a closet door and it was filled with men's and women's clothing, including some children's garments.

"If there isn't a funeral or a wake I don't clothe the bodies. They usually get buried in a plain pine box," Bailey said. "That's why I have all these clothes. Pick something out."

David took a man's suit, three shirts, a pair of trousers and a tie. He held the pants up and they looked to be his size.

"Since you just got into town, why don't you take the clothes with you and come back dressed tomorrow. Be here at 8:00 a.m. I have a body coming in the morning and the funeral is at 1:00 p.m. outside of town at a country church. After that we take the body in the coffin to the town cemetery for burial.

David thanked him and left. He couldn't believe his luck: A new identity, a new town, and a new job. David walked back toward town and saw a sign that said vacancy, weekly rates. He stopped and rented a room for three dollars and fifty cents a week. It looked respectable enough. He did not want to be associated with a brothel, he thought. He needed to project the right image. The room was small, with a bed, a chair, and a small table. The water closet was small, too, but it had a shower, and the outhouse was just outside behind the building. David took off his clothes and took a shower.

The soap was a cheap bar of lye soap, but it did the job and it felt good to wash his hair. He decided he would let his beard grow out and he combed his hair back with his hands. He dressed in his used suit and he had to admit he looked darn good. David smiled to himself when he walked down the street and several ladies turned and looked at him. He walked down to the saloon he had been in yesterday to get a beer. The same lady was there and came up to him.

"Did you have a good time last night?" she asked.

"Sure did," David answered.

"My name is Darlene," she said.

"I'm David Billings. How much do you want for the little Chico?" David asked her.

"I can't do any better than the fifty cents you paid last night," Darlene answered.

"I meant to keep," David said.

"She's not for sale," she said.

"Everything is for sale," David snapped back.

"She's young and should bring a high price," said Darlene.

"Tell you what I'll do. I'm coming into some money very soon, but for now I'll just pay you by the week."

Darlene thought for a few minutes. "She's only been doing this for a few weeks and she doesn't have much experience; perhaps you could train her for me. You can have her in the evenings for five dollars a week, but she needs to keep her job at the café."

David told Darlene where he was staying and to send her over when she got off work.

"What's her name?" David asked.

"Consuelo," she answered. "Be nice to her. If you treat her badly, the deal is off," Darlene said.

"Why so protective?" David asked.

"She's like family. She was dropped off at the edge of town when she was six and I took her in."

David took out five dollars and paid Darlene.

It didn't take long for David to look the town over. He stopped at the barber shop and had his hair and beard trimmed a bit. The local gossip was that a group of investors had gotten the money together to drill for oil a mile or so from town, at a place called Spindletop. Everyone was laughing at them because they had been at it for months and had found nothing except mud, salt and rocks.

Main Street had a small general store that carried a little bit of everything, from smelling salts, tobacco, and coffee, to larger items like clothing and chicken feed. There was a rice mill, a livery stable, a local diner and several saloons. There were several offices, and of course, a small county courthouse.

Later that day, David was waiting in his room when someone knocked at the door. It was Darlene, and Consuelo was standing behind her. David smiled and held out his hand for Consuelo to take. She did not look up, but took his hand. Darlene left and David closed the door.

"Hablas mucho Ingles" (Do you speak much English) asked David.

"Un poco (A little), she answered.

David smiled at her. *"Desnudarme."* (Undress me.)

Consuelo walked over to him and took his jacket off him and hung it on a hanger. She began unbuttoning his shirt. She still did not look at him. David sat on the bed and she continued unbuttoning his shirt. He put his hand under her chin and tilted her face up to him, forcing her to look in his eyes.

"Tiene unos ojos previosos," (You have beautiful eyes)

She smiled up at David and he kissed her. He helped her take his pants and shoes off and then he undressed her. He pulled her onto the bed beside him and took in every beautiful inch of her pale brown skin.

"Mucha belleza," (much beauty) David said.

She smiled and touched his face with her small hand. David took her hand and kissed it and they spent the next hour making love.

After that they showered together and then went to sleep. David woke in the middle of the night and watched her sleeping. She had such an innocence about her, he thought. David smiled to himself and knew Consuelo would be easy to train. She would do for now. He was reluctant to bed a lot of prostitutes for fear he would catch syphilis and he had too much to do to go hunting. One of the prisoners at the camp had syphilis and it was a terrible way to die. He needed to be cautious and Consuelo would be able to take care of his enormous sexual appetite. At least until he could get Catherine.

Beaumont seemed to be a dream come true for David. So far he had not run into anyone he knew and there were enough strangers coming in and out of town for him to become obscure and except for the ladies, no one seemed to pay much attention to him. It couldn't be a more perfect place for him to get down to business.

CHAPTER 3

For many days after the powerful storm swallowed up one of the most beautiful cities in the United States, the twenty thousand or so people who stayed were fed and cared for daily in Galveston. By October first, this number was cut at least by one-half. Supplies, goods, and food were sent to their aid by the mainland. Cleaning up the wreckage, cleaning the streets, and digging for bodies was an everyday occurrence. The business and shop owners whose property survived with the least amount of damage tried to open their businesses and shops, but few people had flood or storm insurance so the lack of money made it difficult to carry on business as usual.

The sailing and steam ship vessels that originally brought the immigrants in through Galveston's wharf were rerouted to Houston, New Orleans and Florida.

Galveston was grieving the loss of over six thousand lives. Hundreds of people left Galveston to build a new life in other cities. The businessmen got together and decided to do what they do best, make more money, and they tried to conduct business as usual. The Galveston News wrote an editorial with the caption, Galveston Shall Rise Again. Changes in the city government were slowly made. A new, more honest mayor was elected and he brought in a new police chief to help clean up the town. The city was determined to rebuild itself, however long it took.

Catherine and John Merit, along with John's invalid sister,

Amelia, had been living in Minnie Wyman's boarding house since the destruction of the city. It had taken weeks before the house was totally dried out. Much of the house sat eight feet off the ground on stilts, and storm shutters over the windows minimized a lot of the damage. John and Catherine worked side by side, hammering siding back on the exterior and John replaced many missing roof tiles. The upstairs bedroom where they now made their home was cramped and for the first time since their marriage two years earlier, Catherine and John were sharing a bedroom. Catherine had made up her mind that the flood waters had washed away all of the sins of her past, and she concentrated on what was most important to her, her husband. Minnie's other live-in boarder, Profession Gordon, moved to the upstairs garage apartment in the back of the house so that John's sister, Amelia, could have the bedroom on the first floor and not have to walk up the stairs. John paid for all the repairs since Minnie had no insurance and he didn't mind. He knew that with the housing shortage, Minnie could have tripled the price for their boarding, but she didn't. They were her family now, she thought.

John Merit went back to his job at the bank as soon as the water damage was removed. The bank was back in business a month later and John spent his days trying to dry out files and sort through papers. He spent long hours at the bank. Since he was the trust officer, there were hundreds of deaths he had to sort through, and finding their heirs would take months. Catherine worked extra shifts at the hospital and then returned to medical school as soon as it reopened several months later. She continued to work when she could at the hospital.

It was nice living in the boarding house. Minnie prepared their evening meals as best she could on a small oil burner. Catherine and John were rarely there for a sit down dinner, because of their irregular hours. Their plates of food were always in the kitchen waiting for them to pick them up. Catherine was only working two nights and Saturdays at the hospital and on the other nights when John worked late she would always go down and sit with Minnie, Amelia and

Profession Gordon and drink hot tea while they ate. Catherine would wait until John came home so they could eat supper together.

It was always nice when they could all sit down with the family to eat, but Catherine loved the intimate evenings, when it was just her and John having supper. Catherine enjoyed listening to John talk about his busy day and watching him eat. After Catherine's brutal attack a year ago by David Brooks, she had reservations about whether or not she would ever enjoy her love-making with John again. When she thought John had perished in the flood, she vowed that if he survived, she would put everything behind her and concentrate on their marriage and having John's baby. She knew John wanted the same thing. She worried that he might not be able to put the indignity of the rape behind him, but he did. Now they had their whole lives ahead of them and their love for each continued to grow stronger.

John loved Catherine more than anything. He had been told by Sgt. Husky, with the Galveston Police Department, that he had received a wire from his brother-in-law with the Houston Police Department that David Brooks had perished in a tornado in Sugar Land the day of the flood. They no longer had to be concerned about David coming after Catherine, and that was a huge relief. It meant that Catherine no longer had to worry that he might come back and try to abduct her or kill her. She still had occasional dreams about that horrible night a year earlier. He had overcome her with a rag soaked in chloroform when she had left the hospital late one night. He tied her up and put her in a coffin and took her miles from town and brutalized her most of the night. He had gotten drunk and when he passed out; she escaped and led the police to where he was. It was behind her now, and she vowed she would not allow the memory of the ordeal to take over her life.

Still, John treated Catherine like a fragile china doll. She had been broken once and had slowly mended her life back together, and they both loved each other. He didn't want to risk hurting her again and he was going to make sure no one else did.

When the city of Galveston had finally cleared the main streets Catherine had asked John if they could go to the cemetery to see the damage that had been done to her mother's grave and see if it was still there. It nagged at her that her mother's final resting place had been disturbed, and she just wanted to see if she could find it again. John rented a horse and buggy for the day, one Sunday afternoon, and they rode to where the old cemetery had been. There were mounds of debris and remnants from the storm scattered all over the place. John could see by Catherine's face how disturbed she was. John's first wife and child along with his parents had been buried in the same cemetery and he was concerned, too. They were both shocked by what they saw. They sat on the wagon for a while taking in the immense damage that lay before them. They saw a black grave digger off in a distance and John drove the wagon over to where he was working.

"Any idea when they plan to clean up this mess?" John asked.

The grave digger stopped and gave him a hopeless look. "The caretaker of the cemetery died in the flood. Don't know where the plan to the cemetery is. You might check with the church or the city," he said. "You lookin' for a special grave?" he asked John.

"Yes, several of them," John answered.

"Well the headstones have been found all over the city and people have been bringing um back here and dumpin' back there," the grave digger said and pointed.

John and Catherine rode to the back of the cemetery where fifty or so headstones were lying side by side. They found all but two: John's father and Catherine's mother, Anne's, headstone. Catherine wanted to cry, but she didn't want John to know how upset she was. John could see the anguish in her face, and promised her that when the cemetery was re-platted, that they would find Anne's grave and put a new head stone on it along with his own father's. Catherine knew that the rebuilding of the city would take some time. It was unfortunate, though, that the cemetery would probably be last on the list.

The most precious thing that John and Catherine had now was their love-making. John always tried to subtly build up to the moment. He would bring her flowers and small gifts and if Catherine didn't initiate their love-making first, John would always start by rubbing her feet and moving his hands up her thighs. He could always sense if Catherine was too tired or just wasn't in the mood, but John knew Catherine wanted to please him, too. The best times were when they both wanted to be intimate at the same time.

One night when John came home late from work, Catherine was waiting for him dressed in a new nightgown that looked similar to the one he had given her on her birthday. When she greeted him she took his briefcase from him and then undid his tie. Neither said anything, they didn't need to. John waited, enjoying the luring look in her eyes.

"Could I interest you in an appetizer before dinner?" Catherine asked, grinning. She stood in front of John and unbuttoned his shirt.

"Depends on whether I can afford it," John responded with a smile. "Maybe I'll just skip the appetizer and go straight to the main course," he whispered in her ear.

"I was hoping you would say that," Catherine answered and pulled him over to their bed.

Catherine took John's jacket and shirt off and then undid his pants and slipped off his shoes. She turned and threw the covers back on the bed and pushed John down on it, pulling his pants and underwear off. She crawled in bed and crouched next to him. She was still wearing the nightgown, but there was nothing underneath. John was already excited, but waited to see what Catherine wanted to do next. After all it was Catherine's conquest and he was more than happy to oblige her. She bent down and kissed John on his neck and fondled his ear with her tongue.

"My turn," he said.

Catherine smiled up at him and said, "Whatever your pleasure, Mr. Merit."

She knew that John's masterful hands would bring out all of her erotic energies and she gave herself to him. John followed with equal pleasure, and then they fell asleep in each other's arms. A short while later Catherine got up and went to the kitchen to get John's supper. John watched her every move. She turned and looked at him and smiled over her shoulder.

"Stay where you are," she commanded.

John didn't move. Before she brought the tray to his bed, Catherine picked up two pillows and propped them behind his back. John grabbed her hand and pulled her close to him.

"Will you marry me, again?" John asked.

"Hmmmm, I'll have to think about that," she teased.

When John had finished, he went into the tiny bathroom they shared. Before the storm the bathroom only had a small bathtub, but during the renovations John had the plumbers install an overhead shower. He had just turned on the water and was about to get in when Catherine pulled on his hand and said, "If I marry you again, may I get into the shower with you now?"

He grinned and picked her up. She had already taken off her robe and she was naked, so he lifted her into the shower and then stepped in behind her. It was an evening he would never forget.

The lot where John's house once stood was empty now. It had been demolished during the storm and all the bones of the house that were once there had been removed. John and Catherine were standing in front of the lot and they were talking to an architect about building a new house. Catherine let John do all of the talking. She liked the old house and hoped that John would want to keep it pretty much the same. This time he told the architect that he wanted three bedrooms upstairs with two bathrooms and a large open bedroom downstairs for Amelia along with a full bathroom and, of course, a study, parlor, large kitchen, and dining room. The previous house only had two bedrooms upstairs but she knew John wanted at least two children and so did she.

John had received a substantial raise at the bank and he now had an assistant. They could pretty much afford whatever they wanted. One day John came home from the bank and gave Catherine an envelope. Inside the envelope were theatre tickets to an opera in Houston, Texas, in two weeks. Catherine stared at them.

"I thought we would take a weekend off and spend it in Houston. We could pick out some furniture and things for the house. Minnie can look after Amelia for us and we won't have to worry about anything," John said enthusiastically.

The tickets John had bought were for the weekend before Catherine's finals at the medical school. John could sense that Catherine did not seem to be as excited as he was.

"What is it, Catherine? I thought you would be pleased." John said.

"Well, I am," she said. "It's just that my finals start the next Monday and I was planning to study all weekend."

John didn't say anything but walked over to the trash can and threw the tickets into it.

"John," Catherine said. "I'll study on the train ride if you don't have a problem with that."

"Look, Catherine, I know that part of the agreement when we married was that you would go to medical school and become a doctor. But all that seemed to change after the storm. I had hoped by now you would be pregnant and that hasn't happened yet. You work under so much stress. I just thought maybe if we had a weekend away together with no obstacles before us, maybe you could relax and get pregnant."

Catherine walked over and picked up the tickets out of the trash can and then put her arms around John.

She reached up and kissed him. "You are right; you always are. I don't mean to be so selfish. Please forgive me," Catherine whispered to him.

He held her and kissed her. That night Catherine tried to get into their love-making and had to pretend she had been satisfied.. She knew that women were expected to marry and breed lots of children. It was her conjugal obligation. She just did not see it that way. Even though she loved John more than anything, their ten-year age gap had a lot to do with John wanting children more than she. She would have preferred waiting until she was through with medical school.

Catherine still missed her mother deeply and longed to ask her for her guidance. She died so young, Catherine thought. She also knew that her mother and father loved each other and that her mother would have done anything to make him happy. Catherine made a decision. When school was out and she didn't pass her finals, she would not return in the fall. She was qualified as a nurse and felt she could pass that exam with no problem. She would just let fate take over. John was in his late twenties and she understood that he wanted and needed children now. Catherine decided to make an appointment with Dr. Copeland soon for a medical exam. They no longer tried to schedule their love-making around the calendar, and she was surprised she had not gotten pregnant. She felt there was no medical problem on her part, except the fact that when she had been abducted by David Brooks previously, she had gotten pregnant. She miscarried two months later.

"Everything seems to be as it should be," said Dr. Copeland, after giving Catherine a complete physical.

"Your periods are normal and there is no reason whatsoever that you should not get pregnant. When you miscarried there was nothing unusual about it and you bounced back rather quickly. It's my opinion that you will probably be pregnant by the end of the year," Dr. Copeland said.

Before Catherine was to leave on their trip to Houston, she spent all of her free time studying. Sometimes, after she and John had gone to bed and she heard him breathing deeply, she would go in the bathroom and study. Catherine wanted to be as focused on John on their trip as she possible could, and if she had the studying behind her it would make it more pleasurable for both of them.

John left work early on Friday to go home and pick up Catherine and their bags. He had bought tickets for the express leaving Galveston at 4:00 p.m. Catherine was not home yet and it was already 3:00 p.m. John began pacing the floor. At 3:10 Catherine came in and ran upstairs to where John was sitting.

"I'm so sorry," said Catherine.

John didn't say anything and he picked up their two bags and walked downstairs. Catherine made a quick change into one of her nicer dresses, grabbed her shawl and hurriedly went downstairs. She followed John out the front door and had to run to keep up with him. The trolley was just pulling up. They were at the train station at 3:50 and the train was blowing its first whistle.

John had purchased tickets in the club car where they had a small private room. The porter took their bags and showed them to their state room. Catherine walked in first and heard John say something to the porter and give him a tip. She closed her eyes and wondered how she was going to make amends with John. He didn't seem to have the patience with her he once had.

John came in and took the seat across from her but didn't say anything. He just looked out the window.

"For God's sake," Catherine said. "Say something. Scold me for being late. Tell me how childish I am for not being on time. I didn't mean to be late, I'm sorry." Catherine had tears in her eyes and willed herself not to cry.

"I guess I just realized that you really didn't want to go on this trip and I'm sorry I made you come," John said.

Catherine's heart sunk. She knew he was right. They both sat in silence for a while and the train began to move. John laid his head back and he pretended to take a nap. Catherine stared at him. How two people could love each other so much, but yet be so far apart on what they both wanted out of this marriage, was impossible for Catherine to understand. A short while later there was a knock on the door and John got up and opened the door. The porter had brought John a double shot of scotch and some hot tea for Catherine. John gave him a tip and closed the door. Before John could pick up the scotch, Catherine grabbed it and started drinking it like a glass of milk. She had almost drunk it all before she stopped and coughed.

John was stunned and then he started laughing.

"Damn, Catherine," he said. "I've never seen you drink like that before."

Catherine started laughing too.

"I guess I should have ordered a bottle," John teased.

Catherine jumped on his lap and straddled him, pulling his face to hers and kissing him hard.

"You, John Merit, are my life and I would do anything for you. I'm quitting medical school after I take my exams," Catherine said.

John was taken by surprise. "Are you sure?" he asked.

Catherine shook her head, yes, and kissed him again.

They had finally come to an understanding, John thought to himself. Now he was feeling guilty. He took a deep breath, happy that the tension was gone. Catherine sat beside him now, with her head on his shoulder. He smiled to himself when he thought about Catherine drinking her first scotch. He wondered what possessed her to do it. She was always surprising him, and he liked that about her.

Catherine had fallen asleep on John's shoulder and he was glad that they were no longer angry with each other. He finished off what was left of the scotch and wanted another, but did not want to wake Catherine, so he put his head back and went to asleep. The both woke up at the same time when the porter hollered out the Houston stop. John picked up their two bags and they walked through the station to a waiting carriage.

John had made reservations at the famous Lancaster Hotel,

which was located in the heart of Houston's business, financial, and theatre districts at 701 Texas Avenue at Louisiana. It was a beautiful hotel and John spared no expense on the room. Catherine walked around the room touching everything and smiling back at John as she did.

"Shall we go down and have dinner before we turn in?" asked John.

Catherine bit her lower lip and started undressing.

"Maybe we could just order some champagne and—" Catherine couldn't finish her sentence because John had grabbed her, kissing her passionately. They were hungry for each other and neither wanted to wait. Catherine was pulling at John's clothes and he gripped her buttocks and drew her close to him. They were kissing each other so passionately that they were both gasping for breath. Catherine unbuttoned John's pants and they were having their way with each other. It was the best sex they had had in months and it was over in a matter of minutes. They lay together on the bed trying to catch their breath when someone knocked on the door and said "Room Service." Catherine jumped up and ran to the bathroom. John pulled up his pants and tried to straighten his shirt before he opened the door.

"You can put the cart over there," and he pointed.

The bellboy smiled and thanked John for the nice tip and left.

Catherine stuck her head around the door and said, "All clear?"

"All clear," answered John. Catherine walked out half-dressed and smiling.

"I didn't know you had already ordered room service," she said.

"You didn't give me a chance," he laughed. "You better put on some clothes unless you want me to chase you around the room," John teased.

"I think I would like a glass of champagne first, and then you can chase me around the room," Catherine teased.

It was a memorable night and in the morning, they made love again. They fell back asleep and when they woke up they were tangled in each other's arms.

"If you want to go shopping we need to get going," John said, stroking Catherine. "I love you, Mr. Merit," Catherine whispered.

"And I love you, too," John said back.

They ate a late breakfast and left to explore the stores and shops. Catherine had never seen such beautiful merchandise in the stores. The windows were dressed with some of Houston's finest clothing, many items imported from abroad. John bought Catherine a beautiful evening dress to wear to the opera and matching shoes. She had asked if she could buy some new earrings and they found a small jewelry store a few blocks around the corner. They were looking in the window and Catherine said, "Oh my goodness!!"

"What is it?" John asked.

"The watch. See that gold watch that's to the right of the necklace?"

John looked. "I thought you wanted earrings," he stated.

"I need to take a closer look at the watch," she said.

They walked in and asked the jeweler if they could look at the gold watch in the window. The jeweler took a key and unlocked a door to the window and took the gold watch to the counter for them to look at.

"Oh, John, it's my mother's gold watch that went missing when she worked at the Grande Opera House. My mother had given my father this watch when they married. See the inscription?"

John asked the jeweler where he had purchased it. He told them he did not like to give out his sources.

"Are you sure, Catherine?" John asked.

"Their wedding date is just below it. I'm positive."

"How much is the watch?" John asked the jeweler.

"Its 14K gold and it is a fine watch," he answered.

"I can see that," John said, getting a bit angry.

"Since you seem to be familiar with the watch I could let you have it for eighteen dollars."

"We'll take it," John said and handed him a twenty dollar bill.

The jeweler put the watch in a small box and tied it with a ribbon and handed it to John. Before they left, Catherine had also picked out some tiny pearl earrings, and she clipped them on her ears.

John and Catherine stopped and looked at some things for the house and picked up several catalogs with furniture and draperies in them. John knew Catherine would be anxious to return to the hotel so she could look at the watch, so they caught a carriage and made it back to the hotel in ten minutes. John stopped at the desk and ordered a bottle of scotch and some snacks to be sent upstairs.

"Would you rather have hot tea?" John teased Catherine.

She shook her head no. When they got to the room, Catherine opened the tiny box. She couldn't believe the watch-fob was still attached. The velvet pouch was gone but that was all right because she didn't intend to keep the watch. Room service came and they sat down together to have a drink. John only poured Catherine a small glass of scotch and a tall one for himself.

"My mother gave my dad this watch on their wedding day and nothing would please me more than for you to have it," Catherine said as she handed John the watch.

John sat looking at her and they both took sips of the scotch.

"Are you sure?" John asked.

"With all my heart and soul, John, nothing would please me more," she answered. John took the watch and leaned over and kissed her.

"I would be happy to accept it on one condition," he said. Catherine looked puzzled.

"That if you ever want to take it back or borrow it, you can," John said. Catherine was pleased and kissed him back.

The opera was wonderful and Catherine looked beautiful in

her new evening gown. They had lots of stares and John was pleased to have Catherine on his arm. It was a beautiful weekend and so was the ride home.

Catherine took her finals when she got home and went back to medical school. She surprised herself by scoring in the top fifteen percent. She had not gotten pregnant yet, and she worried about it. She was sure that after their sexually active weekend she would miss her period and they would be expecting in nine months, but it did not happen. She asked John if she should quit school. John knew Catherine would be miserable not finishing out the semester so he encouraged her to keep going. He did request that she not work at night during the Christmas break at the hospital and she agreed. Catherine agreed to work five days, Monday through Friday, and get off at 5:30 p.m.

CHAPTER 4

Over the next few months David learned a lot from Bailey about how he ran the undertaking business. He liked that Bailey worked on cash only and he had a way to always add on extra things so he could up the price; promising a nicer coffin, or extra facial make-up to make the corpse more presentable for the viewing. Bailey also made it a point to always check the teeth and unless the family asked, he kept the gold that he had David extract from the teeth. Bailey had no idea that David always managed to put a piece or two in his own coat pocket. Bailey had a safe in his office and he never opened it when David was in the room. David figured that was where Bailey kept the gold from the teeth and the wedding bands and gold watches he stole off the dead. When the family would ask about an item, he pretended that it was not on the body. "It must be somewhere in their house," he would tell them.

David had also begun ordering their monthly allotment of caskets and chemicals from the medicine man. It wasn't that hard, David thought to himself. Once he knew who the suppliers were and how Bailey manipulated the money, he figured he could do it. David had never attended school, but the girls at the Ringling Bros. Circus where he grew up made sure he knew how to read and add and subtract. One of the circus girls was Mexican and that was where he picked up the Spanish language.

Consuelo continued to stay with David every night and he

grew fond of her. He liked that she never complained and always did what he wanted. He told her she needed to learn English so she had Darlene work with her on that. Darlene always spoke Spanish to her, so Consuelo did not care about learning English until David told her to.   Consuelo was becoming attached to David and hoped that someday she might be his wife. She had no idea that David had no intentions of every marrying her.

David's fascination with Catherine Merit continued to grow and before he made any plans about her future with him, he decided he would take two or three days off and go to Galveston and see if she survived the flood. If she did, most likely she would still be going to medical school or working at the hospital. He told Bailey he needed to take care of some family business back in Houston and needed to take three days off. Bailey agreed, but it would be without pay.

The night before he left, he made Consuelo promise that she would not go out at night and that she would come directly home as soon as she finished at the café.

"I don't want you prostituting yourself with anyone else," he said. "You are mine and I've paid Darlene for you fulltime."

Consuelo shook her head and told David she loved him and would never sleep with another man.

David packed a small bag and left the next morning, stopping at Bailey's office first. David used his own key to get in and take a few things he might need. White shoe polish, a hat and a half-empty bottle of chloroform. It was an old bottle he had saved, and every time he used some, he would pour a small amount from the new bottle into his empty bottle. He figured Bailey wouldn't notice a bottle missing that way. There was a small shaving mirror on the top shelf and David took it down and looked at himself with the hat on. He pulled open a drawer that had eyeglasses in it and he pulled a pair out and put them on. His disguise was complete except for grey hair. That was what he needed the shoe polish for and he would put some in his hair later.

The 8:00 AM train was blowing its whistle when David was

buying his ticket. One hour later he was in Houston. He stooped and looked in the phone book to find a jeweler that bought, as well as sold, jewelry. He found one in the yellow pages and wrote down the address. It was located a couple of streets over from the Fourth Ward and was easy to find. The store was not open until 10:00 a,m, and he was thirty minutes early. He saw a café across the street and decided a good breakfast was just what he needed. The waitress flirted with him, but she had buck teeth and a flat chest. Not his type at all, he thought.

He was almost through with his breakfast, when he looked out the window and saw a scrawny, tall man with glasses open up the jewelry store. He paid the check and went across the street.

"How may I help you?" he heard the man behind the counter ask.

"Some of my family has passed and I have some gold I wanted to sell," David said.

The man weighed it on his jewelry scale and said, "You've got about twenty-one dollars and fifty cents worth of gold here. Do you see anything in the shop you want to buy, or do you just want the cash?

"I'll take the cash, thank you," David said. David collected the money and left quickly so he could try and make the noon train to Galveston.

After David boarded the train he laid his head back and fell asleep. He woke up and asked the porter how long before they got to Galveston. "Twenty minutes," said the conductor.

David got up and took his bag to the men's room. He was alone so he took out the white shoe polish and put a small amount on his handkerchief. He washed a small amount off and then lightly smoothed it on his hair just over his ears. The more he dabbed at it, the more natural it looked.

His beard already had a few grew hairs, so he didn't add any more. David thought he looked more like forty years old than his thirty-three years. He put his hat and glasses on and even he was surprised by the transformation.

It felt good to be back in Galveston and he decided to find a cheap place for the night. Something out of the way and he remembered China town. Nobody would know him there. Even though his disguise was good, he didn't want to chance running into someone who might remember him.

David was shocked at the emptiness of the streets. The usual crowded streets were practically void of any traffic, and there were a number of buildings boarded up with "Out of Business" signs nailed to the doors. He had heard the storm had devastated the city, but he was not prepared to see a city in ruins. It had only been seven months since the storm and there was some construction going on, but he had not expected it to be this bad. Not all the trolleys were running, but the one on the Strand was, so he hopped on it and rode to the west end of the city. China town was only a small two-block area and the buildings there were not in the best condition to begin with. He got off the trolley and walked down China town's main street. There were still a few vendors selling food off a cart and he could see the main bath house was open for business. He didn't want to risk leaving his clothes in a separate room where someone could rummage though his pockets and steal his money, so he walked over to another street. Several young Chinese prostitutes were standing in the doorways of a couple of old buildings that had withstood the punishment of the flood. One in particular caught his eye and he walked over. He had been here before, two years ago. The Chinese girl was probably eighteen years old now.

"You want sex?" she asked in broken English, "fifty cents today."

David nodded his head toward the door and she opened it.

"Money first," she said.

David reached in his pocket and took out the change. The last time he was here, her mother was the madam of the brothel, and he wondered if she died in the flood. The girl showed him into a small room with a rug and chair. She undressed and bent over holding on to the chair. David pulled his pants down and approached the girl. He found his release a few minutes later. She handed him a towel and he took it. He finished buttoning up his pants and left.

When he got back to the Strand he saw a clock that said 4:00 p.m.. He decided that if Catherine were still alive, she would still be at the hospital, so he caught the trolley and rode the twenty or so blocks and got off close to the hospital. He walked into the emergency room and sat in the waiting room. He picked up a newspaper and pretended to look at it. Each time someone came in or out a door, he looked up to see if it might be Catherine. He didn't want to ask for her by name, for fear someone might bring it to her attention. If anyone could recognize him, it would be her. Fifteen minutes later, she walked out of an examination room with a woman who was crying. Catherine stood in the hall talking to her and she put her hand on the lady's shoulder trying to console her. David had his head down, but he kept an eye on her until she turned and left. God, she was even more beautiful than he remembered. He smiled and then got up and left. The memories of his night with Catherine were vivid and he couldn't help thinking about it. Her body was soft and beautiful and her breasts were the perfect size. He longed for her, worshiped her and soon she would be his forever.

He didn't want to carry his bag anymore so he headed back toward the train station and found a sleazy hotel that wasn't expensive. After he checked in, he took his bag to his room and decided to head back out and get something to eat. David's adrenaline was flowing and he was getting excited. Just thinking about Catherine did strange things to him. He felt the need to kill. There was a café a block from his hotel and he decided to eat first. It would be dark soon and he could go hunting. He sat at a table so he could watch the street. There were not many people out and he wondered if he would have to go over to "fat alley" and find a prostitute. He decided that was too risky. Some of the girls from there might recognize him and he couldn't risk that. He noticed that someone had just turned off the lights in a shop across the street a few doors down. David paid his tab quickly and went outside and watched. A young woman about twenty locked the door and began walking down the street. He followed at a safe distance. She turned the corner and David noticed that several of the street lights were out. While he was following her, he took his bottle of chloroform out of his pocket and soaked his handkerchief.

He quickly caught up with her and said, "Madam, you dropped something."

The girl turned around and when she did, David grabbed her and covered her nose with the handkerchief. She passed out in his arms and he quickly picked her up. He looked both ways and saw no one, so he carried her down an alley. There was a badly damaged building that was empty and David kicked the door open. He laid the limp girl on the floor and he put his handkerchief over her face again. He didn't want to risk her waking up and screaming. It only took him a few minutes to undress her. The darkness made it difficult to see her body and he pulled her through the store until he got to the front where a small amount of light was coming through a boarded up window. He stood over her and looked at her while he took his pants off. As he raped her, he put his hands around her neck. He squeezed it tightly for several minutes, then he finally relaxed. He sat straddling her for a few minutes and relived the last few moments. She coughed and opened her eyes. David grew even more excited. She wasn't dead yet. He stuffed the rag deeply in her mouth and watched her struggle for air. He held her hands and arms with one hand over her head, and pushed the rag deeper until it blocked her windpipe. She couldn't move and he could see the horror in her eyes. He loved the kill, and it had been too long since his last one. Her eyes rolled back and she tried to throw up, to no avail. Her life finally ended. David got up and straightened his clothes as he watched, taking in every inch of her beautiful, dead body. He checked his pockets to make sure nothing fell out and he left the same way he came in.

David caught an early morning train back to Houston and made the connection to Beaumont. He did not want to be gone too long, because he didn't trust Consuelo and he never liked hanging around long after a kill. He figured it would take a few days to find the body, and he would be safely back in Beaumont.

He got back to his room at 12:30 p.m. and put his things away. He went into the bathroom and wet his hair, trying to get the shoe polish out. He finally put his head under the sink and used the soap to remove all traces. After he towel dried his hair, he put on a clean shirt and walked over to the café where Consuelo worked.

When she saw David come in, she looked away. David figured something was up and he walked to the far end of the counter. The lunch crowd had thinned out, and he was glad, so he could ask Consuelo about her evening. She walked down to where he was sitting, and said she was glad to see him.

"It's nice you got back early."

"What did you do last night?" he asked.

"I work here till late," she said.

"What did you do after that?" he asked.

"I go home," she said, looking away.

"When do you get off work?" he asked.

"Six o'clock," she answered.

"Good, I want you to come straight to my room. If they tell you to stay later, tell them you can't. Do you understand?"

"Yes, is everything all right?" she asked.

David smirked and said, "Get me the special. I'm hungry."

Consuelo brought David his lunch and she tried to smile like everything was good, but she knew better. He couldn't possible know what she did last night. He wasn't here, she thought. It worried her all day.

Consuelo had just taken her key out of her purse when the door opened. She reached up to kiss David but he pulled away.

"Undress," was all he said.

Consuelo took off her dress and was standing in front of David with her slip on.

"Everything," he said.

She obeyed him and stood in front of him naked. "Lay on the bed, face down."

She did what he said. David walked over to the dresser and took something out. He straddled her on the bed and tied each of her hands, extending them to the posts on each side of the bed.

"Why do you do this?" she asked.

I'm going to ask you one more time. Where did you go after work last night? Did Darlene whore you out?" he asked.

She shook her head, no. David took a small rag and forced it into Consuelo's mouth. He got up and took off his belt. He struck her across her buttocks and she grimaced and tried to scream. He hit her two more times, hitting the back of her legs. She was struggling trying to move out of his way, but each blow knocked the wind out of her. She was crying and groaning.

"Shhh, be quiet and I'll take the gag out of your mouth," David said. "I really don't want to hurt you, but you are lying to me. How many men did she make you sleep with last night? He waited and when she didn't answer he began putting the rag back in her mouth.

She shook her head no and said, "I tell you, please don't hit me again." She was crying and couldn't stop.

"I'm waiting," David said.

"Five," she said.

David untied her and pulled her into his arms. "I don't blame you. Did she give you any of the money?" he asked.

"No, two of her girls left her. She asked me to stop by last night when she heard you were out of town. She said she needed the money and would pay me another time. I so sorry. She made me promise not to tell," she confessed.

"Stay here," David said and left.

David walked down to the saloon and ordered a whiskey at the bar. He saw Darlene come down the stairs. She walked over to David and said hello.

"I thought we had a deal," David said.

"Here's your five dollars back. I need her here. She can make more money for me in one night than you pay in a week," she said.

"I don't think so. The deal's off when I say so and I won't let her come back. Try and do something stupid and you'll regret it," David said.

He finished the drink and walked over to the café. He got a couple of sandwiches and put them in a paper bag.

Consuelo was dressed and waiting for him. David put the food on the table and poured himself a drink. Consuelo looked at him and waited for him to say something.

"Do you like me, Consuelo?" David asked.

"Yes, very much," she answered.

"Would you rather be with me or go back to Darlene and sleep with a dozen or so men every night and get the disease?" he asked.

"No, Mr. David, I want to be with you," she said.

"All right then, the next time Darlene asks you to come by the saloon again, I want to know about it," David said. "Understood?"

"Yes," she replied.

CHAPTER 5

It was three days before the body of a young shopkeeper was found. The smell of human decomposition had finally seeped through the cracks in the doors and windows, making its presence known to the people on the streets. The owner was called and he almost passed out when he saw her body. Before he made his way back out he had to stop and vomit several times.

Sergeant Husky was called to the scene and he brought another officer from the police department with him. It was difficult to stay inside the building, much less examine the body closely. It was murder, and there was no question in Sergeant Husky's mind that she had also been raped. You didn't usually leave a body naked unless it was a sexual assault. He shook his head and began talking to potential witnesses. He was told the lady had not lived in Galveston very long, and that she had only opened the store about a month ago. Sergeant Husky found himself at a dead end and it was only one of many tragedies that had happened since the flood. The looting, murders and stealing were coming close to an end, and now this. He wondered if it had been associated with a robbery, but then again, she had been raped. Maybe it was a lover getting back at her for leaving him. He knew this one would never be solved. This was an innocent woman, simply going home from work and minding her own business. If he wasn't sure David Brooks was dead, he would have considered him a suspect, but many new people had come to Galveston on the pretence of helping rebuild Galveston. He hoped he wouldn't have to come up against another David Brooks. The likes of him were evil, thought Husky.

Beaumont was beginning to grow on David. It was several degrees hotter than Galveston but it was nothing like the heat in Sugar Land. He would never forget the devilish heat that singed his skin and burned into his insides. That was behind him now and he decided it was time for him to make his move on Bailey.

It had been a slow week so David decided the time was now for Bailey to have a heart attack. He had already ascertained that Bailey had no close relatives. He mentioned a nephew who lived out of state, but that was it. Bailey liked David, and trusted him enough to give him a key to the building. Bailey was at his desk and David was in the morgue area cleaning up some things. Bailey did not hear David when he came up behind him and put a rag soaked in chloroform over his face. David locked the front door and picked up Bailey's limp body and carried it to the embalming table. He tied his arms and ankles securely to the table and stuffed another rag deep into his mouth. David put smelling salts under Bailey's nose, and he blinked his eyes a couple of times. When he woke up, he saw David and realized that he was tied to the table. His bladder was full and he fought the urge not to pee but he could feel dribbles leaking between his legs. He was panicked and wanted to scream. When he tried to swallow he almost choked as he sucked the rag in and blocked his windpipe. He coughed and felt the bile coming up from his stomach. Was David going to kill him, he wondered. How could this be happening?

David stood ginning down at him. If you want to live you'll give me the combination to the safe. Bailey was in shock and shook his head back and forth indicating no. David picked up a bottle that had arsenic written on it. He held it in front of Bailey so he could see it. One more time David said, "What's the combination? Do it with your fingers." Bailey lifted one hand and showed three fingers.

"Left or right?" David asked.

Bailey raised his left hand.

"Next number," David said. Bailey used both hands and showed four on one hand and two on the other.

"Forty-two?" asked David.

Bailey shook his head yes and raised his right hand.

"Next," David demanded.

Bailed raised two fingers on one hand and then five on the other. He lifted his right hand and then made a circle twice.

David thought for a minute. "Twenty-five right, making two turns and stopping where?" he questioned.

Bailey held up four fingers.

David left to go try the numbers on the safe, which opened on the first try. David quickly wrote the numbers down before he went back to Bailey. David placed the chloroform rag over Bailey's face and knocked him out again, then removed the gag over Bailey's mouth and picked up a short twelve-inch tube and stuck it down Bailey's throat. David carefully measured out the amount of arsenic needed to end Bailey's life and began pouring it into a funnel connected to the tube that would empty the contents into Bailey's stomach. Bailey's eyes opened immediately and he began to gag. He was heaving up and down in spasms, and after a couple of minutes he wet his pants and succumbed to his death.

David had left to see what was in the safe. He counted over $1400 in cash, twenty-three gold watches, a large bag of gold fillings and another bag of gold wedding bands. He also took out some papers and found Bailey's will. He did have a nephew, and he had left everything to him. David took most of what was in the safe but put back $400.00 and placed the papers back in the same spot where he had taken them and locked the safe behind him. David took the stolen goods and put them in a small leather suitcase he had purchased at the general store and put the suitcase on the floor of the closet. David went back to Bailey and untied him. He wrapped some rags around

Bailey's neck to catch any fluids that might drip from his mouth when he moved the body. He took Bailey into the main office and placed Bailey in his chair in a slumping position making sure to keep Bailey's eyes looking at the ceiling. David cleaned up Bailey's face of any evidence and removed the rags from his face. He unlocked the front door and then picked up his suitcase and walked out the back door.

Trying not to be seen, David walked down to the opposite end of the alley and came around the front of the general store. He purchased some tobacco and paper wrappers and visited with the clerk for a few minutes. On his way back to Bailey's, he spoke to a few people on the street and made sure they saw him walk through the front door of Bailey's office. A second later he came running out.

"Help, Help, Mr. Bailey must have had a heart attack. Someone get the doctor." Five minutes later the town doctor was putting a stethoscope on Bailey's heart.

"Sorry, he's dead. His heart must have given out," said the doctor.

David said, "What should we do with the body?"

"You're the new undertaker now, bury him," the doctor said.

David had sent word to the pastor at the country church letting him know that he was going to bury Bailey's body at 2:00 p.m. in the afternoon at the local cemetery. He also posted a notice on the front window of the newspaper, letting people know about the funeral. Next David stopped at the attorney's office. After introductions, David told Bailey's attorney about his death and funeral at 2:00p.m. and that he was welcome to pick up Bailey's safe. David couldn't believe his plan was working so well. He smiled to himself and pulled one of the less expensive coffins from the warehouse in the back and placed it on the funeral wagon. David put Bailey on a rolling cart and rolled him to the back where the funeral wagon held the coffin. He lifted Bailey's body and put him in the coffin. Grabbing some nails, David hammered the top shut and added a few more nails for good measure.

About twenty of Beaumont's citizens showed up for the funeral and the pastor spoke for about twenty minutes before the grave diggers put Bailey's coffin in the ground. Afterwards they all came up to David and asked him to please stay on as Beaumont's new undertaker. They told him that he could continue to use Bailey's office and embalming building as it was leased to Bailey by the city and the lease could be taken over by him. David assured them that he would stay and it would be business as usual.

The next day David ordered a new sign for the front of the office. Billings Undertaking Services. He was proud of his new business. Bailey's attorney came by and asked David if he could pick up Bailey's personal items and his safe. David was happy to oblige. He said he didn't know the combination, but that he was welcome to take the safe with him. It must have weighed seventy-five pounds, and it was extremely heavy. David went to the back and got a rolling wagon. Between the two men they loaded it on to the wagon and they pulled it to the attorney's office to be held until the heir had been notified. David pulled the wagon down to the general store and bought a new safe that was a little smaller than the one Bailey had. He didn't want to act too pompous and call attention to a larger safe. It seemed like everyone was watching. After he put the safe in the office, David locked the door and put a note on it that said, "Family death- Back tomorrow". David took his small suitcase and went to the bank. He told them he needed a safety deposit box to put some of his papers in. David emptied everything in his suitcase and put it in the box. He kept out $100. He hated banks, but knew that he had to open an account so money could be wired to his account for his business.

David walked out of the bank with a smirk on his face. Everything was falling into place. He had never had access to this much money and this was just the beginning. He would wait a month before he spent anything so he wouldn't call attention to his new wealth. He also decided he would have some flyers printed out with prices and the services they would receive. It was more professional and he knew that was what the high end funeral homes did. Once he had some burials behind him he would have his own money to use.

It was business as usual the next day. David received a telegram that a body was coming in on the morning train and that the family would be on the same train. David got the funeral wagon ready and went to the station to meet the train. A man and woman got off the train and approached him.

"My father was visiting us in Oklahoma when he passed. My mother is buried in the city cemetery here and his plot is beside hers," said the man. "We would like to arrange for him to be buried next to her as soon as possible. If you have a pastor, I would like for him to say a few words over his grave."

The man helped David load the coffin onto the wagon. David offered to drop the couple off at the local hotel, but the man said his father had a farm about three miles outside of town. David took them to his office so they could sign some papers.

Afterwards, the man asked David if he knew of anyone who might be interested in buying his father's five-acre farm. David said he might be interested, and they all got into David's wagon and rode the three miles to the farm. It had a small, understated frame house with two bedrooms that was probably twenty years old and a good-sized barn that had been added a couple of years earlier. There was water well between the house and barn, and a corral with a shed for livestock. David liked it a lot and asked how much he wanted for it.

"Well, if you throw in the cost of the funeral and burial of my father, I'll let you have it for $300.00, furniture and all. The men shook hands and David agreed to pay him in cash after the funeral.

A few weeks went by and it was business as usual in the undertaking trade. Word on the street was that oil or gas might be discovered in the not too distant future, and that meant more and more people moving to the Beaumont area.

Darlene rang the bell at the undertaking office. David opened the door and she went in.

"What if I told you that you could keep Consuelo on a full time basis?" Darlene asked.

"You mean you want to sell her to me?" David asked.

Darlene told David she needed some money and he could take Consuelo on a full time basis if he gave her fifty dollars. It cost him more than he wanted to pay, but he knew Consuelo would keep her mouth shut and he could trust her. He needed help and he would teach Consuelo what she needed to know about preparing the bodies. They agreed and David paid Darlene her asking price on the condition that she would never try and get Consuelo to work for her when he was out of town. Darlene promised she wouldn't.

David spent his spare time fixing up a small room across from the embalming room as an apartment inside the business and put in a bed and dresser in it. He added a shower in the small water closet himself and was pleased with his handiwork. Consuelo was now his full time live-in.

David liked owning his own farm. It was a bit run down and also needed some work, but in time that could be taken care of. He kept two of his horses and wagon in town and then had ordered a new funeral hearse that would be delivered to Galveston for him to pick up in one month. On weekends, David would bring Consuelo to the farm to help him make repairs and improvements to the house. She wanted to move into the house with David, but he told her he wanted her to stay at the business and look after things when he was gone.

David's plan was to take five days off and go to Galveston, with a stopover in Houston to pawn some of his watches and rings. He meticulously showed Consuelo the procedures for the burial process. He also made arrangements for one of the black grave diggers to help Consuelo do the necessary procedures to prepare the bodies for burial. There would be no embalming while he was gone. Only he could do this. Consuelo worked with David for weeks as he patiently showed her the process, including extracting the gold fillings. David was going to leave a small amount of money in the safe and gave Consuelo the combination. Everything was in place now, and David told Consuelo he would be going to Houston, Texas, on business and would be home sometimes the next week.

Consuelo was scared and nervous the night before David was to leave. It made David angry and he hit Consuelo across her cheek, leaving a bruise. This was the second time she had seen this demon inside of him, and she was terrified His love-making was rough and tense that evening. He was not the David she knew, and she begged him not to hurt her. She was on the bed crying and he ordered her to stop crying.

Consuelo tried but couldn't stop whimpering. David slapped her with his open hand and told her to stop crying and she bit her lips trying to hold her cries in.

"You'll do as I say and never tell anyone what I did to you, understand?" Consuelo shook her head yes.

"Why do you do this to me?" she asked in a whisper.

"Because I can. I own you now. You do everything I tell you to do," David said. "You be a good girl always, and I won't need to hit you again."

Consuelo shook her head yes. She loved David and she would do anything to make him happy and David knew it.

The train ride to Houston only took a couple of hours and he mentally made a list in his mind of things he needed to do in Houston. Once he got to Houston, David stopped for a shave and haircut. He kept his beard but had it trimmed neatly and his haircut made David's wide eyes pop out. Next he stopped at a local pawn shop and took out six watches and four gold rings from his leather suitcase. He was paid a good price for them. The tailors were next on his list of things to do. Once David was fitted in his new business suit and tie, he hardly recognized himself. He looked handsome and all the ladies on the street smiled and stared at him.

When David got off the train in Galveston, he noticed that not many improvements had been made since he was here a couple of months earlier. There were gaps in between buildings where businesses once stood, and many were still boarded up. The trolleys were up and running but the streets that used to be filled with automobiles and carriages looked like a Sunday afternoon instead of a Tuesday.

He registered as David Billings at an out-of-the-way mid-priced hotel that wasn't too far from the hospital. The hotel was still under construction and there was a lot of activity going on. He had no idea if Catherine was working that day at the hospital, so he thought it would be a good place to start. Like the rest of the city, the hospital was under construction too, and there were stacks of new lumber, bricks and building material everywhere lining the streets. This was a good thing, David thought, because he could disappear into the fabric of the city.

CHAPTER 6

Catherine was asked to work at the hospital during her Thanksgiving break and she agreed. John had encouraged Catherine to re-enrol for the next semester at medical school. She had not yet gotten pregnant, and John knew she loved being a doctor. He had decided, after their last trip to Houston, he was no longer going to fight with her about her job, her schooling, or their future children. He loved her so much; he just wanted her to be happy. They moved into their new house over the weekend and it was perfect timing so they could enjoy the Thanksgiving holidays in their new home. All of the furniture had not arrived yet, but the beds, kitchen table and some of the living room furniture was already there.

John let his sister, Amelia, decorate her own room and she loved the furniture John had bought for her. Catherine and Amelia worked together selecting the wallpaper and furnishings for the rest of the house. They had spent Sunday moving their things from Minnie Wyman's boarding house and getting everything settled. After supper, Catherine went upstairs to their bedroom. Catherine loved playing tricks on John, so she told him she was tired and going to bed and he could take a shower first. After John had stripped and gone in the bathroom, Catherine removed her clothes and got in the shower with him. John smiled. He knew she had something up her sleeve and he hugged her tight.

"After we get through with our shower, I'm going to get

even!" John teased.

"I would hope so, Mr. Merit," Catherine teased back.

They took turns drying each other off and John carried her to bed. Their love-making had escalated to the next level. Catherine no longer dreamed about her earlier abduction and brutal torture. She had made peace with her demons. She desired John's love more than ever and he felt the same. It was as if they were one. Catherine was in the middle of her monthly cycle and she prayed this would be the night she would get pregnant.

The next morning when Catherine woke up, she looked around her new home and smiled to herself. She loved their new home and she knew once everything she had ordered for the house came in, that the small essentials would make it even more wonderful. She was excited about preparing her first thanksgiving meal. Amelia had promised to show her how to make dressing and bake a turkey. She was more worried about that than being in surgery with one of the doctors. She looked down at John just as he opened his eyes.

"What?" he said with a grin.

Catherine kissed him and said, "I'm just so excited about our new home. It's beautiful. Thank you."

John looked at his gold watch beside the bed and said, "You can thank me tonight. I've got to get ready for work."

Catherine reached for him as he tried to get out of bed and John laughed, "Tonight!"

David had difficulty sleeping the night before. He was anxious and nervous. If Catherine was not working today, he guessed he would stake out their house and try and abduct her when she left. David took a trolley over to the stables to buy a horse and tack so he could pick up his new hearse. He also purchased some additional rope, a knife, some bullets and a small hand gun and holster that he could carry under his coat. The hearse David purchased was similar to the one he used when he worked for Barker Funeral Home over a year ago, when he lived in Galveston before the storm. The hearse was waiting for him when he arrived at the stables, where he also bought a strong mare. After he hitched it up he went to another area in the stables to claim a large box with a coffin in it. He had specially ordered one that was similar to the one he used before when he had abducted Catherine. The small air holes had been drilled and when he finished with it, it would make the perfect tomb for Catherine's trip to Beaumont.

David had already checked out of the hotel and he knew he had to make his move that night or the next. He didn't want to leave Consuelo alone any longer than that, and it was a day's trip home in a one -horse hearse. David had collected everything he needed for their journey: jugs of extra drinking water, non perishable food and enough water and food for the horse to keep him at a steady pace. David found a place on the side of the hospital between some roof tiles to leave his hearse. He wore a derby and tilted it towards his face. He waited around the emergency room lobby for about ten minutes when he saw her. She had come out of one of the patient rooms and was writing something on a chart. She walked right by him and didn't look up She was more beautiful than ever and he felt his blood rush when she walked past him. It was mid afternoon and he figured he had less than two hours before she quit work. He walked to a café not far away and ate a big meal. If everything went according to plan, once he had Catherine, he would leave the city in a steady trot and be in Texas City within an hour after he left.

David hid behind a stack of roof tiles and waited outside the emergency room doors. He wanted a cigarette and he took out his tobacco and rolled a couple while he waited. He had rolled three and figured that was enough to get him to Texas City where he would make his first stop.

Catherine had become accustomed to using the emergency room exit when she left. It was closer to the trolley. She was off at 6:30 that evening but it was closer to 7:when she left. David had gotten a little drowsy sitting on a stack of roof tiles, but he quickly became alert when he saw the doors swing open and Catherine Merit walked out.

Catherine was already thinking of her menu for Thanksgiving and doing the grocery shopping with John. They both were going to be off on Wednesday and Catherine was looking forward to their evening together. She crossed the street and walked past the roof tiles and hearse, not noticing the man standing beside it. She did notice that the hearse was different from the one that usually waited outside the hospital, but thought that they may have gotten a new one.

David was quick and methodical. He grabbed her and put the handkerchief soaked in chloroform over Catherine's face. She went limp as David opened the back door and heaved her inside. He got in, closed the door and picked up Catherine, placing her in the coffin. He tied her hands and pulled them down in front of her, extending the rope to her feet, and then tied the end to a hook he had put at the base of the coffin. She was gagged and David put the handkerchief to Catherine's face again leaving it on longer. It was going to be a long trip and he wanted her unconscious.

They travelled across the wagon bridge from Galveston to the mainland and David felt relieved once he was on the other side. Her husband was probably missing her by now and had gone to look for her, he thought as he laughed to himself. By the time her poor husband figured out she was gone, David would be at his farm in Beaumont.

John looked at the grandfather clock at 7:25p.m.. Catherine had made her usual call earlier, letting him know that she would be leaving the hospital by 7:00. She was normally home by now, but he figured she missed the first trolley and would be home in the next ten minutes or so.

He visited with Amelia for a while and he started getting upset that Catherine had not come home, as she said she would. He dialed the number for the hospital and after waiting for about ten minutes, one of the nurses came on and told him that Catherine had signed out and left at 7:00p.m. John put the phone down and was white as a sheet.

"What did they say?" asked Amelia.

He told her what they said and he grabbed his jacket and told Amelia he was going to look for her. John walked in the direction Catherine always used, and boarded the trolley. He was angry because Catherine had promised that she would always leave before dark. He got off the trolley and started walking towards the hospital. He had not noticed all the mess that was on the streets by the hospital before. Building materials, roof tiles, pipes, and who knows what else, John thought. It was a perfect place for someone to lie in wait to abduct someone. Why hadn't he paid closer attention to this? He scolded himself. There was a nagging pain in the pit of his stomach when he went into the back entrance of the emergency room. He stopped and asked those closest to the exit if anyone had seen Catherine leave.

One nurse said that Catherine waved goodbye to her when she left. Another said he passed her on the street, when he was approaching the hospital. John's eyes began to tear. He was in a state of panic. He ran outside to the middle of the street and screamed Catherine's name at the top of his lungs. There was a deafening silence.

John went to the front of the hospital and went in to the use the phone to call Amelia. Catherine was not at home. John went outside and found a police officer patrolling the streets. John was hyperventilating and he could barely talk.

"Take it easy," said the officer. "Tell me what's wrong."

John told him his plight and the police officer listened intently.

"Are you sure she didn't go meet someone else for dinner or something?"

John grew angry and tried to keep calm, but he knew Catherine didn't leave willingly with anyone. After fifteen minutes of questioning, John could not contain himself.

"Damn it!" he said. "Someone has taken her. She would not

leave with anyone but me," he insisted.

There were several people gathered around John and the policeman. Someone must have called the police station, because two more officers arrived at the scene. John had to repeat his plight again. Just then, Sergeant Husky came up and took John by the arm and led him into the hospital waiting room. This was not their first interview. It was déjà-vu all over again. After interviewing everyone at the hospital, Sergeant Husky told John to go home and get some sleep. They would work on the case all night and get back with him in the morning. John walked home as it began a misty rain. He cried most of the way and when he got home, he sat on the front porch of his house and damned God for allowing this to happen to Catherine again. Amelia opened the door and tried to get John to come inside. He finally walked in and collapsed on the floor. John crawled over to the sofa and watched the front door, willing Catherine to walk in. He must have finally fallen asleep.

When he woke up it was 6:00a.m. John called the police station. Sergeant Husky was out and would not be back for another hour. John put on his coat and left to go to the station and wait. He was slumped in a chair in the waiting room of the police station when Husky walked in. John could tell by looking at him that they knew nothing.

"I've had my men out all night looking. It's like she disappeared into thin air," Husky said.

Husky was at a loss of what to do. He knew people didn't just disappear. John put his head down in his hands and then looked up.

"Is there any possibility David Brooks survived that tornado?" John asked. "Did they ever find his body?" he continued.

Husky shook his head no.

"I don't see how anyone who wasn't in a storm cellar could have made it through that one. My brother in Houston, who is with their police department, said the Sugar Land tornado struck a path straight through that plantation where Brooks was and the only survivors were the ones in the storm cellar. I've already sent a wire to my brother in Houston to see if they can turn up anything else on Brooks," Husky said.

John used Sergeant Husky's phone to call the bank and tell them he would not be in the rest of the day. Next, he called Amelia and gave her an update, and said he would be home later. John gave Husky his home phone number again and then left to go to St. Mary's Catholic Church.

John lit a candle and was on his knees in front of the statue of Mary Magdalene. Father Jonathan walked up to him and put his hand on his shoulder.

"When you have finished," he said, "come into my office."

John made the sign of the cross and got up, following Father Jonathan into his office. The priest offered John a chair, and he sat in it. John broke down again and confessed that he had cursed God out loud for whatever had happened to Catherine. Father Jonathan listened to John talk about how happy they had been and their plans to have children. John talked for over an hour about how he felt and that the last time this happened, it had taken Catherine over a year before she was able to move on.

"I just don't know what to do," John said.

Father Jonathan knew there was nothing he could say that would make John feel better, so he just listened.

"We must continue to pray and I will ask the sisters to pray a special prayer for Catherine. We are here for you, John," Father Jonathan said.

CHAPTER 7

David was making good time, and he was passing through Texas City. He wanted to put some distance between him and Galveston, and decided to cut around through League City and Baytown, bypassing Houston. It had been over a year since the tornado. He didn't think they could possibly suspect he was still alive, and that he had come back for Catherine, but he did not want to leave anything to chance. There was a half-moon, but with the winding roads, he decided to pull off when he saw a grove of trees just about seventy-five feet off the road. He needed to water his horse and give it a rest and he did not want to chance an accident.

Catherine woke up about an hour after they had left Galveston and the same horror flooded her mind that she had experience before. She had a terrible headache and she thought she might be dreaming. They had hit a bump in the road, and it moved the coffin up and down. She knew she was inside something and that her hands and feet were bound. Her mouth was dry from the gag and she could still smell the chloroform. She did not smell human decomposition that she had smelled in the box before. In fact, the box smelled of new wood. Her body was aching and she was thirsty and scared. David Brooks was dead, she thought, or was he? she questioned.

The ride was rugged and extremely uncomfortable. She was tossed around inside the box and every time the carriage hit a pothole, she would bounce from side to side. The ride seemed endless and she prayed for it to be over soon. She had no idea how long they had been travelling, but knew they must be far away from Galveston, She knew John was probably looking for her by now and there was a feeling of helplessness. No one would ever think of looking outside of Galveston for her. Sheer panic crept through her body and her insides felt like they were frozen in ice.

The wagon, or buggy, she was in stopped, and she listened intently. She heard the horse lapping water and a man's voice. Then the back door opened and she felt weight move the wagon down. Oh God, she thought, he's in here now. She heard the latches snap open and the lid came up. There was some light coming from a candle and she smelled the sulphur from the burned match. David untied the rope at the base of the coffin and lifted her out. She recognized him immediately and her heart skipped a beat. Why, after all this time, did he come back for her? She tensed and waited in fear.

"My little Catherine," David said. "Welcome back. I'm going to take your gag off so you can have some water. Do not scream, or there will be consequences."

David poured some water in a tin cup and pulled her gag down. Catherine drank all of it. She was breathing hard and she wanted to spit into his face, but knew it would lead to a beating, so she resisted. David took the bindings off her feet and left her hands tied in front of her. Visions of the last abduction appeared before her and she wanted to die.

"Where are you taking me?" she asked.

"To our new home," he answered.

He got up on his knees and began unbuttoning his pants and she gasped when she saw his manhood. David blew the candle out and pulled up Catherine's dress. He jerked off her pantalets and moved on top of her.

"No, please......no," she begged.

He unbuttoned the top of her dress and began kissing her breast as he began violating her. She started crying and the cold emptiness of the moment encased her body, leaving her frozen in despair. Her only comfort was numbness. Relief was unimaginable. She cried softly as David rolled over and fell asleep. He was half on top of her, making it difficult for her to move. The night seemed endless and sleep would not come. Her life was over now. She knew in her heart David would never let her leave alive.

David woke up about 5:00a.m. and unlocked the back door. He got out and went over to a tree to take a leak. He jerked Catherine up and carried her over to a smaller tree and tied her hands to a branch.

"I took your pantalets off so you can just squat," he said.

She stood there and moved her legs apart feeling the warmth run down her legs. Tears were falling down her cheek and she felt the indignity of the moment. David gave the horse some oats to eat and some water and left Catherine standing by the tree. She looked around and saw no one. Not that she expected to.

David untied her from the tree and carried her back to the hearse. He gave her some more water and broke off a piece of bread and told her to open her mouth. She didn't and it made him mad. He grabbed her hair and pulled her head back. He made a fist, like he was going to hit her and she opened her mouth. The bread was hard to chew, but she forced herself to eat it. When David finished eating, he went outside to check on the horse and get it ready for their trip. Catherine lay still, listening, wondering and praying. She heard the key in the lock again and the door opened. David was again in a kneeling position and opened his trousers, pulling them down. He lifted her dress up and entered her once more, violating her body and she couldn't help but scream. She had never felt such indignity, such disgrace, and the humiliation was painful. David gagged her again and placed her in the coffin. After he finished tying her up, he closed the lid and locked it. She began kicking and hammering at the box. David opened it and picked up his gun and put it between her eyes. She stilled. He closed and locked the lid again and left, locking the door behind him.

Catherine lay in the darkness, willing herself to die. The bindings on her hands and legs were tearing into her flesh and beginning to burn. The carriage heaved up and down the faster they drove, and she wondered if the nightmare would ever end.

David pushed the horse to its limits and after a couple of hours the horse began snorting and slowing down. David cursed and pulled off the road into another cluster of trees. The horse probably wasn't used to traveling long distances, so he needed to give it a rest. One hour, he thought. It was almost 9:00 a.m. He took out a cigarette and smoked it while giving the horse some more water. The water was almost gone, so he figured he better look for a cistern or a river to refill the can. He was getting close to civilization so he had to be careful. David unlocked the hearse again and took out his bottle of chloroform and wet the handkerchief. He crawled in and opened the lid to the coffin and saw Catherine's pitiful face. He took the gag off, and gave her some water and she drank it all. He pulled the gag back up and then placed the handkerchief soaked with chloroform over her face for a couple of minutes. She tried to resist, but finally passed out. It was easier this way, he thought. He needed to stop at the next town and get something to eat and replenish the horse's water.

A couple of miles further he passed through a small town. Catherine would probably sleep for at least another hour, so he stopped at a café and ate a big meal. Afterwards, he asked if he could use their cistern outside and fill his water can. Everyone was nice to him and asked where he was going. Everyone respected the undertaker, he told himself. He found out he was about an hour's ride away from getting home. He checked his horse and gave it more water. He could slow down now. After all, he did not want to kill his horse.

David finally made his way to his farm outside of Beaumont. It was almost 3:00p.m.and he was relieved that everything went according to his plans. He was even home a day early. He opened the door to his barn, removed the tack and straps from the horse, and put it in the stable. He filled up the water can and put some hay and oats in the stable for his horse. David unlocked the back end of the hearse and crawled in, unlocking the coffin. Catherine was awake. He lifted her out and took the gag off.

"Aint nobody around for miles, but if you scream, you will have consequences," David told her.

He lifted Catherine out of the coffin and placed her beside it. Once he got out, he picked her up, threw her over his shoulder, and carried her into the house like a sack of potatoes. He took off the gag and untied her. He grabbed her hand and pulled her through the small house and to the water closet. He put her in it and closed the door and locked it.

It was dark and the window had been boarded up, but a small amount of light crept through two small openings between the cracks. She looked at her image in the medicine cabinet and then looked away. Her hair was a mess and there was a bruise on her forehead from smashing into the side of the coffin. She went to the bathroom sink and carefully washed her face. She had no idea where she was. She waited and listened. David did not come back. Where was he, how long was he going to keep her here, she thought to herself. She tried the door and it was locked. There was a towel and her body hurt, so she filled the old bathtub with water. It was cold and she could only stay in a few minutes before she began to shiver. She washed her body quickly, scrubbing every inch of it, all the while shivering. She couldn't stand the cold any longer, so she got out and dried off. She looked in the medicine cabinet for something to put on the burns from the ropes, but there was nothing in it. She put her dress back on and sat on the side of the tub and started to cry.

David locked up the farmhouse and saddled up his new mare. He decided he would take the hearse into town the next day so his horse wouldn't be so stressed. He rode up to his office, and when he opened the door, Consuelo ran up to him and kissed him. He grinned at her and gave her a small box. She opened it and inside was a small pair of pearl earrings. She put them on and told David how happy she was he was home.

"Tell me what's been going on," he said.

Consuelo told him they had only one burial and that she put the gold from the teeth and the money in the safe.

"Good girl," he said.

He gave her a few dollars and told her to go get some food from the diner. While she was gone, he checked his safe and the rest of the building. He locked everything up and went back to his desk. He read the newspaper Consuelo had put out for him, and waited for her to bring the food back. His mind was on Catherine. She would be fine for now in the water closet, but he knew he had to work on something more permanent. In time, they would get married and she would be his wife. He still had to break her spirit and he wasn't sure how long it would take. She was strong willed, but he felt that a few beatings would bring her around.

Consuelo returned with the food and she was in a good mood. They ate at his desk. He knew Consuelo would expect him to stay the night with her, but he had to get back to Catherine.

When she finished, she got up and came around the back and started massaging his shoulders. He began to relax and told her to bring him a glass of whiskey. She obeyed and David drank it down. He got up and walked back to the small apartment where Consuelo lived now, and he undressed. Consuelo began taking off her clothes, too. She crawled under the covers and waited for him. David stayed with her for about an hour and then he got up and dressed.

"Can I come, too?" she asked.

"Not tonight," David said as he left and closed the door.

It was dark and about 8:00 p.m. when Catherine heard the gallop of a horse. She was scared, but relieved that she might get out of the water closet. The room was tiny and there was very little room to walk around. She had spent her time in the small room thinking of

John in between crying and screaming. She knew John would be crazy with worry, and she feared she might never see him again. The thought was agonizing. She tried to calculate how much time had passed, but she slept and was knocked out so much of the time, it was impossible to try and calculate.

David unlocked the door and pulled Catherine into the kitchen and pushed her into a chair.

"There is some bread and cheese in the icebox if you want to make a grilled cheese sandwich. I know your mother liked them." Catherine just looked at him and didn't say anything.

David began taking off his belt and then he slapped the table with it, just missing Catherine's arm. It scared Catherine so much she fell off the chair. David grabbed her hair and pulled her up and sat her back on the chair. She wanted to strike back at him, but his powerful hands were holding her tight and hurting the burns on her wrists.

"When I tell you to do something, I mean for you to do it, understand?" he shouted at her. "Now feed yourself," he ordered.

Catherine got up and opened the icebox. The ice had melted and nothing in the box was cold. She took the bread and cheese out and asked where a knife was. He laughed and picked up the cheese. He took out his pocketknife and cut two slices and handed them to her. His hands were dirty and Catherine brushed off the cheese with her fingers before putting it inside the bread. David poured himself some whiskey and sat drinking it and watching Catherine.

"Is it all right to drink the water?" she asked.

"It's a clean well. Hasn't killed me yet," he answered.

She got up and pumped some water into a cup. David poured himself another drink and continued to stare at her. She had only taken a few bites of her sandwich when David said, "Take off your clothes."

"Now?" Catherine asked.

"Now, unless you want me to do it for you," he said.

He watched as she began removing her clothing, taking off her skirt and underclothes and then her blouse. She was standing naked with her arms folded and she looked at the floor. There was no heat in the house and the room was dank and had a musty odor.

David knew it wouldn't take long to break her spirit. He had seen it at prison camp. If a convict didn't respond to the whipping, they were stripped and forced to stand naked in front of all the prisoners for hours. It was intimidating and demeaning. He could see it in Catherine's face now. He sat watching her, and she stood paralyzed, afraid to move, wondering what he was going to do now. Catherine was afraid to talk, so she stood and waited. She stared down at the table, not wanting to make eye contact with David. She was humiliated. He made her stand there for over thirty minutes and she willed herself not to cry. Still, tears ran slowly down her cheeks. She did not look at David.

"Pick up your sandwich and eat it," he demanded.

Catherine obeyed, taking only small bites. She gagged and prayed she wouldn't throw up. David got up and took off his shirt. He stood in front of her and then walked over and tilted her chin up to his, kissing her hard. She did not respond. He slapped her and she almost fell, but he caught her.

"I thought you were smarter than that, Catherine. When I kiss you, you're supposed to kiss me back."

She was humiliated and she wanted to run, but knew he would just catch her. David told her to undress him. She walked over to where he was now standing, and unbuttoned his shirt, taking it off of him. David's muscular frame was overpowering and she tensed as her hands touched his body. David kissed her again and she tried to kiss him back, so he wouldn't hit her. David helped her finish undressing him, and then picked her up and carried her to the bedroom.

He was nicer to her this time and she tried to act more willing, hoping that by being more consensual, he wouldn't be so rough. Afterwards, Catherine lay under the covers after David went to sleep and she wondered how she would ever survive this. She had no idea where they were, but she knew it was at least a day or so ride from Galveston. Even if she could escape, there was no light and the room was dark. Where would she go? Catherine couldn't imagine another night with David, and she prayed she could just die. She quietly got out of bed and tried to open the door, but it was locked. It was cold and she was naked, so she got back under the covers. She began praying and finally drifted off to sleep.

The next morning when she woke up, David was gone and when she moved her legs, they were chained together. She stood up and looked down. She was in shackles and the chain between her feet only extended about ten inches. She could only take small steps. She sat back down on the bed and felt totally isolated and alone. She looked around the room for something to wear and hobbled over to the closet. There was a long sleeping gown and some men's shirts hanging up. She grabbed the sleeping gown and put it over her head. Her shoes would not fit over the chains, so she opened a drawer and found a pair of David's socks and put them on. She was cold and wrapped the blanket around her. She tried to remember what day it was and then sat back down on the bed when she remembered. It had to be Thanksgiving. She and John were planning to spend their first Thanksgiving in their new home. She was unable to cry anymore. She decided to walk herself through the happy Thanksgiving they had planned. She and Amelia would be in the kitchen getting things ready. John would bring flowers and help prepare the table. They would drink wine and enjoy their meal and later that afternoon she and John would go upstairs to their room and make love. Oh, John, I miss you so much, she thought. She knew they would never be able to spend another Thanksgiving together, and now she had to concentrate on trying to survive.

Catherine hobbled into the kitchen and opened all the drawers and cupboards looking for something, anything she could use to get the chains off. The house was sparsely furnished and most of the cabinets and drawers were empty. There were some tea bags on the counter and Catherine filled the pot with water to boil. She did find some oatmeal and once the water boiled she made herself some breakfast and hot tea. She would feel better after she ate, she thought.

She had eaten so little over the last few days. She could starve herself, but knew that was a horrible way to die. She could provoke David enough to kill her, she thought, but he didn't want her dead, and his beatings would only make her more miserable. Her mind was racing, and it came to her that she could hang herself. She looked through David's things to see if she could find a belt. She looked around the house for something she could tie into a noose. There was nothing. Even the doors were taken off the hinges except for the bathroom and his bedroom. She heard the key in the front door and turned around. David came in with some groceries and put them on the table.

"I'm glad you found something to wear," he said.

She didn't answer.

"Make me some breakfast," he ordered.

Catherine hobbled over to the table and started taking the groceries out. David grabbed her hand and twisted her arm behind her. He started kissing her neck and he put his other hand on her breast. Catherine stood frozen. She didn't want him to slap her and figured that if she just submitted to him, he might be gentler. David picked her up and put her on the table. He took out a key and removed the shackles from her ankles. He pulled her gown up and opened his pants. He raped her again and she begged him to stop, but he didn't. Afterwards, he told Catherine to make his breakfast and he went into the water closet. Catherine tried to get up, but fell to the floor. She was broken and she knew in her heart she could never face John again.

Catherine went to the door and tried to go outside. It seemed stuck and she pulled with all her force trying to open it, but it wouldn't open.

"Give it up, Catherine," David said. "You're mine now and I will never let you go."

She ran up to him and started hitting his chest with her fist.

"I hate you, I hate you," Catherine cried, and she fell to the floor.

"Sit," he ordered. Catherine slowly got up and sat in the chair.

"You have a choice, Catherine," David said softly. We can repeat this every night and day and I'll lock you in the water closet during the day, or you can just accept your fate and be content as my wife.

"I'm already married," she said.

"That's just a piece of paper. I'm going to ask you one more time. Are you going to mind me? Or, I could come up with a few more ways to torture you to break your spirit. What will it be?" he asked.

She started crying and he pulled her into his lap. He held her and stroked her tenderly.

"Oh Catherine, I really don't want to see you hurt," David told her softly.

David carried her to the bedroom and pulled the covers back and crawled in bed with her.

He raped her again and she did not fight him.

Catherine began mumbling something and David couldn't understand her.

"Please kill me," she whispered. She began sobbing uncontrollably. David left and poured himself some whiskey. He wondered that maybe he had gone too far. He locked the door to the bedroom and left again.

Catherine lay on the bed staring into space. She must have fallen asleep, because when she woke she heard someone in the kitchen. She didn't get up, and she really didn't care. If it were David, he would just have to come and get her. She was dying inside and she was afraid it was going to be a long, slow death.

David walked over and sat down on the bed beside her. He had put a cup on the side table.

"I'm sorry I had to do it this way, but I had to break you. I think you have learned your lesson now. I brought you a warm cup of soup."

David pulled her up on her pillow and put the other pillow behind her. He put the cup of soup in her hand and told her to drink. She sipped from the cup.

"In time, you will grow to depend on me and maybe even love me," David said. "I feel sure that after what you have been through, you won't want to go back to your husband."

Catherine sat mute, drinking the soup. She knew he was right about the fact that she would not go back to John. It was difficult the first time when she had gotten away, and now she knew she would never be good enough for John. David made sure of that.

CHAPTER 8

It was difficult for John to go back to work after Catherine's abduction, but he had no choice. He had gotten the name of a private detective firm in Houston, Texas, from Sgt Husky at the Galveston police department.

"Maybe a private investigator could talk to some of the people at that plantation where David Brooks was," Husky said. "If he survived the tornado, maybe someone saw something. Sugar Land is out of the jurisdiction of Galveston and Houston where my brother-in-law works. It may be pricey, but that's the only thing I can suggest."

John made an appointment with one of their top men at the investigation firm of Conner & Hopper by the name of Larry Conner, and they were to meet on Saturday at 1:00 p.m. in Houston.

Larry was waiting in the lobby of the hotel when John checked in. The two men went to the bar and ordered drinks while John filled him in on the details of the first abduction, and also the death of Catherine's mother. John had given Larry David's name earlier in the week, so Larry could do some investigative work before they met. John told Larry about the night Catherine went missing, and realized he had very little to tell him.

Larry finished his drink and they both order another one.

"I've been doing some checking, and Brooks has a record a mile long. He is wanted in New York for murder, and also Denver, Colorado, for rape and murder. The Houston police think he may have been involved in the murder of three, maybe four prostitutes in the Fourth Ward. They have finger prints matching him to the murders, and also the murder of a prostitute in Galveston.

"What has taken the police so long to find this out?" John asked.

"They were still putting the pieces together when Brooks went missing at the prison farm. They dropped everything when they assumed he was dead," Larry began. "The first place I'm going to check out is the prison farm in Sugar Land. Someone there saw something, and I won't leave until I get answers," Larry said.

Larry told John he needed $250.00 up front and the rest would be billed. He would stay in touch. John was willing to do whatever it took to find Catherine, and he would go to the poor house, if necessary.

Alex Cooper was sitting in the lobby of the Lancaster Hotel waiting on a telegram. He had been there for two days, and figured he might have to just pack up and go back to Dallas, Texas, where his offices were. He opened the Houston Daily Post newspaper on January 11, 1901, and he smiled. The headlines clearly gave him notice of what his next assignment would be:

Oil Struck Near Beaumont
A stream of petroleum shot into the air for One
Hundred Ft. About three miles south of the city there
is spouting an oil well the equal of which cannot be
seen in the United States or elsewhere in the World.

Alex knew it was just a matter of an hour or so before he would get the telegram that would instruct him to go to Beaumont, Texas, immediately. He had already checked on the train schedule and there were two more trains coming though in route to Beaumont, the last one leaving at 5:00p.m.

He got up and went into the bar to get a beer while he waited.

He sat at the far end of the bar and saw two men sitting at a table close to him, heavy in conversation. He could see one of the men out of the corner of his eye and he couldn't help but hear parts of the conversation. He felt sorry for the poor guy who was obviously talking to a private detective. He caught the part about the wife being abducted from Galveston, and that he was looking for her, but had no idea who took her. He heard another name, David Brooks, and something about a prison farm, and that Brooks might have died during a tornado at the same time Galveston had the devastating storm that killed over six thousand people. It was a pitiful story, he thought. He had heard similar ones before. After all, he worked for an oil company and he was around a lot of men. Most of the time, the wife had run off with another man. When he heard the fee of the private investigator, he almost spit out his drink. The poor soul must want her really bad, he thought. He did catch the name, Catherine, and that she was just eighteen years old.

"You have a telegram, sir," said the bellman.

Alex took out some change and tipped him.

It was short and immediate:

Gusher hit, Beaumont, Texas.
Leave Immediately, Boss

Alex folded it carefully, and stuck it in his pocket. When he got up, he took a look at the two men. They didn't notice him. He noticed the man telling the story was probably about thirty. Must have been an arranged marriage, Alex thought to himself. There's a good twelve years difference in their ages.

Alex packed his small suitcase and checked out of the Lancaster. It was cool outside and he flagged down a ride. He looked at his watch and knew if he hurried, he would have just enough time to make the 3:00 train and get into Beaumont before dark.

Alex was twenty-eight years old and had only lived in Dallas,

Texas a short while. He had started his career in oil after he finished college with a degree in engineering and traveled as an oil scout, never staying too long in one place. He had moved up the ladder in his company and his job was to coordinate everything between the land owners, the oil leases, the attorneys and the oil company. Being gifted with good instincts and the ability to be a good negotiator, he was well respected in his field, and he made an effort to be fair to everyone. He detested dirty deals and the scum that tried to squeeze one more dollar out of the innocent land owner. There was always enough to go around and this new discovery was going to put a lot of money in a lot of people's pockets. His job was to get his piece of the pie for his company, before the vultures started scratching at the cavities of the deals.

Alex was tall, with wide shoulders and a lean body and he always sported a tan on his face from riding the hillsides and pastures on his horse. He had an engaging personality and he was not only strong, but extremely good looking. His exceedingly good looks made the ladies pay attention. Alex had come close to getting married once, and was going to ask his sweetheart to get married when he got back from one of his long trips. Before he had a chance to ask her, she married someone else. He got over it, but he never seemed to stay in one place long enough to develop another relationship. Alex's mother and younger sister had been killed in a fire when he was sixteen, and his father could not stop grieving. His father had died a year later. Alex's dad had left him a small amount of money and a $5,000 life insurance policy that Alex used for college. He promised his dad before his death that he would make something of himself.

The train was packed with people and Alex wondered how many were headed to Beaumont for the same reason he was. He got the last seat in the dining car and ordered a scotch from the bar. He had called ahead and reserved a room at the Ambassador Hotel in downtown Beaumont. Alex was told in a previous letter that there would be several horses reserved at the stables in his company's name and it looked like his company had taken care of everything else he needed. Alex liked to use his own horse, Pilgrim, and since he would be in Galveston for a while, they agreed to send Pilgrim to Beaumont by train before the end of the week.

Word was all over the streets in Beaumont about the gusher that had exploded out of the ground that morning. The main street was bustling with activity and people were being turned away from all the hotels and boarding houses. Beaumont just wasn't prepared for the overwhelming number of people who were now migrating in from everywhere. The train continued to carry people from every direction into the now overflowing Beaumont. In a matter of days, thousands of people flocked into the already overcrowded town, and it was an everyday occurrence. Alex had settled in at a nice boarding house, beating the crowd by only one day, and he was ready for action.

David was busy working in the embalming room. There were two deaths from the explosion of the oil well at Spindletop and the company wanted them embalmed and placed in coffins to be shipped back to each deceased person's hometown. Consuelo was helping David as much as she could, but knew nothing about the embalming procedures. David was short with her and was yelling at her a lot. He had stopped staying overnight with her in the apartment she lived in behind the morgue, and she wondered if there was another woman. He had been different since he came back from his business trip to Houston. Their intimacy was no longer tender, and he slept with her only to pleasure himself. When she would ask him to stay, he would get angry and often hit her. She was so in love with David, and was worried that she might lose him.

It was late in the evening when David finished preparing the bodies and dropped the two coffins at the train station. He was going to charge the company double because they wanted it done quickly, and to certain specifications. It was done now, and he was ready to go home to Catherine. Consuelo came up to him and asked what he wanted her to get for dinner.

"Nothing, I'm tired and going home," he said.

"You have a new woman?" asked Consuelo.

David didn't answer. He didn't want to get into it right now.

Catherine had been in David's captivity for almost eight weeks, and she had finally accepted the fact that David would never let he go. She felt like she was living in a vacuum and would do almost anything to get out of the prison she was in. Catherine tried not to antagonize David, but she was always doing something wrong. She tried to remember how long she had been a prisoner in the house and she calculated at least a month or more.

One morning she woke up sick at her stomach and she made it to the bathroom just in time. David did not put the shackles on until right before he left, so she ran as fast as she could. She threw up a couple of times and David came in and asked her if she was all right.

"I think I'm pregnant," she said. David figured in his mind how long she had been there.

"Is it his?" David asked.

"No!" Catherine said. "It's yours."

David hadn't thought about having kids, but he grinned at the thought of it.

"How can you be so sure?" he asked.

"You got me pregnant the last time, and I miscarried. I have not been able to get pregnant with my husband."

David seemed to be pleased with the answer. Actually, Catherine had no idea which man was the father. She had slept with both of them, but she was afraid if David knew that, he might hurt her or force her to lose the baby.

Her future was dismal and now she was pregnant. She wondered if she would be able to keep the baby to full term. They had come to an understanding when she found out she was pregnant and told David it was his chid. He agreed he would not hit her anywhere that would hurt the baby. Perhaps she could have some kind of life if she had a child with David, she thought. It would not be a perfect life, but it was all she could think about now. She was having a baby, and even though it may not be with the man she loved, it would be hers and she had to protect it.

Catherine tried to please David in every way. She stopped resisting the rapes, and always imagined being somewhere else with John when it happened. The days seemed endless and the boredom was overwhelming. David had brought her a catalogue and she spent most of her idle time looking at baby things and praying. She tried to keep her mind occupied by recalling what she had learned at medical school. Her mundane existence created a lot of opportunity to think about what motherhood would be like. She thought of her mother and younger sister and she ached for John. She knew he was devastated. Their love was so great she worried he might never get over losing her.

Catherine heard David open the barn door and the tension rose in her upper body. She tried to appear busy when he came in. She could see he was tired and irritated. He grabbed her and pulled her back to the bedroom.

He hadn't said anything to her when he came in, but his demeanor projected anger, and she hoped he wouldn't take it out on her. She knew what was coming so she began taking off the nightgown. She wasn't doing it fast enough, so he started pulling at her gown. He twisted her arm behind her back. She tried not to scream, but it was extremely painful. He was rough and was only thinking of his immediate needs and pleasure. When he finished, she was crying. She turned over and put her face in the pillow, trying to muffle her cries. She wondered if the madness would ever stop. David got up and went into the kitchen to eat supper.

After he finished he went into the bedroom and sat on the bed beside her. "I'm sorry," he said. "I hope I didn't hurt you or the baby."

She turned and looked at him and said, "You are going to kill our child if you continue to batter me for no reason. Is that what you want?" she asked still crying.

David didn't answer and went back into the kitchen. Catherine put on a robe and followed him.

"I've done everything you have told me to do, but I can't live like this. You are going to kill us. Please, just stop."

Catherine knew she had crossed the line and waited for David to hit her. He got up and drew his arm back and Catherine blocked her face with her hands waiting for the blow. He stopped and looked at her and then went outside.

Catherine was sitting at the kitchen table with her face in her hands when David came back in.

"I know I have a violent temper, and I'm sorry," he said. "Are you willing to do anything I demand from you?" he asked her.

Catherine said yes, afraid that a no would provoke him. David went on to tell her about the discovery of the oil well and that he needed more help at the morgue. He wanted Catherine to help him, but only under certain conditions. Catherine listened intently. She would do anything to get out of this prison she was in.

"I will introduce you as my mail-order, mute wife. You will talk to no one and do as I say," David finished. "Understood?" he asked.

Catherine answered yes.

"The consequences will be severe if you talk or even look at anyone, understood?" David asked again.

Catherine said yes. "What will I do for clothes?" she asked.

"You can wear Consuelo's clothes. You can put something on when we get there."

Catherine had no idea who Consuelo was and was afraid to ask.

The next morning Catherine tried to piece together the skirt and top she had worn when David took her. Her laboratory coat was missing a few buttons but it looked presentable. David looked at her and took one of his coats out of the closet and handed it to her.

"It's cold outside and you'll need this. Remember, you can't speak. At the morgue if you have a question, write on paper and give it to me," David reminded her.

Catherine would have done almost anything to leave the walls of the house she was imprisoned in. She had not been outside since she was taken. The ride into town on the wagon was cool, but she enjoyed the fresh air. They pulled up to the back of a wide building with a large door. David got out and unlocked it, pulling it open enough for them to take the horse and wagon in. He closed and locked the door behind him. When David and Catherine walked in, Consuelo was just coming out of her apartment. She looked at Catherine and then David. "Consuelo, this is my wife, Catherine," David said.

Consuelo did not answer, but turned and ran back into the apartment. David followed her and closed the door. Consuelo said something in Spanish and David slapped her. Consuelo cried out and David began yelling at her. Catherine looked around wanting to make a run for it but she had no idea where to go. She knew David locked the door they came in. She heard another slap and a cry. Catherine was paralyzed with fear. She had no idea who this Consuelo was. Had he taken her, too? She wondered. The door to the apartment was not closed all the way and she could see David standing over Consuelo, and then he was on top of her on the bed. Catherine wanted to scream. She opened the door to the office, and before she could make an exit, David ran after her and grabbed her; he pulled her back in, and dragged her into the apartment where Consuelo was. He slapped Catherine hard and he caught her before she fell. He slapped her again and she cried out. Consuelo watched in shock.

"You try that again, and the baby's gonna be gone," David said.

Consuelo looked at Catherine, not sure she understood about the baby being gone. David grabbed Consuelo and told her to go back into the apartment and close the door. She left David and Catherine alone.

David turned to Catherine; pulling his hand back like he was going to slap her again and she flinched. She was crying. "I guess I made a mistake bringing you here." David said.

"No! I wasn't trying to leave, I thought it was a closet and I was looking for some clothes," Catherine said, not sure David believed her.

"All right, I'll give you one more chance. We have another body coming in, and I want to show you the embalming process. Your medical school education should help you with that," David told Catherine.

He walked over to the closet and opened it. "Take some of the clothes home when we leave tonight."

David opened the door to the apartment and told Consuelo to get to work cleaning up after his embalming from the day before. She eyed Catherine, but did not speak to her. David told Catherine to help Consuelo sweep up and put the chemicals back on the shelf. They both worked in silence. Catherine did not look at her but could feel Consuelo watching her.

Not a day passed that Catherine didn't think about escaping. Had she not been pregnant, she might have chanced it. But now, she had to look out for her child. Bailey had left behind several volumes of books on the human body, and the history of embalming. She asked David if she could take a couple of them home and he said she probably wouldn't have time to read them, but to help herself. The more she learned about the undertaking business, the better she can do her job, David thought.

CHAPTER 9

The discovery of oil in Beaumont catapulted its status to a new level and thousands of people infiltrated the city. The sleepy town of ten thousand tripled in three months and the Billings Undertaking Business was now a full-fledged undertaking business. There were tents and barns turned into living quarters. New saloons, restaurants, supply shacks, offices and of course, the riffraff.

New buildings that were erected had gambling houses on the second floor and they operated twenty-four hours a day, never closing. It was impossible to keep peace in the now expanded little city. The sheriff and small law enforcement could not keep up with the problems, and they gave up trying. The constant bar fights and gun slinging standoffs kept the undertaking business going from dawn to dusk.

David was handling all of the money and Catherine and Consuelo were doing the preparation and embalming. Catherine worked with surgical skills and was respectful of the bodies. She refused to remove the gold fillings even when David tied her up and put her in the dark closet for three hours. Consuelo said she would do it and begged David to untie Catherine and let her go. Consuelo and Catherine never spoke to each other and Catherine would point or make motions with her hands. It was difficult not being able to give her verbal instructions, but after a while, Consuelo caught on and the two became good at their non-verbal communication.

Catherine had made surgical masks to wear so the formaldehyde would not be so strong. They were not only breathing in the fumes of the chemicals but the oil companies had begun drilling more wells and the sulphur and oil sprays from the hills made it difficult to withstand. Catherine detested the smell, but eventually grew accustomed to it. David was beginning to give Catherine a little more freedom and would sometimes take her with him to the dry goods store. He had told everyone that Catherine was a mail-order bride and that she was deaf and mute. He rarely left her alone and watched her like a hawk.

Alex Cooper had settled in and had taken up residence at a nice boarding house, paying more than triple in price, since he had gotten there. He had seen ghost towns rise into big cities if a barrel of oil was discovered, and Beaumont was no different. The source of Spindletop's oil was the biggest ever discovered in the United States. He spent most of the days at the rig, working out of a dilapidated building that had been abandoned on the site before the oil was discovered. It was more of a hut than a building, and the conditions were as bad as working in a trench. Frogs, spiders and a few bats had to be removed but there was little time for comfort.

The climate in Beaumont was humid and the southern sky indicated a chance of showers over the area. Since mud was needed for the daily operation of the drill, everyone was praying for rain. The showers also washed away the sulphur-laden air that loomed over the little town on a daily basis.

Today, Alex had to come into town to take care of some business. He stopped in at the dry goods store to pick up some tools he had ordered, and while he was waiting to pick them up, he noticed a pretty brown haired girl browsing through some fabric. She was stunning to look at and he hated to stare, but she had a mesmerizing grace and she was really beautiful. He figured she was around twenty years old, more or less, and he thought she looked out of place. She was really striking and he almost spoke to her. Out of nowhere, a man came over and grabbed her by the arm and shook her. She looked up at the man.

"What the hell is taking you so long?" he demanded.

The girl did not say anything. The man pulled his hand back like he was going to slap her, but he didn't. He pulled her hard and then pushed her in front of him. They walked out of the store. Alex was stunned when he finally noticed the girl was pregnant. He walked over to the window, and watched as the man was pulling the girl through the streets. When Alex paid his bill, he asked the clerk if he knew who the couple was.

"That man is Beaumont's undertaker, and the woman is his mail-order bride. She is a deaf-mute. I think she might be a little daffy, too," said the clerk.

Alex didn't see that in her. She seemed perfectly normal to him, except she did not speak. "Do you know their names?" Alex asked.

"David Billings and his wife's name is Catherine, I think," he said.

It bothered Alex that any man would treat his pregnant wife the way that man had treated Catherine. If Alex hadn't been in a hurry he might have said something, but figured it would be best if he minded his own business. Alex had enough on his plate. The negotiations were going slowly and the competition was strong.

The next morning at the morgue Catherine tripped and spilled some fluids on the floor. She made the choice to drop the bottle of fluid and grab onto something so she wouldn't fall and hurt the baby. David got mad, because it was an expensive bottle of embalming fluid. He struck Catherine in the face with the back of his hand and hit her in the eye. Consuelo was stunned and told David not to hit Catherine. David yelled at Consuelo and told her to go back to work or he would hit her, too.

The tension rose and Catherine feared he would hit her again. He pulled her up off the floor and told both women to get back to work or there would be more consequences.

They both looked at each other in a helpless way. They knew very little about each other, but yet they knew everything. They were both subject to the same treatment, although Catherine could tell that Consuelo really liked David.

Catherine's eye began to swell and it throbbed and she did not make eye contact with David. He didn't notice Catherine's eye beginning to swell, and an hour later it was black and blue. They worked late that evening so David took Catherine over to his favorite café at the Crosby House.

Alex Cooper was at the counter when he saw them come in. David walked in first and Catherine followed. Alex looked up at Catherine when she walked past him. For a moment they made eye contact. Alex was surprised when he saw Catherine's black eye. He finished what he was eating and decided it was time to introduce himself to David.

The waitress had just taken their order when Alex walked over to their table. "Excuse me," he said. "My name is Alex Cooper and I'm with the Glacier Oil Company. Someone told me you were the undertaker here in Beaumont."He took off his hat.

David stood up and shook his hand. "I'm David Billings, nice to meet you," David said. "This is my wife, Catherine. She doesn't talk because she can't hear."

Catherine didn't look up. David had just noticed Catherine's eye for the first time and then said, "Catherine helps me in the morgue and she had a little accident today."

Alex said he was sorry to hear that and then left. He didn't believe for one minute that Catherine had had an accident. He had met men like David before. They liked to use their wives as punching bags. There was something about the couple that haunted Alex. They were such an unlikely couple, he thought. David was crude and uneducated, and Catherine seemed more sophisticated; there was something about her that drew him to her. He couldn't put his finger on it. Maybe he just felt sorry for her.

Alex Cooper spent most of his time either at the rig or out scouting the land and talking to the owners. Pilgrim, his horse, was his closest companion. He had bought Pilgrim five years earlier in Corsicana from a rancher who had sold his land and was selling his livestock. Alex wasn't really looking to buy a horse, but Pilgrim seemed to take to him and after riding him a few days, it was clear they were meant for each other. When Alex had to ride the trails and stay overnight on the prairie, Pilgrim always let him know if someone was coming and one time, when Pilgrim refused to go up a hill, Alex looked up and saw a mountain lion. He had just enough time to get his rifle and shoot it before it jumped them. Alex was told he would be staying for a while in Beaumont, and it made sense to have his company bring Pilgrim, too.

The boarding house Alex was staying in wasn't the nicest in town, but it was fine for the little time he spent there. Dianne Mason, the owner of the boarding house, was a widow and was a few years older than Alex. She had a twenty-year-old son, but he had moved away. Alex could tell she had an interest in him from the beginning and they had dinner together on a couple of occasions. Lately, she had been inviting him to her own room and cooking dinner for him. He could tell she wanted the relationship to go to the next level, but Alex made excuses and always left after coffee. He avoided relationships because he never stayed more than a few months in any one place, and he wasn't good at saying goodbyes. It was lonely, he confessed to himself, but he didn't consider himself a ladies' man.

One Friday evening, Dianne invited him to dinner and they had a bottle of wine. Alex had just begun to relax when Dianne made her move. She began kissing him and before the evening was over, Alex was in her bed.

"I hope you don't take this the wrong way," Alex said. "You're a really nice lady, but I'm not good at relationships. My job moves me around a lot and I don't want you to think I could be more than just a friend. I could easily be gone tomorrow."

Dianne smiled. "I am aware of that. Not many men coming through Beaumont stay for long. I just found you attractive and hoped you found me attractive, too. I won't expect anything more than your friendship."

Alex was relieved, but decided not to stay the night. He preferred to have monogamous relationships and especially ones where he did not feel like he had to make a commitment. If Dianne was willing to be just close friends, he was happy to be just that. They began seeing each other two or three times a month, when Alex was able to stay in town. The sex was good, and he hoped she wouldn't expect anything more than that. Alex knew that at some point in his life he would want to settle down, but until he found the right girl, occasional affairs with consenting adult women worked just fine for him.

CHAPTER 10

It had been seven months since Catherine had gone missing, and the Galveston police didn't know any more than they did the day of her abduction. John Merit went through the motions of trying to stay focused on his work. For some reason he felt he hadn't done enough and he blamed himself. He was a hard worker and he threw himself into his work, glad that it kept him occupied. The nights were the hardest. He tried to concentrate on all of the happy times he and Catherine had had together, and he wasn't ready to give up yet. He had already spent $550.00 with the private investigation firm and they were only finding dead ends. He had used some of the money from Catherine's trust fund. John could not understand how anyone could just disappear the way Catherine had. He anguished over it every day and was devastated that it was out of his control. John had just finished working on one of his customer's file at the bank when his secretary brought in a letter from Larry Conner. John tore it open and read it.

Dear Mr. Merit:

I made my third trip back to the prison farm to talk to a man who had come forward and told one of the guards that David Brooks had escaped and survived the tornado. He said that after the tornado was over, he saw Brooks crawl out from under a bridge and run toward the railroad tracks.

I've notified the Houston police department.
    I will keep you informed if I find out anything else.

    Larry Conner

John read the letter several times and he pounded his fists on his desk. If that son-of-a-bitch did take her, and if she were still alive, she would be broken. Seven months with that evil man would ruin her for life. John got up and left the office. He walked over to the hospital and stood at the emergency room exit where Catherine was last seen, and he felt tears on his cheeks. He knew in his heart he would never see her again.

John caught the trolley, rode to the end of the line, and walked the six blocks to the cemetery. It had been cleaned up since he and Catherine had last been here, and some of the tombstones that were found had been reset. The city had located the old plat and there were markers with numbers on them. He didn't know what they meant, but figured he could check with the city and get the names that matched the numbers. His wife, child, and mother's markers were back where they were supposed to be, but his father's was still missing. He walked to where Catherine's mother, Anne, had been buried. The stone was apparently gone forever with everything else that the storm had taken. John felt empty without Catherine and wished the storm had taken his life. He sat down beside Anne's grave and put his head in his hands and cried. That was going to be the last time he cried for Catherine. He had to move on, he decided.

Several people had encouraged him to give up and he figured it was time. When John got back to his office he wrote a short note to Larry Conner.

Dear Mr. Conner:

    She is gone. Look no more.

    John Merit

John put his final payment inside the envelope and mailed it along with the letter. At 5:00 he called Amelia and told her he would be late coming home. The trolley dropped John off within half a block of St. Mary's Catholic Church. There was one more thing he had to do and that was to talk to Father Jonathan. It was important to him to cleanse his soul. Father Jonathan was closing the door to his office when he saw John approach. The two men exchanged greetings and then John said, "Have supper with me, Father."

"I was on my way to make some rounds at the hospital. Walk with me and we can stop and eat along the way," Father Jonathan said.

They stopped at a small family-owned café. The atmosphere was grim with wallpaper peeling off in one corner and none of the plates or coffee cups matched, but the food was really good. John opened the letter that Larry Conner had sent him and read it to Father Jonathan. He also told him about the note he wrote back. John told him that he just couldn't take it anymore, and he was going to stop looking for Catherine.

"I know David Brooks took her, and if she is still alive she will never come back."

"Why do you think that?" asked the Father.

"Catherine told me one time, that if anything like that happened to her again, she would die before putting me through the torment we suffered during her healing from her last abduction. She also said the indignity of another abduction and rape would make her go mad. I know her, Father, and I know she would want me to move on."

Father Jonathan pondered a minute. "Catherine is a strong woman and she is a woman of God. Her faith will overcome anything she endures."

"I feel in my heart that I have lost her, and she is gone," John said. "I have cried my last tears."

Father Jonathan knew John had made up his mind. After all,

he had been praying that John could find peace again, and he figured this was John's way of dealing with the pain. He would not try to change his mind.

"I will continue to pray for you, my son," said the Father.

Father Jonathan always thought Catherine was special. He also felt that John had been used as an instrument by God to marry Catherine and save her from dying in the storm, had she stayed at the orphanage. He felt God had something special planned for her. Father Jonathan never told John that he had sent out over fifty letters over the last six months to surrounding Catholic parishes, notifying them of Catherine's disappearance, and her abilities has a medical doctor.

Father Jonathan felt that if Catherine were with Brooks and if she escaped, she would find shelter at a Catholic church. He would continue to pray for both John and Catherine, and placed their future in God's hands.

Moving around the cramped quarters at the morgue was difficult for Catherine and she worried that the fumes she was inhaling might threaten her health or the baby's. She was eight months pregnant and although she had not gained a lot of weight, she felt awkward and fat. She liked Consuelo and even though they never spoke, they developed a mutual fondness for each other. David used Consuelo more to feed his huge sexual desires and even though Catherine had figured out that Consuelo loved David; his abuse was less than tolerable. He would use Catherine to get him excited, pulling her hair and kissing her, and then take Consuelo into the apartment and have intimacy with her. He had been gentler with Catherine during her last month, and she did whatever it took to please him, so as not to put herself or the baby in danger.

Catherine had thought a lot about escaping, but she was so afraid of David and knew if he caught her, both she and the baby would die. She had surmised that David was a monster with killer instincts and he was good at it. If this child were David's she prayed that it would not inherit his evil spirit. She knew they lived in

Beaumont and it was close to Houston, but she still felt like she was in a foreign land and besides, where would she go? If she were carrying David's child, she couldn't ask John to raise it. She wrestled with her own identity and felt so alone. The baby had begun to move a lot and it was the only thing that got her through the long hot days. In another month, he or she would be born. It was the one thing keeping her going.

David's business had more than doubled since he became the owner. He knew it would be impossible for Catherine and Consuelo to continue working the hours he was forcing them to work, and he had to do all the moving, transporting and lifting himself. The grave diggers were constantly digging new graves and were not able to come in to town to help them. David found a young Mexican man by the name of Emanuel Perez to help dress, pick up and move the bodies and transport them to the cemetery. Emanuel was about twenty-two years old and was nice looking except he had a long scar on his face. He told David that he had gotten it in a fight. "Manny" as David called him, also took care of the horses and kept the hearse clean and David agreed to pay him ten dollars a week. Emanuel would have been able to make more than what David paid him, if he worked for one of the oil companies at the rig on Spindletop, but he was not very smart and he was smaller than most of the oil field workers. He had tried working there first, but he was constantly being hit upon and had been raped by two men in the field house. He told no one, but he did quit his job.

David had already given Manny the strict rules he would be working under. Absolutely no one was to talk. David had also learned that at the prison camp. No talking and socializing, because the men would form alliances with each other and cause problems for the guards. When Catherine was finished with her part of the embalming and preparation, she would have to sit in David's office or sometimes in the apartment. Consuelo and Manny always did the clean up. David couldn't be more pleased with himself. He was making over $500.00

a month and Consuelo and Catherine did not make a salary. David figured that with the additional gold fillings and jewelry he took off the bodies, he was making well over $650.00 a month.

David was in his office one day when Alex Cooper came in. David figured there was another death at the derrick, but Alex said it was another matter. Alex tried to explain to David that the reason why he was there, was that his oil company was interested in doing a subsurface lease on David's farm. There was no way to tell right now, without doing some studies, whether or not oil was present, but the first step would be for David to sign an agreement with his company that would give them rights to drill if they wanted to at a future date. If oil were found, David would be able to collect royalties.

It all went over David's head and he didn't want to sound ignorant so he just said, "Hell no, nobody is coming on my land to drill for shit."

Alex tried to reason with David and gave him a final offer of $100,000, if he would sell the land outright. David thought for a few minutes and turned down the offer. Alex left a sample of the paper work he would need to sign, and asked David to think about it. David was not surprised by the offer. He had heard on the streets that land was going to become very valuable and he was willing to wait awhile for a much bigger offer. Besides, Alex was not the only hustler out there and he was in no hurry, he thought to himself. David was going to wait it out as long as he could to get top dollar, and then he might take Catherine and move to Florida, or even New Orleans, and never have to work again. He would decide Consuelo's fate later. She knew too much to ever let her go free.

The August heat in Beaumont was unrelenting and even with a fan blowing in the workroom of the morgue it could be unbearable. Catherine's back was aching and she was constantly thirsty. Some days she was standing on her feet five and six hours with only short breaks for lunch. She had just finished her last corpse, when she felt a sharp pain and water trickling down her legs. Consuelo was busy cleaning up and had her back to Catherine. She heard a weak cry and turned and saw Catherine's face.

"Baby?" Consuelo asked.

Catherine shook her head yes.

"I go get doctor," Consuelo said and she ran out. David and Manny had not come back from a funeral yet. Catherine managed to walk over to the apartment and lay on the bed.

Another sharp pain took Catherine off guard. She knew with the pains coming that close together, it would not be long before the baby would come. She tried not to push, but the labor was intense. Ten minutes had passed by the time Consuelo brought Doctor Martin in. She knew deaf-mutes did not make a sound, and it was hard for her restrain her cries. Consuelo assisted Dr. Martin and one hour later Catherine gave birth to a six-pound baby boy.

It was a joy that Catherine did not know existed. She had been living in a vacuum of dissolution and heartache and never thought she could feel happiness again. She smiled at her new son and then up at Consuelo and Dr. Martin.

"You did good, Miss Catherine," Consuelo said.

"The baby seems to be healthy, and you will be fit as a fiddle in no time," Dr. Martin told Catherine, as she looked at him and pretended to read his lips.

David got back to the office just as Dr. Martin was leaving. "Congratulations, Mr. Billings, you have a fine son there."

David was surprised and didn't say anything. He went back to the apartment and saw Catherine holding the baby. David walked over and took a closer look, parting the blanket so he could see the baby's body, as though he didn't believe it to be a boy. He smiled when he confirmed that it was a boy. David knew Catherine had already picked out the name, Daniel, and he really didn't care what the baby was called. Catherine had silently selected Daniel because it was John's father's name.

Consuelo asked if they had picked out a name and David said,

"Daniel.""That is a strong name for the young man," she said, pleased. Catherine smiled.

"Go find Manny and tell him to get the wagon ready," David told Consuelo.

Consuelo helped Catherine get cleaned up and dressed again. Consuelo was cooing at the baby and deep down, she wished it was her and David's baby. Maybe her time would come, she thought.

David took Catherine home and he hardly spoke to her. He knew it changed things. He had never been around babies and he knew the crying would get on his nerves. He was feeling anxious again. He got Catherine settled, and told her he was leaving for a few days and wouldn't be back until Monday, late.

"Could you ask Manny to bring us some groceries? I'll nurse the baby, but I have to have food," Catherine said.

David walked over to the closet and got his leather suitcase. He threw a few things in it and left without answering Catherine.

Catherine was exhausted and she lay down on the bed with the baby and fell asleep. The baby started fussing a few hours later, and when he woke Catherine up, it was dark. She lit the candle and went to the water closet before she came back and nursed the baby. She was mesmerized as the baby so willingly and naturally sucked at her breasts. She wondered if this was how her mother must have felt, when she had her first child. Daniel's sweet, tender fingers kneaded her breasts instinctively, and Catherine smiled. She studied his face. At first, nursing was painful, and she would have to struggle not to cry. But now her tears came because there was no doubt that Daniel was John's son and he would never know. She only hoped that David would not notice.

Catherine had not eaten all day and was hungry, so she picked up the baby and went into the kitchen. They usually stopped at the store on Friday afternoons to get groceries for the weekend, but the delivery of Daniel interrupted their routine. She found some oatmeal so she put a kettle of water on the burner and found some tea bags.

Oatmeal it is, she thought to herself. Daniel was stirring, so she changed his diaper while the kettle heated. She looked around the sparsely decorated room and saw nothing that would work for a cradle. She and David had never talked about what they needed after the baby came. Catherine had picked up diapers and a few gowns for the baby, but that was all. Catherine finished eating and went back into the bedroom.

She opened the bottom drawer on the chest and it was empty, so she pulled it all the way out and put it on the floor on her side of the bed. She grabbed a clean sheet and a towel from the bathroom and folded it several times to fit the drawer. She smiled as she put Daniel in it.

"Sleep, my precious angel," she said out loud.

It was already dark when she heard a wagon outside the farmhouse. She walked over by the window and pulled the curtain back to see if she could make out who it was. Consuelo and Manny came to the door. Catherine was happy to see them and almost said something, but caught herself. Consuelo had a bag in her arms and Manny had two bags.

"Mr. David gave us money to get you some things for you and the baby," Manny said. Catherine touched her heart and smiled.

"Can we see the baby?" asked Consuelo.

Catherine took them into the bedroom where Daniel was sleeping in the drawer. "Mr. David, he did not make Daniel a cradle?" Manny asked.

Catherine looked down and didn't say anything. After Manny and Consuelo left, Catherine couldn't help but notice that Manny had touched Consuelo's arm and lingered when they were looking at the baby. They were perfect for each other, she thought. But she knew that would never happen. David would kill them both before he would ever let Consuelo leave. She wished she could warn them, but Consuelo knew of David's violent temper and what he was capable of. She had enough to deal with on her own. She was as much of a prisoner as Catherine was and neither would ever be able to escape.

CHAPTER 11

David has just barely made the last train leaving for Houston. Before he left, he had gone back to the morgue to get some money out of the safe and give Consuelo and Manny their instructions of what to do while he was gone. He had noticed the way Manny had started looking affectionately at Consuelo and he was going to talk to him when he got back. Right now he just needed to get away.

David was anxious as he waited for the train. Because of the influx of people still migrating into Beaumont, the railroads had added more times to their already busy schedule and he did not have to wait long. He walked to the dining car and ordered a double shot of whiskey. It was almost like old times, he thought. He still couldn't put a finger on what was eating at him. Maybe it was the fact that Daniel didn't look anything like him, but it was hard to tell about babies. He would wait and see. If he didn't notice any likeness between him and Daniel when he was three or four months old, he might have to do something.

David had always thought that if he had money, his anxieties would go away, but they were worse. Even Catherine and his position in Beaumont's society had not brought him the peace he thought it would. David never expected that he would have access to this amount of money, and he had no conception of how to manage it, and right now all he wanted to do was spend some. He had not made a kill in a long time, and he began to get aroused at the thought of it. The brothels in Beaumont were always busy and he didn't think it was a good idea to be seen there. He had also heard they were filthy and that did not set well with him. There were murders in Beaumont every day, but it was just too crowded and he did not want to risk getting caught there. He knew Houston well and could fade into the background. He just needed some time to get away and think.

When David got to Houston, he told the driver to take him to a nice hotel and that he needed a woman. They were at Houston's red light district known as the Hollow in ten minutes, and they stopped in front of the Auditorium Hotel. David tipped him and went inside. It was bustling with business men and there were lots of beautiful women. David smiled and knew he was at the right place. He checked in and went upstairs to his room to clean up a bit. He decided to keep his gun in the holster under his jacket. He had over $100 on him and he didn't want to chance getting robbed. David had also brought some gold jewelry and fillings that he was going to pawn the next day.

The bar was dark and loud. David ordered a double shot of whiskey. It felt good to be there. He had barely gotten his drink when a pretty, light-brown-haired girl about twenty came up to him.

"Got a light?" she asked.

David took out a match and lit her cigarette.

"You from around here?" she asked.

"Beaumont," David said.

"Are you in one of them oil wells they found there?" she asked.

"Maybe," said David. The prostitute smiled.

"I like oil men," she said. David didn't answer. "How about buying me a drink?" she asked.

David picked up his drink and moved to the other end of the bar, and sat next to a pretty red-headed girl also about twenty. She was much better looking than the one he had been talking to, and besides, he thought, red heads were usually better in bed. David looked at the red head and noticed her drink was empty. He motioned to the bartender to replenish the girl's drink.

When the bartender put the drink down in front of her, she turned to David and said, "I'm not cheap and I don't like rough men."

"Understood," David said. "I don't like cheap either, that's why I moved down here."

"Five dollars," she said.

"For how long?" David asked.

"An hour," she answered.

David took a drink of his whiskey. "How much for the night?" he asked.

"Twenty dollars," she said as David whistled.

"I intend to get my money's worth," he said and paid the bill. "Drink up," he demanded.

The hooker followed him through the hotel and took the stairs to the third floor. David unlocked the door to his room and waited for her to go in first.

"You got a name?" David asked.

"Rita, just Rita."

"OK, just Rita," David laughed and said, "Get undressed."

She walked over to start taking David's coat off. He stopped her.

"You first," he said.

David walked over to the small bar and poured himself another shot of whiskey. He turned around and watched Rita. She was smiling and taking her time, licking her lips with her tongue. David took off his jacket and then his gun and holster. Rita was tall with long legs and she had taken everything off except her garter belt and stockings. Her body was almost perfect and she had beautiful breasts. David walked over to her and started moving his hand up one of her arms and then he put his other hand on the back of her buttocks and pulled her to him. They kissed. Rita took the lead and David could tell she had been at this for a while. He closed his eyes, enjoying Rita's every move and David savored the moment. They were both exhausted when they finished. David walked over and got his wallet and gun and put them under his pillow. "I need to sleep for a while and you better be here when I wake up," David said. "Any attempt to leave with any of my things and you won't make it out of here alive, understood?"

She shook her head yes.

After Manny and Consuelo left Catherine's house they headed back to the morgue. Manny had noticed early on the way David treated Consuelo and Catherine, and he did not like it one bit. He decided to talk to Consuelo about it. "Mr. David, he is very mean to you and Mrs. Catherine," Manny said.

Consuelo did not answer him.

"Why do you let him treat you like that?" Manny asked.

"Mr. David has a bad temper and I guess we provoke him sometimes," said Consuelo.

"That does not give him the right to hit you," Manny said.

Consuelo started crying and told Manny that Darlene had been paid a lot of money by David Brooks to buy her as his personal muse, and that if she left he might hurt her or Darlene.

"And what about Mrs. Catherine?" Manny asked.

"I'm not sure. He bring her to morgue one day and say she is his mail-order bride," answered Consuelo. "She is very nice to me, but I think she can hear better than she lets on," Consuelo continued saying.

Manny put his arm around Consuelo and asked, "Does Mr. Billings pay you?"

"No," answered Consuelo.

"Does he make you have sex with him?" asked Manny.

Consuelo did not want to answer him. She really did not have to say anything; Manny already knew the answer. He just wanted to see what Consuelo would say. Manny could tell she was terrified of Billings and so was Mrs. Catherine.

When they got back to the morgue, Manny and Consuelo

unhitched the horse from the wagon and put the mare in its stall. Manny grabbed Consuelo's hand and pulled her close to him.

"When the time is right, I am going to take you away from here. I am saving my money so that we can start over in another town," he told her.

She hugged him.

"You are very kind, Manny, but Mr. David would kill both of us if he suspects we are planning to leave."

She started crying again. Manny took his fingers and dried her tears and then he kissed her very softly and tenderly.

"Mr. David is a big man, but I am not afraid of him," Manny said.

They both were attracted to each other, and they also knew that if they gave in to their desires, they would be putting themselves in harm's way. At the moment it didn't matter. Consuelo began kissing Manny back and they went past the point of no return. Afterwards, Consuelo cried and begged Manny to forget it ever happened. Manny stroked her hair and held her tenderly.

"We must be strong," said Manny. "When the time is right we will leave and go far away. Mr. David will never find us," he assured her.

Manny spent that night with Consuelo in the apartment, and the next day they worked together, doing their routine chores and talking. They both knew that they had to be careful and not look at each when David got back. Consuelo was worried the most because she had seen David's violent temper, and he would not hesitate to kill either of them.

Catherine did not get much rest over the weekend. She was extremely tired and she was up every three hours nursing Daniel. She had only ordered a couple dozen diapers from the mail-order catalogue and she knew they would not last over the weekend. Later that morning, when she put Daniel down after nursing, she forced herself to get a bucket and soak the dirty diapers. Once she scrubbed and rinsed them, she went out on the front porch to let them dry over the banister. Catherine was surprised when she saw a man on a horse approaching their farm. She squinted but she could not make out who it was. She placed the last diaper over the banister and went inside and locked the door.

Alex Cooper was out on a scouting expedition when he saw Catherine come outside with the basket of clothes. He watched her through his binoculars and decided to approach her and talk to her. He figured he must have scared her, because she ran into the house when she saw him approaching. He really had not intended to scare her. He just wanted to be friendly. Alex had seen David get on the train the night before, when he had dropped off one of his own men to catch the train. Alex also couldn't help but notice that Catherine did not look pregnant anymore, and the clothes she had hung on the banister looked like baby diapers. He thought it seemed odd, if Catherine had given birth the day before that her husband would leave her alone so soon.

Alex sat on Pilgrim outside the farmhouse trying to think of how he could approach Catherine. He had almost decided to leave, when the door opened. Catherine was holding a baby. Alex tipped his hat to her.

"Do you read lips?" Alex asked slowly.

Catherine nodded her head yes.

"I'm sorry to come unannounced, but I was wondering if Mr. Billings might be home?" Alex lied.

Catherine shook her head no.

"I see you had your baby; boy or girl?" Alex asked.

Catherine pointed at Alex.

"A boy?" Alex asked.

Catherine smiled and shook her head yes.

"May I see?" Alex asked and got off his horse before Catherine could answer.

He could see her grow tense. Alex walked over and took a

closer look at Daniel. His strong hands pulled the blanket away from Daniel's face and he smiled at him.

"He has your eyes," Alex said.

Catherine smiled at him again. She had never looked closely at Alex and she felt secure and safe standing beside him. He projected a gentle mannerism and he reminded her of John, her husband. She did not see a ring on his finger, but not all men wore wedding rings, and she wondered if he were married.

Catherine wanted more than anything to talk to Alex and tell him everything, but she did not want to put Alex in danger. There wasn't anything he could do for her now. It had been nine months since she was abducted, and she had already reconciled with her demons. Besides, she had Daniel to protect and she knew David would kill Daniel first and then her, before he would let her go. Her fate was already obvious and she had to accept it. The consequences would be too great, she thought.

"When will your husband be back?" Alex asked.

Catherine thought for a minute and held up two fingers.

"Two days?" Alex asked.

Catherine shook her head yes. The baby started fussing and Catherine automatically reacted to his crying. She realized what she had done and looked at Alex with panic in her face.

Alex tipped his hat and said, "Good day, Mrs. Billings."

As Alex rode off, he wondered how a beautiful woman like Catherine ever got involved with Billings. Alex had suspected Catherine was not deaf. Maybe she could not speak but he knew two things. She was terrified of her husband and she had excellent hearing.

David had enjoyed his evening with Rita, and they both woke up at the same time. After they played a while in bed, David paid her and she left. He felt more anxious than even and knew there was only one thing that would calm his nerves. He had to make a kill, and he felt eager to do it. David dressed and left the hotel after he had a huge breakfast. He decided to take care of his business first and headed over to the other side of Houston to buy some plans to build his own coffins. He met with the casket makers and purchased a set of plans. His intentions were to keep Manny busy building the coffins and thus save him money. David knew that the nicer coffins had to be ordered from the casket makers but that was only about twenty percent of his business. He figured that by making the most popular wood coffins himself it would save him hundreds of dollars every year and having Manny build the coffins, he wouldn't have time to lust after Consuelo. David also ordered some shrouds and a case of embalming fluid before he left.

David took a trolley over to the business district to see the jeweler to whom he had previously sold his gold. He was there for almost an hour and finally accepted a price from the owner that he could live with.

David needed to waste some time, so he stopped at a nice restaurant and had lunch. Afterwards he decided to find a poker game. He spent the afternoon winning for a while and then losing most of the money he brought. He stopped when he was down to his last twenty-five dollars.

David hung out in the bar until about 9:30PM and then left. He walked over to the diner in the red light district where he first met Vicki. He missed her and wondered if her old man had actually killed her or if she did commit suicide. He would never know and it really didn't matter. She was gone and so was her old man. The streets were busy with hookers looking for customers and David stood back in a door way and watched. The stalking was part of what made the kill so much fun for him. It had to be the right girl. The younger the better, thought David. He saw a young girl walking toward him and he figured she must be about fifteen. She reminded him of Vicki, as they were built the same way; big bosoms, short, and not too fat. The girl stopped a few feet away from David.

"Are you just looking, or are you just trying to get up your nerve?" she asked David.

"Are you offering?" he asked.

"Maybe," she said. "You a policeman?"

"Nope," answered David. "Do you live around here?" he asked her.

"I got a room not too far from here," she answered.

"How much?" he asked.

"Normal is one dollar; anything else is another dollar."

David smiled and said, "Let's go."

He followed behind her a couple of feet until they turned down an alley. He made sure no one was watching. He was just one more customer walking behind his lady of the night and few people paid attention to them.

The girl unlocked a door and they went upstairs. They walked down the hall and she unlocked another door. It was dark and musty and when they walked into her room it smelled of cigarettes and sweat. She walked over to the bed, sat down, and took off her shoes. David asked where the water closet was and she pointed. He went in and closed the door behind him.

David took out a small vial of chloroform and soaked his handkerchief, then put it back in his pocket. He flushed the toilet and came back out. She had undressed down to her garters and stockings and was lying in bed in a lascivious position. David walked over and lifted her head like he was going to kiss her, and then covered her face with the handkerchief. She struggled for a minute and then went limp. David took another handkerchief and gagged her, then proceeded to tie her up to the bed, using some rope he had previous cut into thirty-inch lengths. He watched her as he stripped naked and straddled her on the bed. He reached over to his pants pocket and took out some smelling salts and put them under her nose. She woke up. She was groggy, and at first she wasn't sure what had happened. When she tried to move, she realized her hands were tied. She wanted to scream and she became frantic. She struggled and tears came to her eyes.

"Just relax," David encouraged. "It won't hurt that much."

David had already taken a surgical knife out of his pants pocket and he was holding it. Her eyes widened and she shook her head back and forth. He put the knife down and said, "I'm going to save the best for last."

He straddled her and tears were coming down her face. David placed both of his hands around her neck and began squeezing as hard as he could. Her eyes bulged open and David took the surgical blade and slit her throat. He fell over panting and then he laughed with relief.

David untied the girl's hands and took off the gag. He took the rope, gag, and knife and put them in a paper bag. After he cleaned himself up, he dressed and checked to see that he left nothing behind. He picked up the bag and slowly opened the door, leaving quietly. David was back out on the street in a matter of minutes. He felt invigorated and complete. His anxiety was gone and he felt like a new man. It was as if he had cleansed himself of every bad thing that had happened to him in his life. He wondered about his own mother. If he ever found her, he thought, he would kill her, too. She had made him into the man he was now and he hoped she had been paid back.

David no longer was concerned about Consuelo and Manny. He would deal with them when the time was right. Catherine was another story. He was still obsessed with her, and the one thing nagging at him, was whether Daniel was really his. David decided to leave early the next morning. He would make Catherine tell him the truth.

David caught the early bird special leaving out at 5:00 a.m. He was back in Beaumont by 7:00 a.m. The only sleep he got was about two hours on the train. David walked over to the barn behind his morgue and saddled one of his horses. He was back home before 8:00 a.m.

CHAPTER 12

The crime scene was disgusting. Blood was splattered all over the sheets and onto the wall above the bed. Sergeant Jack Shaker had been promoted to sergeant a year earlier and he was called to the scene of a dead prostitute in the red light district. The girl's sister had found her the next morning, and had called the police. The wound on her neck was clean and he figured it was some kind of surgical knife. It was easy to buy them. Farmers used the thin knives to bleed out the hogs when they slaughtered them. Sergeant Shaker searched around the room to see it there might be something the killer left behind, but the man was smart and had cleaned up after himself. Shaker could see bruises on the girl's wrists where she had been tied up, but the ropes were nowhere in sight. Shaker had ordered a fingerprint kit from a new company in New York and it was the first time he had to use it. He took some prints off the door knob and by the sink in the bathroom. He also noticed a peculiar smell in the bathroom and decided to get closer to the pillow underneath the girls head.

"What is it?" asked one of the officers.

"It smells like some kind of chemical. After the girl is removed I want to put the pillow case in a bag to have it checked out and evaluated," Shaker said.

Sergeant Shaker knew the Houston Police Department spent little time investigating the deaths of prostitutes or vagrants, but this girl was somebody's daughter and she had a sister. He always gave his job one hundred percent, no matter who it was and he was not going to treat this one any differently.

Catherine had enjoyed getting to know Daniel over the last two days, even though she was exhausted. She sang songs to him while she nursed him, and for the first time in a year, she felt like she really had a reason to live. She had just put Daniel to sleep in his makeshift bed, when she thought she heard a noise outside. Before she could get out of bed, the door to the front of the house swung open and David was standing in the bedroom looking at her like a mad man. Catherine sat up in bed, glad that Daniel was asleep.

"What is it?" she asked David.

She was scared and tried to think if she had done something she wasn't supposed to. She remembered Alex and wondered if he had talked to David. Maybe that was why he was upset. David grabbed her arm and pulled her off the bed. She was still in her nightgown and he was pulling her so hard she tripped several times before he got to the door.

David pulled her up and hit her with his open hand across her face. It stunned her and she fell. When she got up, she found it hard to keep up with him as he dragged her outside. She begged him to stop and she asked him again why he was doing this to her. Halfway to the barn, she fell and he dragged her the remainder of the way. David tore her gown, ripping the sleeve, and tied her hands together. He lifted her up and tied her hands to a pulley that was hanging down in the middle of the barn. It was a pulley that the previous owner had used to slaughter his hogs. David had seen it and left it there thinking it might come in handy some day. David yanked Catherine's locket off and threw it over to the side, and then grabbed the whip he used sometimes on the horses.

"David, please tell me what's wrong," she pleaded. She could barely touch the ground with her feet, and her arms and hands were extended above her head. It was difficult to breathe and she pleaded with him.

"Tell me who Daniel's father is," David demanded.

"You are his father," she shouted at him.

David stuck her on her back and she screamed in pain. He hit her again, this time hitting her legs. She grimaced in pain and cried, "He's yours."

David lashed her several more times, striking her randomly on her body, each time tearing at her skin. He left her there and went back into the house. The barn was hot and Catherine was sweating. She kept praying that David would not kill Daniel.

"Please, God," she said out loud. "Please don't let him kill my baby." She was in agony and the pain in her arms was excruciating.

David went into the house and walked over to where Daniel was sleeping. He picked him up and looked him over carefully. He still couldn't be sure. Maybe Daniel was his kid. He did have dark hair and brown eyes, but so did her husband, he thought to himself. He couldn't be sure, so he carried the baby to the barn and laid him at Catherine's feet.

The barn had been closed up, and the dense air smelled of hay, blood, and sweat. Daniel began crying. Catherine had passed out earlier, but when she heard Daniel cry, she woke up and looked down. She had never in her life felt so hopeless. She began to cry, too.

"David, David, David," Catherine screamed. "He is your son." David was standing behind her, and she did not know where he was. "He's your son," she said in a breathless whisper.

David left her hanging from the pulley, forcing her to listen to Daniel cry. She was numb and she wanted to pray for death, but she would not leave Daniel at the mercy of David. Catherine passed out again.

Catherine was dreaming, and she dreamed that Alex Cooper had offered to take her and Daniel away from David. She was sorry that when she had the chance to tell Alex that she had been kidnapped, she did not tell him. She most likely would not get another opportunity. She dreamed of John, her husband, and he told her he no longer wanted to be her husband. She dreamed she was back on the ship, and that the body of the child they buried at sea was Daniel. She saw the devastation of the wreckage from the storm in Galveston, and that she was being swept away along with the children at the orphanage and the sisters. She was drowning and she gasped for breath. Catherine woke up and looked down, and Daniel was gone.

She screamed, "Daniel!" She felt her body being lowered and she went limp on the ground. She looked up.

"I'm asking you for the last time, is Daniel my son?"

"Yes, yes, yes!" she screamed.

David untied Catherine and left her there. She watched as David got up on his horse and left. Catherine saw her gown lying several feet from where she was and she crawled over to get it. Her arms hurt too much to try and put the gown over her head, so she wrapped it around her body. She crawled over to the stable and used the wood rail to try and pull herself up. She screamed in pain, but she finally was standing. Catherine hobbled as best as she could, the forty or so steps to the house. She willed herself not to fall, afraid that she might not be able to get up again. She made her way to the bedroom and saw Daniel asleep in the drawer, and she was overcome with tears. Catherine wanted to pick him up, but was afraid she might drop him, because her arms were hurting so much. She touched his tiny neck with her two fingers and found his pulse, and cried with joy that he was still alive. Catherine curled up on the floor beside him and passed out.

Catherine's nightmares began to haunt her again, and she woke up. She looked at Daniel and he was awake. She smiled at his obvious happy spirit. He fussed a bit, but rarely cried. She forced herself up against the wall and pulled the drawer toward her so she could support her body. It was time for his feeding, and she grimaced as she leaned forward to pick him up. It was painful, but she lifted Daniel onto her lap and up to her breast. She used her torn nightgown to clean the blood from both of their bodies. There was none on her breasts, and Daniel was already searching for her nipple so she held him up to her. She smiled as he hungrily enveloped her nipple in his mouth and began sucking.

The throbbing in Catherine's arms began to ease and she looked up at the ceiling. She knew what she had to do. She had to save Daniel and sacrifice herself. It was the only way she knew of that Daniel would be safe from David. Meanwhile, Catherine continued to hold Daniel and he fell asleep. She watched him, as she wanted this moment to be planted in her heart forever.

Catherine put Daniel down in the drawer and walked slowly into the bathroom to clean up her wounds. Her jaw still hurt from where David had hit her and it was beginning to swell.

She dressed and went out to the barn. David always kept the horse and wagon in the same place at the barn, and Catherine began to hitch the mare to the wagon. When she finished, she went inside and picked up Daniel. She wrapped him in a blanket that she had embroidered prior to his birth with the name, "Daniel." She printed a note that she pinned to his blanket:

My mother is dead; please see that I am taken to Father Jonathan at St. Mary's Church in Galveston, Texas.

Catherine put the sleeping Daniel in her small laundry basket and put him under the seat of the wagon. She climbed up into the wagon, grimacing from the pain, and drove the mare as hard as she could. She prayed she would not meet David along the way. Catherine approached the outskirts of town cautiously, and left the mare and wagon behind a building. It was Sunday and church was already out, so she walked to the building where the sisters lived behind St. Louis Catholic Church and left Daniel in the basket at the door. She cried as she made her way to the wagon. She had made the trip into town and was back home in just over an hour. David had not come home yet.

Catherine had made herself some oatmeal and hot tea while

she waited in the kitchen for David to come back. She was ready now. Daniel was safe and she knew her punishment would probably be death. It would be easy to have a funeral with two coffins. Her body would be in one, and perhaps a log put in Daniel's to give it some weight. She could almost hear Alex telling everyone that they both died in childbirth. She really didn't care what he told everyone. Catherine's took a deep breath when she heard David at the door.

When David came in, he looked at Catherine and was surprised she was fully dressed. He walked into the bedroom and the drawer had been put back into the chest. He came back into the kitchen and calmly sat at the table.

"Do you want to tell me what is going on, Catherine?"

She did not look at him. "I had slept with my husband the night before you took me away. I really don't know whose son Daniel is, but he is my son and I have taken him someplace you won't be able to hurt him," Catherine said calmly. "I left him in a basket at the church. We will have a burial for him tomorrow and tell everyone he died shortly after I gave birth to him. It happens all the time," she said.

"You think you are so smart," David said. "Perhaps I could have two coffins, one for you and one for Daniel," he continued.

"That is your choice; I am prepared to die," Catherine said.

"No," David said. "I'm going to put you through hell first. I'll decide when you die. Get in the wagon."

Consuelo was in the apartment when she heard David come back for the second time. When he came back to the morgue earlier, he did not say very much to her and stayed in his office for awhile before leaving again. Consuelo waited for a few minutes and peeped around the door. She saw David and Catherine place a baby coffin on the hearse and she did not see Daniel. She saw David turn towards the office and she ran back to her apartment and stood at the door. Catherine followed David in and watched as he took a woman's black hat and mourning scarf from the closet and handed it to Catherine.

She put it on and did not look at Consuelo.

Consuelo asked, "Is Daniel......?"

"He's dead," David said. "Catherine killed him, and you are not to tell anyone. We will tell them he died in childbirth."

Consuelo was stunned and wondered if David was the one who killed the baby.

David hitched up two horses to the front of the hearse and he and Catherine got up on the front seat. He pulled the hearse around to the far end of town and slowly drove the hearse down Main Street. Catherine was wearing the mourning scarf and looked down. Dozens of people came out into the street and watched as the hearse paraded by. Several made the sign of the cross, as men took off their hats and women and children watched. Alex had just come out of the café when he saw the hearse approaching.

"She must have lost the baby," Alex heard someone say.

Alex took off his hat and watched as Catherine looked down.

When they reached the cemetery, David stopped at two freshly dug graves. Catherine looked up at David.

"I was going to kill you both when I came back, but you solved the problem for me. You are worth more to me alive than dead, and I am going to see that you pay," David said.

David motioned for the grave digger to come over. He pushed Catherine out of the way and she stood and watched as they took the tiny casket off the hearse and dropped it into the ground. She was numb, and watched as they shovelled dirt on top of it. When they finished, David grabbed her hand and lifted her up onto the seat of the hearse. They did not speak.

Alex couldn't help but feel sorry for Catherine. He had seen both Catherine and the baby the day before, and the baby looked healthy. He knew it was not unusual for a baby to die after childbirth, but the baby was at least a day old and he couldn't help but remember the way Catherine had smiled at him. Had the baby been sick, she might have acted differently. He didn't know why it mattered to him.

It was none of his business, but there was something drawing him to Catherine. He felt he needed to save her, but he wasn't sure from what. She wouldn't accept his help, and without proof that she was being held against her will, there was nothing he could do. He shook his head as if to shake away the thought of her.

CHAPTER 13

It was around 5:00 p.m. on Sunday afternoon, when Father Jonathan was resting in his room before going to make his calls at the hospital. There was a knock on his door and one of the sisters said, "There's an important phone call for you, Father."

He walked down the hall to his office and picked up the phone.

"This is Father Jonathan," he said. He listened intently and asked the caller to repeat what he had just heard. He listened and wrote down what was said. "I will get back with you in the morning with instructions," he replied into the phone. Father Jonathan looked at the message he had written down from the caller:

My mother is dead; please see that I am taken to Father Jonathan at St. Mary's Church in Galveston, Texas.

The caller also said the name on the baby's blanket was, "Daniel." Father Jonathan pondered a moment and then said "Daniel Merit," out loud.

The next morning, Sister Caroline Arnett, who had come to St. Mary's Catholic Church and Hospital after the storm, boarded the train leaving for Beaumont with a short stop in Houston. She was a nurse and had been sent to Galveston by the bishop to assist with the survivors from the storm. She had explicit instructions from Father

Jonathan to meet another sister from St. Louis Catholic Church to pick up a baby at the Beaumont train station.

When the train arrived in Beaumont, Sister Caroline was approached by a sister dressed in the traditional habit of a nun. Sister Caroline was also dressed in a nurse's habit and the two sisters approached each other. They exchanged a few words, and then the baby was given to Sister Caroline, along with a small bag with two bottles of milk, plus a few diapers she would need for the return trip home. The trip took a bit longer because there was a layover in Houston, but Sister Caroline didn't mind. She was fascinated with the tiny baby. He had big brown eyes and watched Sister Caroline. He cried very little and when he began chewing on his fist, she scolded herself for not asking what time he had last been fed. She decided she needed to space the two bottles of milk out long enough to make the trip home. The baby finally began crying after an hour into the trip and he willingly latched on to the bottle of milk.

Sister Caroline wondered what might have happened to the baby's parents. Perhaps the mother died and the father just couldn't take care of it. Father Jonathan said nothing about the parents. She thought it a bit unusual to go so far to pick up an orphan when there were so many left after the storm, and they were already at capacity at the makeshift orphanage they were using in Galveston. But whatever the case, she knew Father Jonathan had his reasons. He always knew best and she greatly respected him.

Sister Caroline's instructions were to take the baby directly to the children's ward at the hospital for a complete examination. The porter from St. Mary's was waiting in the church's wagon when Sister Caroline got off the train.

Father Jonathan was already at the hospital making his rounds when he was told that his package had arrived. He smiled to himself, and went to the second floor to the nursery. Sister Caroline was feeding the baby in one of the rockers when Father Jonathan approached her. She smiled up at him when he told her that he hoped she wasn't too tired from her long trip. He just stood and looked carefully at the baby.

"The doctor said he is a very healthy baby, and that he believes it to be no more than three days old. He weighs almost seven pounds."

Father Jonathan nodded his head approvingly.

"We'll keep him here overnight and I will arrange for one of the sisters at the orphanage to pick him up in the morning." Father Jonathan thanked Sister Caroline, and then went back to his office at the church.

Father Jonathan sat in his office contemplating what he needed to do. He picked up the phone and called John Merit. He asked John if he could stop by the church after work on Monday and that he needed to visit with him about an important matter. He told John he did not want to talk about it on the phone, and John agreed to come.

Mondays were always busy at the bank, and John was glad. He had no idea what Father Jonathan wanted. Maybe he found out that John had begun seeing another woman and she was not Catholic. John had been introduced to a woman by the name of Carla Beranger by his boss. She was his boss's niece and a widow with two young girls. She was pleasant, but not particularly good looking. Not like Catherine at all. Carla was a bit pudgy and she relished all of Galveston's latest gossip. John was not interested in marrying again, but he needed the companionship of a woman and she was available. At first it was dinner at her house, and then John took her on a real date to a new restaurant that had opened up. They began seeing each other twice a week and within a month she was already mentioned the "M" word. John had already told her that until Catherine was declared dead, he would not be able to marry, but that didn't seem to stop her from suggesting it might happen down the road.

At 5:00 p.m. John put his files away and locked up his desk. He jumped on the trolley and made his way over to the Catholic Church. Father Jonathan was waiting in his office when John arrived.

Father Jonathan had all day to decide how he was going to approach John about the note and the baby, and he decided the best approach was to be direct. John listened intently as the details of the phone call from St. Louis Church in Beaumont were given, and that the baby was at the orphanage here in Galveston.

"And why does this concern me?" John asked.

Father Jonathan was surprised at his hostility but finally said, "Catherine has been gone about nine months now and the name on the baby blanket is, "Daniel." That was your father's name."

"That doesn't mean anything. It's probably someone playing a sick joke. A lot of people left here after the storm, Father, and it was all over the newspaper that Catherine had disappeared," John said angrily. "I'm sorry if I sound so uncaring about some orphan, but I had previously told you I was moving on with my life. I can't keep waiting. Once a year has passed, I'm planning to have Catherine declared dead, and then I will probably remarry."

Father Jonathan was going to ask John if he wanted to see the baby, but it was clear John's mind was made up. After John left, Father Jonathan prepared a birth certificate for the baby:

Date of birth: August 27, 1901, Place of Birth: Beaumont, Texas, Mother: Unknown, Father: Unknown, Faith: Catholic, Baby's Name: Daniel Merit.

Father Jonathan looked at the certificate for a long time before he signed his name at the bottom.

After the empty coffin was buried, Catherine and David rode back to the morgue in silence. David closed the door to the back entrance, turned to Catherine and grabbed her by her arm and twisted it behind her. He led Catherine into the apartment and put her in a chair and told her to stay there. She did not move. A few minutes later David came in with Consuelo. He started kissing her and told Consuelo to take her clothes off. Consuelo looked at Catherine and then at David.

"Do as I say," David demanded.

Consuelo began removing her clothes. David poured himself a glass of whiskey and proceeded to take his clothes off, too. He stood in front of Catherine and told her she was to watch, and if she looked away there would be consequences. David began tormenting Consuelo and making her do things she did not want to do. Catherine tried to block the images from her mind as she sat staring at them. She felt sorry for Consuelo and hated that David was taking his anger out on her. She knew it was only a matter of time before it would be her turn.

Images of Daniel came to her mind, and she prayed he was safe and that Father Jonathan had been given the note. She knew David would not risk trying to get him back, especially when it was uncertain whose son he was. She did not regret what she had done. Her only peace now was that Daniel was safe, and with people who would love him. David had sex with Consuelo for over an hour, forcing Catherine to watch. When he had finished he took Catherine to the barn and chained her wrist to the wheel of the hearse. Afterwards, he went back and spent the night in the apartment with Consuelo. It was hot in the barn, but Catherine was exhausted and sleep finally came. Catherine woke an hour later from another nightmare. She was drenched in sweat and she was thirsty. She heard the sound of some mice and she grimaced at the thought of one biting her and she started crying. She forced herself to sit up against the wheel, and she tilted her head back and rested it on one of the spokes. She had visions of a mouse eating at her face and she shivered.

David threw water in Catherine's face and woke her up the next morning. He unlocked her chains and told her it was time to go to work.

"I need to pee," she said.

"Go ahead," he said and opened the barn door, motioning Catherine to use the outhouse. She went in and closed the door.

When she went into the morgue, there was a body lying on the embalming table so she put on her laboratory coat and mask. David grabbed her mask and yanked it off. "You can smell it now, Catherine. Get used to it," he said.

Consuelo came out of the apartment and Catherine noticed her black eye. David gave Consuelo some money and told her to go get breakfast for two, and bring it back to the office. When Consuelo got back she was told by David to join him in the office where they would eat breakfast together. Consuelo was not very hungry and only ate half of her food. David finished his plate and lit his cigarette and smoked it while Consuelo sat with him. After he finished, he put the cigarette out on Consuelo's uneaten food and told her to take it to Catherine.

Consuelo took the plate into the morgue and sat it on the table beside where Catherine was working.

"Mr. David said this was for you," she said apologetically.

Catherine gave her a quick smile. She didn't blame Consuelo. Catherine knew David was going to make her life a living hell. She would expect nothing less. Manny had come in and was given instructions by David to pick up another body outside of town. Manny looked at the two women and knew things were not right. When he saw Consuelo's eye he wanted to kill David, but he knew he was no match for him. In time he would take her and leave.

It was a busy week at the morgue and David would wake Catherine up at 5:00 every morning and make her go into the morgue and work, and sometimes she would not finish until six or seven in the evening. David would chain her to the wheel each night and then sleep with Consuelo. Her period had finally stopped and what she wanted most was a bath. She did not ask, because David would prolong it, if it was something she desired. It was Friday and she wondered if they would go to the farm. She was exhausted and longed to sleep in her bed. David began going to the café every night for his meals by himself and occasionally he would bring his leftover food or a cheese sandwich back for Catherine.

Alex took most of his evening meals at the café, too, and

noticed that after the baby's funeral David came alone, often asking for something to take his leftover food in. After watching David come in several evenings alone, Alex walked over to David's booth.

"I hope the Mrs. is not ill," Alex said.

"She's fine, what is it to you?" David said.

"Nothing," Alex said. "I just noticed that you had been eating alone lately, that's all."

"Well, she's still upset about the kid and doesn't want to get out," David replied.

Alex tipped his hat and left. Later when Alex was walking to the stables to check on his horse, he saw David and Catherine leave town in their wagon. They did not notice him, but he noticed Catherine. She looked dirty, her hair was in tangles and she looked unkempt. She had a hopeless look on her face and Alex felt sympathy for her. Catherine was glad they were leaving the morgue, and that she might be able to rest on Saturday. She was exhausted, and she had a terrible headache from breathing in the chemicals.

When they got home, David said, "Clean yourself up and come to bed."

Catherine was relieved that she could finally bathe and wash her hair. She had just put some soap into her wet head when David banged on the door and told her to hurry up. She scrubbed quickly and then rinsed it out.

She quickly dried off and walked into the bedroom. David was lying naked on the bed waiting for her. She was getting into bed when he grabbed her hair and twisted her head towards his, kissing her hard on the mouth. The evening was like a bad dream and nothing she did pleased him. He was brutal and unrelenting in his treatment towards her and she prayed again for death.

The September heat was stifling and after Catherine prepared David's breakfast the next morning, he gave her his orders.

"The stalls in the barn need the manure shovelled out. After that, throw in some fresh hay. Then after that you can do the laundry." Catherine shook her head yes. "I have to go into town on some business and when you finish with your chores, have my supper ready."

Catherine knew it was going to be ten to twenty degrees hotter in the barn so she decided to take care of the stalls first. She grabbed some gloves and a shovel and began shovelling up the manure in the stalls.

Alex had just finished breakfast at the café when he saw David come into town. Alex paid his check and went to the stables to fetch Pilgrim. He was at the Billings farm in less than thirty minutes. Alex noticed the barn door open and he watched from behind a cluster of trees.

He put his binoculars up to his eyes when he saw someone coming out of the barn. It was Catherine, and she was pushing a wheelbarrow. He saw her take the wheelbarrow behind the barn, empty it and go back towards the barn. Before she went back in she took her apron and wiped her face with it, then walked slowly over to the well, pumped some water on to her apron, and wiped her face again. When Catherine went back into the barn he took off towards the house. Alex got off his horse and walked into the barn.

"Catherine," Alex said. She looked up, startled. She almost collapsed, but Alex caught her. "You shouldn't be doing this. You just had a baby."

She didn't answer him. "Look, I know you can hear me and I think you can also talk. Tell me; is you husband making you do this?" Alex demanded.

"You have to leave," Catherine said almost in a whisper.

"Tell me what happened to your baby," Alex pleaded.

"He's gone, please leave now," Catherine begged him.

"I can help you," Alex said.

Catherine shook her head no and said. "It's too late. You have to go now before he comes back and sees you."

Catherine picked up the shovel and began working again.

Alex stood there watching. He couldn't help but notice the rope attached to the pulley and saw fresh blood on the ground. He looked back at Catherine and she stared at him. There was nothing he could do if she were not willing to help herself.

Alex took out his card and forced it into her hand. "When you are ready, I'll help you," he said, and left.

Catherine took his card and hid it under a rock. She had just finished cleaning the stalls when David came back home.

"I heard some news today that might interest you," David teased. Catherine looked at him. "Seems someone dropped off a baby at the church and he wasn't found until the next morning. He was dead," David told her, and Catherine fainted.

David poured some water on her face. She opened her eyes and David continued saying, "How does it feel to know you murdered your own baby?" he asked her.

Catherine started crying. David laughed at her. It took a few minutes before she realized that David was lying to her, and she went into the house and gathered up the laundry. David's verbal abuse often hurt as much as the beatings. She should have known that he would do everything in his power to make her life miserable, including lying to her.

CHAPTER 14

Carla Beranger had invited John Merit and his sister, Amelia, to join her and her daughters at her uncle's house for Thanksgiving dinner. Carla's uncle was John's boss and he was happy to accept. Amelia had only met Carla once, and she really did not care for her, but she would never tell John that. Carla's two daughters were eight and eleven and they were not well-behaved. They both were a bit overweight and had pudgy cheeks. It was no wonder, Amelia thought. They had huge appetites and terrible table manners. Carla said they were just going through puberty and they would grow out of it. Amelia wondered about that and hoped that John would see through Carla's innuendos.

"Have you talked to your lawyers yet about getting that death certificate?" Carla's uncle asked John.

He almost choked and wondered how he knew.

Carla said, "I hope you don't mind, John, I might have mentioned to him about the death certificate."

"No, no, that's all right, uh, I filed the petition last week," John answered.

Amelia looked at John and was hurt that he had not told her. After dinner, Amelia said she was tired and asked John to take her home

"I'll have my driver taker her home," Carla said. "John, you can stay a little longer, can't you?" Carla asked.

Amelia glared at John when she left.

When John got home later that evening, he knocked on Amelia's door. "Hey sis, can I come in?" he asked.

Amelia had a book in her hand and she was sitting up in bed.

"I know I should have said something to you about having Catherine declared dead, and I'm sorry you had to hear about it from someone else. I know you loved Catherine, too, but I have to move on. A year is long enough," John said.

"I understand," Amelia said.

"There's one more thing," he said and hesitated. "I've asked Carla to marry me."

"Will she and her daughters move in with us?" Amelia asked.

"No," John said. "She wants me to move into her house because it is much bigger than ours. I know you don't really care for her, and I am hoping we can find someone to move in with you and take care of you. This is your home and I want you to have it."

John didn't wait for an answer. He heard Amelia softly crying after he closed the door.

It was close to Christmas before the judge signed the papers declaring Catherine Merit dead. It had been over a year and John felt that was long enough. Carla went with John for the signing and then they left to get their marriage license. Carla had planned their wedding and it would be a small affair at her house with about fifty people.

"I thought it was just going to be a small wedding," John teased when he heard the number of people who were coming.

"Fifty is small," Carla said.

They were to be married on Sunday, December 22nd at 4:00 in the afternoon by the pastor of her church, so they would be together on Christmas morning. John would have preferred a Catholic wedding, but since Carla was a Protestant, he knew it was out of the question. He did send Father Jonathan an invitation but his RSVP said he was unable to attend.

John interviewed several ladies who had expressed an interest in the ad he had placed in the newspaper for a live-in companion for Amelia. There was one lady he liked and set up a meeting at his house with Amelia. The lady was a widow with no children and she was a member of St. Mary's Catholic Church. She was forty-two and only a few years older than Amelia. Amelia thought the lady to be pleasant and approved John's choice. She moved in the week before the wedding.

John spent most evenings after work with Carla, and only came home to sleep at nights. Amelia still felt that John was abandoning her, and she couldn't help but resent Carla. She really did not want to go to the wedding, but she wasn't sure she could disappoint John like that.

John spent the Saturday before the wedding packing up some of his things from his study and getting his clothes together. He made several trips back and forth to Carla's house, taking his possessions, and was disappointed that Carla did not make very much room for his things. He had to use the small hall closet for his clothes and there was not a study for him to use. Carla apologized that the study was full of her personal things, and she would try and move some things around so he could use it too. Carla hollered at the girls several times about picking up things and keeping the house nice for the party the next day. John felt tense and out of place, but he did not say anything. When John left, Carla kissed him on the cheek and said she couldn't wait until they were married. She would see John at 4:00 on Sunday afternoon.

When John woke up Sunday morning, he had a terrible feeling in the pit of his stomach. He was beginning to have second thoughts. He had the run of his whole house when he and Catherine shared it with Amelia. Now he felt like he was going to be a visitor in a new house, with three women he barely knew. His thoughts went back to Catherine and their wedding night, and he hated himself for allowing her to be taken. He had promised himself that he would not cry again, and then a terrible thought came to his mind. What if the baby Father Jonathan had picked up was really his? John tried to put the thought out of his mind. After lunch, John put on his new suit that Carla had picked out, and out of habit, he picked up his gold watch Catherine had given him and he opened it for the last time. He closed it and walked over and opened Catherine's jewelry box and put the gold watch in the box. It wouldn't be right for him to keep it, he thought. He picked it back up and kissed it and whispered, "Goodbye, Catherine, I will always love you."

When John went downstairs, Amelia was not dressed and he asked her why she wasn't ready.

"I have a headache and I just don't feel like being around a lot of people I don't know."

"I'm sorry." John bent over and kissed her and said, "I understand. If I weren't the groom I wouldn't be going either." Before John walked out the door he turned and said, "You know you can call me anytime, all right?"

Amelia smiled and said, yes.

The house was packed with people when John arrived. There were fresh flowers everywhere and Cindy, Carla's oldest daughter, met him at the door. "My mom said I should tell you that she won't be down until straight up 4:00." She turned and ran upstairs.

John went into the kitchen to pour himself a drink and he could hardly make his way over to the bar. There were caterers and people everywhere. He found the scotch and poured himself a stiff drink to take the edge off.

"There you are," Walter, Carla's uncle, said. "Big day ahead of you. Carla sure knows how to throw a party."

John lifted his glass as if he was making a toast, and he took another drink.

John and Carla exchanged vows in front of the fireplace, and after a few words by the pastor they were told they could kiss. The whole thing was over in fifteen minutes. Carla couldn't have been happier and she did look lovely in her designer evening gown. Carla had hired a professional photographer from Houston, Texas, to take pictures and that seemed to take forever. John wondered how much that was going to cost.   The drinks and food was constantly replenished and people began to leave around 7:00 PM. John was tired and relieved when it was finally over. Carla began shouting orders to everyone. John tried to stay out of the way, and it was close to 8:30 PM when the last caterer left. Carla ordered the girls to bed and there was a huge fight about having to go to bed early. John decided not to say anything, but knew he would have to make some suggestions to Carla at some point about the girls' behavior.

They were finally alone in the bedroom and John felt awkward. He and Carla had only kissed prior to their wedding, and he wasn't sure if he should undress her or just put on his pyjamas. Carla answered his thoughts.

"For heaven's sake, John, put on your pyjamas."

Carla went behind her dressing screen and began taking off her clothes. John took his pyjamas and went into the bathroom to change. Carla was still behind her dressing screen when he came out and looked at the bed. He didn't know which side to get on.

"Mine is the right side," Carla said.

John walked around the bed and crawled under the covers. Carla was in the bathroom for a long time and John was afraid he was going to fall asleep before she came out. Finally, Carla walked over to the bed and turned out the light and crawled under the covers. She had put on a long gown with long sleeves, and when John reached over to kiss her, she said, "Look, I don't know about you but I'm exhausted. Can we just do this husband and wife thing another night?"

"Sure," John said and he turned over, facing away from her.

If John had reservations earlier, they were certainly confirmed now. He had made the biggest mistake of his life. Carla was like a different person. He knew he was not madly in love with her, like he was Catherine, but he thought if he remarried it would help him forget about Catherine. It was too late now, and he was just going to have to make it work.

Father Jonathan had not regularly visited the orphanage at St. Mary's. He knew the children were well taken care of by the sisters, and his visits were usually short. He now made it a habit to check on Daniel daily. The sisters loved tending to Daniel, because he was such a sweet baby and did not cry like some of the other newborns. Daniel was easy going and his piercing dark eyes automatically drew you to him. Father Jonathan loved sitting in the rocking chair and cradling him in his arms. He knew he should not get too attached, but he felt a strong bond with the child. Father Jonathan had also put a note in Daniel's file. "Cannot be adopted without consent of parents." He had made the decision that Daniel would live permanently at the orphanage, until his mother or father came to claim him. Father Jonathan could see Catherine's nose and John's strong eyes in Daniel.

"Someday they will come for you, my son," he whispered to Daniel.

Several days had passed since the wedding and John still felt like a stranger in Carla's house. After dinner, Carla would help the girls with their homework and John would sit in the living room and read. There was always a fuss before bedtime, and then Carla would go into her study for a while. On the third night John followed Carla into her study.

"Oh," she said, "I'm glad you came in. I have a few bills here for you to pay."

Carla handed John some papers and he looked at them one at a time.

"Carla," John said. "There's over $400 worth of bills here."

"I know," Carla said, "I guess I went a little crazy on the wedding."

"You should have discussed this with me first," John said.

"I know and I'm so sorry, I just didn't think you would mind," Carla protested.

John left the study and went upstairs. Carla knew John was angry with her and decided she needed to try another approach.

John was already in bed with the light out when Carla crawled under the covers. He really didn't want to talk to her, and he pretended to be asleep. Carla put her arms around him and started kissing him on his neck and then moved her hand down, touching his navel. It had been over a year since John had been with a woman, and he was surprised when he became aroused. She fondled him and he responded to her touch. He turned around and he kissed her.

She had pulled her gown up and moved his arousal inside her. John came quickly and he apologized to Carla, telling her it had been a long time since he had been with a woman. She said she was glad it was quick, and she hoped he wasn't mad at her anymore. John took a deep breath and let it out slowly. He lay on his back and stared into the dark. He felt the emptiness of the moment, and he wondered how his life had come to this.

It was two days before Christmas when Alex Cooper got a telegram from his company telling him that he needed to leave Beaumont and go to Amarillo for a couple of months. He wasn't expecting to leave Beaumont so soon, as his job was not finished. He had only signed up two-thirds of the people he had interviewed, and being away could cost the company thousands of dollars. He knew there were problems in Amarillo and wondered why one of the other men could not be assigned to it. He figured that since it was so close to Christmas and he did not have a family, he would be the likely choice. Normally, Alex would welcome the change and not question it. His thoughts went immediately to Catherine Billings. He had hoped that she might call him, and now if she did call, he wouldn't be there for her. Damn, he thought, why was he so drawn to her? Maybe leaving for a couple of months would clear his head. Dianne had asked him to stay the last night with her, but Alex excused himself, saying he had work he had to finish. She cried a bit and asked Alex to write her. He said he would, but he no longer had any interest in

Dianne. Catherine was on his mind constantly.

The next morning Alex packed up his suitcase and started walking to the train station. He had made arrangements for Pilgrim to be on the same train, so he checked to make sure the stables had taken care of their end. He was at the corner when David and Catherine rode by in their wagon. Catherine saw Alex's suitcase and their eyes caught one another. She stared as long as she could at Alex and then turned and looked away. He stopped and watched as their wagon turned the corner and Catherine looked back at him as if to say goodbye. He had a strange feeling that he needed to rescue her from whatever it was she was hiding. He walked back a few steps, so he could see her again, but they were gone.

The train whistle reminded Alex that he had a job to get to. After boarding the train, he settled into his seat and noticed a newspaper someone had left behind, so he picked it up and looked at it. The date was December 23, 1901, and it was a Galveston Gazette. The paper was a day old, but he kept it, thinking it would help pass the time. Alex stared out the window for a while, still thinking about Catherine, and he decided the newspaper might be a good distraction. The news was pretty much the same as it was in most towns. There were articles about local stuff and news about Theodore Roosevelt, the new President of the United States. He had been sworn in after President William McKinley died from a gunshot wound on September 14, 1901. It seemed the president had begun pulling together his new cabinet. David scanned through the first two pages and stopped when an article caught his eye. It was the name that jumped out at him on the first line:

Medical Student, Catherine Eastman Merit
Declared Dead

Catherine Eastman Merit, a local medical student and intern at St. Mary's Hospital, disappeared a year ago, several days before Thanksgiving. After months of investigative work by local police and private investigators, Judge Oval Williams declared Mrs. Merit to be dead so that her husband, John Merit, could wed local socialite Carla Beranger. Mr. Merit and Mrs. Beranger married on December 22, 1901.

Alex read the article several times and remembered the first time he had come across John Merit in the bar of the Lancaster Hotel, when he was talking to a private investigator. Could Catherine Merit be Catherine Billings? He wondered. Alex carefully tore the article out of the newspaper, folding it carefully, and putting it in his wallet. The trip to Amarillo was going to take the better part of the day and Alex would have to change to a different train when he got to Houston. The article haunted Alex most of the trip and he wished there was some way he could find out what Catherine had looked like. Maybe on his way back he could take an extra day or two and detour through Galveston. Perhaps the police could describe to him what she looked like. It was a long shot and maybe by the time he returned to Beaumont, he would have her out of his head. It was going to be a long two months, Alex thought to himself.

Catherine had mixed feelings when she saw Alex leaving with his suitcase. She wondered if he were leaving for good, or just going on a trip. She liked running into him occasionally at the café. When he had come into the barn and they talked, she knew she could trust him not to say anything. It was like they had a secret together. She hoped he would be back and wasn't leaving for good. She had no friends, but for some reason she felt like Alex was her friend.

Catherine had no idea what day it was. She knew it was close to Christmas as there were decorations up in all the windows and people up and down the streets were carrying packages. She saw toys and colored lights in the windows and wondered what Christmas would have been like with Daniel. She remembered Christmas with her own family back in England and it made her happy to think about the happier times. She hoped the memories would see her through the days of pain she suffered. She thought of John and their first Christmas together, and she smiled to herself when she thought of their first kiss and the butterflies in her stomach. She was still daydreaming when David pulled her off the wagon and told her to get to work.

CHAPTER 15

Spindletop had brought the sleepy little town of Beaumont to life and created a dramatic need for the expansion of local services and businesses. Hotel Dieu, Beaumont's only hospital, had begun erecting a second building, adding thirty-six more beds to its current twenty-four-bed capacity. With the influx of an additional twenty thousand people, it was only a matter of time before Billings Undertaking Services would find itself up against a newer, more elegant funeral home that had just opened at the opposite end of Main Street, and had a large show room of professionally made caskets and coffins.

David had already been cutting corners, and his less than professional reputation now put him in second place behind Raymond Porter's Funeral Services, which did not make David happy at all. Not to mention the fact that David's egotistical and heartless attitude did not set well with the townspeople of Beaumont. He had a way of brushing people off and the new funeral home was well received by everyone, excluding David.

Once David found out what Porter's Funeral Services was charging, he cut his prices to be more competitive. He knew he could make up the difference by stealing the jewelry and the gold from the teeth of the deceased. The new place still out-classed David's and David had no intention of trying to compete with that. There were more poor people in Beaumont that rich ones, so he was always going to get his fair share of the dead.

David had known of Manny and Consuelo's little affair for several months now, but he needed Manny to help him until he could find the right replacement. David had gone to the stables to check on one of his horses that had thrown a shoe one morning, and he heard a young man say, "Mr. David, is that you?"

David turned around and it was Jasper Cummings from the chain gang at the prison farm. Jasper was a young colored man who befriended David when he first arrived at the prison farm, and they were friends.

David motioned for him to follow outside. Jasper told David he had been released a month earlier from the chain gang and he had come to Beaumont because he thought he could find work. David confided to Jasper that he had been able to escape, but Jasper already knew that. He also told Jasper that he needed someone he could trust to work in the undertaking business and that he would pay Jasper well if he would keep his mouth shut about David's background and come to work for him. Jasper jumped at the opportunity. David told him to give him a day or so, because he had to take care of the man that was currently working for him.

That evening David took Catherine back to the farm, chained her to the bed, and went back into town. Catherine was surprised when David insisted on putting the chain on. She didn't think she had done anything to make him suspicious of her, or that she might run. With David's unpredictable behavior though, nothing really surprised Catherine.

David had told Manny before he left that he wanted Manny to work late and that he would be back after taking Catherine home. David stopped by the stables first and picked up Jasper, telling him that he could start his new job that evening, and that he needed his help with something. Manny was waiting for David when he got to the morgue. David introduced Jasper as a second helper, since they had so much business. Manny was delighted, thinking it would give him more free time with Consuelo. David told Manny to show Jasper where he kept the woodworking tools and wood for the coffins.

"I'll join you two in a few minutes. I just have to get something in my office," David said.

Consuelo came out of the apartment and David yelled at her to stay inside the apartment, and Consuelo obeyed. David walked over and picked up a rag and soaked it with chloroform. He put it in his pocket and went into the barn. Consuelo watched through the partially open door and wondered what he was doing.

Manny was showing Jasper some plans on how to make a coffin, and when he turned around, David caught him off guard. David placed the rag soaked in chloroform over Manny's face. Manny tried to struggle, but the chloroform was so strong, he went out immediately. Jasper was stunned.

"Help me tie him up," David demanded.

Jasper didn't move.

"Jasper, grab that rope and bring it to me," David said.

Jasper picked up the rope and gave it to David, still unsure about what just happened. David tied up Manny and gagged him.

"Help me get one of the coffins," David ordered Jasper.

Together, David and Jasper put Manny in one of the coffins and put it on the wagon. They hitched up the horse to the wagon and they left the barn, heading towards the cemetery.

Jasper was not sure what to say and David could sense his uneasiness.

"The man in the coffin has been stealing from me. It's time for payback," David said. It was almost dark when the wagon pulled up beside a freshly dug grave at the cemetery.

"You ain't gonna bury him alive, are you?" Jasper asked David.

"Was thinking about it," David said.

"That just ain't human," Jasper said.

"O K," David said, "then you kill him." David opened the

coffin and Manny was looking up at them. Manny tried to sit up and David took a shovel and hit him over the head, causing Manny to fall back into the coffin. He handed the shovel to Manny and said, "finish him off."

"I ain't never killed nobody!" Jasper explained.

"Do as I say or you will be joining him," David said.

Jasper's eyes widened and David took the shovel from him and slammed it down on Manny's throat, cutting his neck half-open. Jasper's mouth fell open and he thought about running, but knew he would be next if he did. David locked the coffin back up and told Jasper to help bury him. Once the coffin was in the ground, David watched as Jasper shovelled the dirt back into the hole.

The two men barely spoke on their ride back into town. Before they got to the barn David stopped the horse and turned to Jasper.

"The way I see it," David said, "you can keep your mouth shut and stay and work for me, or I can tell the local sheriff you and Manny got in a fight and you killed him. What will it be?" David asked.

Jasper tried to swallow and then said, "I'll work for you, Mr. David."

David told him he could sleep in the barn that night, and that he had better be there in the morning when he got to work. Jasper was scared. He was barely twenty and he had seen men like David at the prison camps, but he had never thought David was a killer. He was fearful that if he left, David would make good on his promise to tell the sheriff Jasper killed Manny. Jasper didn't want to go back to the prison farm, so he decided he would stay and work for David.

The next morning Consuelo was already getting things ready. Two bodies had been dropped off by the sheriff. There had been a fight in one of the bars and it ended up in a shootout in the street. They would not have to embalm them, but they had to get them ready for the families to identify and take care of whatever instructions the family deemed to be worthy of the dead. Consuelo was worried about

Manny, but knew better than to ask David. She felt strongly that David had done something to Manny. Catherine was finishing up for the day when Consuelo came in crying.

"Manny is gone," she said. Catherine made a gesture showing she did not understand. "He did not come to work today, and there is a new man working in the barn. Manny would not leave without me," she said.

Catherine put her arms around her and tried to console her. They heard David come in the front door and they both pretended to be working. Consuelo drew in a deep breath and decided to casually ask David where Manny was.

"He gave me notice last night that he was leaving town. I had to find someone to take his place. The black man, Jasper, in the barn, is taking his place. Found him at the stables," David said.

Consuelo wanted to ask more questions, but knew better. David told Consuelo to wait in the apartment and he would join her in a few minutes. David turned to Catherine and told her that when she was through to wait in the front office for him.

Catherine finished up and went into the front office. She heard a scream and then David shouting obscenities at Consuelo. She closed her eyes and prayed for Consuelo. Catherine knew that if David found out that Consuelo and Manny were sleeping together, the outcome would not be good. She also knew that David would remove anybody or anything that got in the way of him and his women. That was one of the reasons Catherine did not accept Alex's offer to help. She would never forgive herself if David killed Alex, or anyone else who might try and help her.

She was doomed and she knew her destiny. David was heartless and Catherine prayed that in the silent reproaches of her consciousness she could someday find it in her heart to forgive him for what he had done to her. For now, she had to accept the penalties of the truth, in silence, and without complaint.

David came into the office and told Catherine to get in the

wagon. She walked to the barn obediently and climbed up on the wagon. She sat there for awhile and when David did not come, she got down and settled into some straw. She fell asleep and was awakened when a young black man tripped over her. She screamed. Within seconds David was in the barn with a lantern.

"I's so sorry," said Jasper. "I, I wasn't expectin' a woman to be laying in the hay."

David laughed and told Jasper it was all right. "She's my wife. She doesn't talk and she can't hear either," David explained to Jasper. "I told her to wait for me and she must have fallen asleep."

David went over and grabbed Catherine's hand and pulled her up. He put her up on the wagon and they left.

It was late when Alex finally arrived in Amarillo. The first leg of his trip seemed long because the private rooms in the club car were already sold out and he had to listen to crying babies and fighting children in the regular car. He did manage to find a place at the bar the last hour of his trip before he got to San Antonio. There was a cancellation on his next leg, and he was relieved to get a small private room in the Pullman car. He stared out the window for a while and then took out his wallet and looked at the newspaper article he had torn out of the paper earlier in the day. He was perplexed as to why he was so drawn to Catherine. Maybe she wasn't that same woman who disappeared a year earlier. Maybe she was a mail-order bride whose family just wanted to marry her off. He had to stop thinking about her. Whatever the case, there was not anything he could do now, and it was going to be a long two months.

Catherine was pleased that David did not stay the night with her, even though he felt compelled to chain her to the bed. He had made the chain long enough that she could go to the water closet, but that was all. She had only eaten an apple and crackers for lunch and she drank a full glass of water that had come from the well. She hoped it would stop her hunger pains. She took her time washing herself and noticed that some of her old bruises were fading. She looked up at her image staring back at her from the medicine cabinet mirror. She looked tired, and she had dark circles under her eyes. She was barely nineteen years old and she looked much older, she thought to herself. She wanted to cry but her tears had stopped flowing months ago. Now she only cried from physical pain, which she could not help. Once Catherine had made up her mind to send Daniel away for his own protection, she vowed to shed no more tears. Her only prayer was that Daniel was under the protective eye of Father Jonathan and her husband, John Merit. At least she felt she had fulfilled one person's dream, and that was a son for John.

CHAPTER 16

John Merit was glad to be back at work after his wedding and the Christmas holidays. All he could say about it was that it was different. His new wife, Carla, lavished her two daughters with expensive gifts and clothes for Christmas and she had a wonderful seated dinner for her family and John's sister, Amelia. Carla gave John a new gold pocket watch, since she noticed he did not carry the one Catherine had given him anymore. Carla also gave Amelia some French embroidery and thread. Amelia had originally declined, but John personally went and picked her up and would not leave until she said yes. The holidays were over, but the bills continued to be left for John to pay.

After a month John decided it was time to have a heart-to-heart talk with Carla about her extravagant purchases and spending.

"But John," she said, "I've always had a full time maid and I have to wear nice things. It is expected of a woman in our rank of society."

John had also found out that he now had to pay for a hefty mortgage on Carla's house, and he was still paying for the house he and Catherine had built, and Amelia was now living in. John had always paid for Amelia's expenses and medicines from a small insurance fund his parents had left, and it was slowly drying up. He was spending more than he was making and he was slowly going through his savings. John had to put his foot down and he told Carla she could not buy one more thing without his consent, or he would cancel their credit at all the stores. She cried and threw a huge tantrum, stomping her foot and yelling at him like he was a child. Their sex life was not wonderful to begin with, and now John had to sleep in the guest room. John rubbed his forehead as he looked down at the papers in his hands. Why hadn't he thought of asking questions before he married Carla? Her uncle gave John the impression that she had her own money and that was certainly not true. John decided to bring the matter up to Carla's uncle, John's boss.

Walter motioned for John to come into his office when he saw John approach. "Wonderful Christmas dinner, John," Walter said.

"Thank you, sir," John said. "I need to talk to you about a little family matter if you have time," John said hesitantly.

"Sure, Sure, tell me what's on your mind," Walter said. John proceeded to fill Walter in on Carla's expensive tastes and that he was led to believe that Carla had her own money.

"Well, that's not entirely true," Walter told him. "You see, when my nephew, Carla's husband, passed away a few years ago, he set up a trust for the girls that would take care of their needs and college, if they go. He felt Carla would probably get remarried and her new husband would take care of her. He had taken out a mortgage on the house he inherited from his father, who was my brother, to pay off some bills but I don't know what he still owed on it. My nephew left her about $10,000 in life insurance and I guess she used that to make repairs after the storm, and live on for the last year. I also helped her from time to time," Walter concluded, and then apologized by saying, "I know she has expensive tastes and I'm sorry about that. My nephew complained about it all the time."

John looked out the window at the street, listening intently. "Then," John said, "I guess I need to put my foot down."

"Good luck with that," Walter said.

John didn't feel any better when he left Walter's office, but he knew one thing; the spending had to stop. When John got home that evening, he asked Carla to hurry and get through with the girls' studies and that he had something important to talk to her about. Carla didn't say anything, but stared at him like it inconvenienced her.

"What is it that is so important that I can't spend time with my own daughters?" she demanded when she approached John.

"I have prepared a budget that sets out the necessary expenses first, like the mortgage payment, food, utilities, etc. The bottom line is what is left. I also have my own obligations which include the mortgage payment on my house, plus the food, utilities, etc. for my sister. I feel that I can give you a generous allowance of $250 a month which should pay for your full time maid, your hairdresser, clothes, and your miscellaneous expenses." Carla's mouth dropped open and before she could respond John said, "Walter told me that the girls had a trust fund for their specific needs and I would appreciate you using that for their clothes and necessities."

Carla grabbed the budget from John's hand and looked at it.

"My first husband never treated me this way. Why are you so cruel to me?" and she began crying.

"Carla," John said, "I'm drowning in debt and if you continue to spend like you have been doing, we will be in the food line in three months."

"Walter told me you were such a great catch and that you had money," she said before she realized how it sounded.

John looked astounded by her statement and walked out. John went upstairs and took his suitcase out of the closet. He began packing up his things from the two bottom drawers. Carla was at the door, still crying. She went over to him and told him how sorry she was and that she didn't mean it the way it sounded. That she really loved him and wanted their marriage to work.

"I'll do anything, just please don't leave me," she pleaded.

John stood and looked at her and took a deep breath before he said, "I want this to work, too, but you have to be willing to make some sacrifices."

Carla promised and then she began kissing him. Their intimacy was always on Carla's terms, and she manipulated her sexual advances to arouse John at his most vulnerable moments. He wanted to pull away, but she had unzipped his pants and put her hand inside his trousers. He closed his eyes and tried not to get aroused. Carla was all over him, teasing him, sucking on his ear and then she jumped on him, straddling him with her legs, knocking him down to the floor. John couldn't help himself. He began kissing her back, caught in the heated moment of his own sexual desires, and then she pulled up her dress and got on top of him. He had come in a matter of a few seconds. Strangely enough when it was over, John felt as though he had been raped. Carla got up and straightened her dress and left the room. John lay there for a few minutes, not feeling anything and wishing he were dead.

Daniel Merit was amazing to watch. He liked the attention he was getting from the sisters, but most of all, he lit up like a Christmas tree when he focused on Father Jonathan. He would waive his hands and kick his feet in excitement. Father Jonathan looked forward to finishing his rounds at the hospital every night and always made Daniel his last stop. He would pick him up and carry him over to a rocker, where a sister would hand Father Jonathan a baby bottle, and he would give him his bedtime bottle. Sometimes Father Jonathan would be late, but Daniel never cried because he was hungry. He would quietly lie in his crib and wait. It was a bond they had created between the two; a dependency that they had inflicted upon one another without a word. Father Jonathan knew he was going somewhere he should not be going, but he loved Daniel, and until Daniel's parents showed up to claim him, he would give him all the love he deserved. Daniel was sleeping through the night by the time he was two–and–one-half-months old. He awoke early in the morning and hungrily sucked on his bottle, often taking an extra ounce or two. He was strong and was developing a sweet personality, like none the sisters had ever seen. Daniel was everyone's favorite. Most of the babies were adopted when they were infants and it was unusual for the sisters or Father Jonathan to ever see them grow beyond one or two months.

CHAPTER 17

Catherine knew when she had skipped her last period that she was most likely pregnant again. She didn't have the morning sickness like she had had before, but there was little doubt that she was pregnant. She was waiting for a good time to tell David, but lately there were no good times. He had become verbally abusive to her and his cutting remarks would slice her equally as bad as a whipping did. Now that she was pregnant, she hoped she would not have to endure the whippings. David usually used the horse whip which was extremely painful, and he used it on her when she did not have any clothes on. She tried hard not to aggravate him, but it was difficult since she was not allowed to speak in public. She couldn't ask questions and sometimes he would assume she should do something that she wasn't aware of. A day without a whipping was a good day. Now that she was pregnant, he might be easier on her, but that did not always hold true. David was equally hard on Consuelo, and it was hard for either of them to please him. Every afternoon he would choose one or the other to join him in the apartment to feed his sexual fantasies. Usually it was Consuelo, because Catherine was more proficient with the embalming procedures and Consuelo usually assisted. Jasper learned the ropes pretty fast and helped carry bodies in and out, and in his off time, he was busy building the coffins or taking care of picking up and delivery bodies. Jasper knew better than to agitate David and tried to please him at every turn. He was afraid of

David, too. He frequently reflected on the night David used the shovel to end Manny's life, and he knew David would not hesitate to do the same thing to him.

When Consuelo skipped her period, she was excited that she might be pregnant. She could not wait until she could tell David. When she told him, it did not set well with him and the two went into the barn.

"What makes you think it is my child? I know you and Manny were sleeping together."

Consuelo was stunned and hadn't thought about that. "It is not Manny's baby. We did not sleep together," Consuelo lied.

David hit her hard with his hand across her face and she fell to the ground. "Don't say a thing about this to anyone, not Catherine, not Jasper, no one. Do you understand?" David asked her. Consuelo shook her head yes.

It was Friday evening and Catherine and David had just finished loading up supplies to take to the farm. They were just out of the city when Catherine told David she thought she was pregnant. David didn't answer. Catherine was sure he heard her and decided not to repeat it. She had no idea what his reaction was going to be, and she wished he would say something. Sometimes his silence spoke louder than his words. They unloaded the supplies and Catherine took the groceries into the kitchen. She heard David several steps behind her. He grabbed her arm and swung her around and the groceries fell to the floor. He pulled her into the bedroom and slapped her across the face and it stung. Her reflexes made her hand come up to her face to protect it from another blow and he grabbed it and twisted it behind her. She screamed from pain.

"Don't get too attached to this one," he said. "I may not let you keep it. We don't have time for kids."

Catherine was stunned by his remark, and wasn't sure what he meant. "But, it would be your child," she pleaded.

David went back outside to put the rest of the supplies in the barn. He was upset that Catherine and Consuelo were both pregnant, and he wondered if there might be a doctor in the county that could do an abortion. The more he thought about it, the more he began to think it was a good idea. Children would take both of them away from being able to work efficiently. He remembered how adoringly Catherine had cooed at the baby and that she was so protective and attached to it. Consuelo would be no different.

David's fervid temper often kept him from thinking clearly. He had a piercing dark side and an inexorable temper. He could be mellow at some point, and then turn on anyone and everyone in a matter of seconds. This often stood in the way of his making good business decisions, and it was clearly the reason why the good people of Beaumont did not care for him. David liked the way things were and he didn't want anyone or anything to threaten his lifestyle. Consuelo was his and he would share her with no one.

When the medicine man came through the middle of the week, David took him aside and asked him about where a woman could get an abortion, and possibly be fixed so she could not have any more children. The medicine man's name was Harry Jackson and he told David that he did abortions from time to time, under certain circumstances, but that it was very expensive.

"What's expensive?" asked David.

"Twenty-five dollars," Harry said.

"That's fine," David said. "Can you be at the back of the barn at 6:00 p.m. tonight? Harry Jackson told him that could be arranged and they agreed to meet.

That evening David told Jasper to take Catherine home and sleep in the barn at the farm and then return in the morning with Catherine at 8:00 a.m. After they left, David had fifteen minutes before Harry Jackson was to come. David went to the chemical cabinet and pulled out a bottle of chloroform and bathed a rag in it. He went into the apartment where Consuelo was and covered her face with the rag. She had fainted in an instant. David removed her clothing from the waist down and carried her to the embalming table and tied her hands to the corners in case she woke up. Harry Jackson was on time and the two men went inside. The medicine man took out another chemical which David was not aware of, and then he put it inside a small oval mask that he placed over Consuelo's face.

"This should make her sleep for a couple of hours," he said.

David watched as the medicine man took out his instruments and began working on Consuelo.

"She won't know what happened to her when she wakes in the morning," Harry said. "You can just tell her she had a miscarriage."

After Harry was finished, he cleaned up his instruments, packed up his supplies, and then helped David get Consuelo into the bed in the apartment. David was relieved that this one was over. He would have to think about Catherine. He may have to let the baby go to full term. Catherine would know better, if he tried to give her an abortion. She knew too much about medicine.

CHAPTER 18

Amarillo, Texas, was a small Texas town located in West Texas, out in the middle of nowhere. Glacier Oil Company had some land leases that they were considering buying, and they needed Alex's engineering expertise before the company made the deal.

When Alex got off the train, it was cold and windy and the dust storm had just come up. He knew immediately that he did not want to stay here for two months, and decided to get the work done as quickly as possible and head back to Beaumont. Alex walked back to the stock car and watched as Pilgrim got off the train. Pilgrim immediately walked over to Alex and nudged him.

Things didn't go quite the way Alex had planned it. He spent hours on horseback, scouting out the various farms and leases, and he had to wear a bandana over his nose and mouth so he would not have to breathe in or eat the Amarillo dirt. He was glad he had brought Pilgrim. It gave him something to talk to, and he knew Pilgrim always had his back. It took Alex just under two months to get everything in place, so he could turn it over to the lawyers to finish up. He couldn't wait to leave.

There was hardly a day that Alex didn't think about Catherine. She was in and out of his thoughts like summer mosquitoes on a cow. He had made the decision early on to make a detour on his trip back to Beaumont, and take a train from San Antonio to Galveston. Alex knew the telegram was coming, so he checked the schedule and decided he would leave on a 5:00 a.m. train. He wasn't sure where he would start his search when he got there, but he would make that decision on the way. Pilgrim was sent directly back to Beaumont and Alex sent instructions to the stable to pick him up.

The instructions on the telegram were simple: Beaumont needs you. The Boss. Alex finished up his work for the day and went back to the hotel to check out early. He knew he would not get much sleep, so he decided after his shower to put his travelling suit on and sleep on top of the bed. He woke up every couple of hours to check the time and when he looked again, it was closed to 4:00 , so he picked up his suitcase and walked to the train station. He felt anxious, and was never so glad to leave a place, and hoped he would not have to come back ever again. Alex hated Amarillo.

There wasn't much to see on his leg from Amarillo to San Antonio, so he dozed off and woke when the porter called out the San Antonio stop. He did not get off since he was staying on the same train and decided to walk back to the dining car and have breakfast. The train was only half full because Galveston had not fully come back from the 1900 storm. Alex had never been to Galveston, since there obviously was no oil there. Just a big sand dune with a city built on it. The newspaper article about Catherine was beginning to get worn because Alex had taken it in and out of his wallet so much. He decided not to open it again. He had memorized every word of it. The only reason he ever took it out was because it somehow made him feel close to Catherine. He was attracted to her, and never in his life had he met a woman who had a way of drawing you to her the way Catherine did. He knew he felt sorry for her and the only reason he could think of for wanting to help her was because of the evil man she was married too. Alex finished his breakfast and went back to his seat. He fell asleep again and woke up when he heard the Galveston stop called.

Alex stopped one of the depot clerks and asked how far the police station was. The clerk gave him directions and told him the trolley stopped right next to it. It didn't take long to get there, and Alex made his exit. He asked the officer at the front desk if he could talk to the man who headed up the investigation of a missing person named Catherine Merit about a year ago. After waiting for twenty minutes, a man came out and introduced himself as Sergeant Husky. Alex introduced himself and asked if the Sergeant was familiar with the disappearance of Catherine Merit.

"Mind if I ask why you are inquiring about something that doesn't concern you?" Husky asked.

"I might have some information about her disappearance and I was hoping you could tell me what she looked like," Alex said.

"What kind of information?" Husky asked. Alex could tell the Sergeant did not want to give him any information so he decided to try a different approach.

"I think she is alive and living in Beaumont. Her name is Catherine and she showed up about a year ago, about the time she went missing from Galveston," Alex told Husky.

"Did she tell you she was the same woman?"

"No... her husband claims she was a mail-order bride and that she is a deaf-mute."

"I think you are barking up the wrong tree, here. Why don't you just go back to where you came from and let us do the police work?" Husky said.

"That's just why I'm here. I was hoping you might look into it. Could you at least describe her to me?" Alex pleaded.

"She was seventeen when she disappeared, just short of her eighteen birthday. Long, light brown hair, about five feet three inches tall and weighed about a hundred and ten pounds. Oh, and she clearly has a British accent, I know that for a fact because I interviewed her when he mother was killed." Husky said.

"Her mother was killed?" Alex asked.

"Look, if you want to find out more you can talk to the newspaper. They have their old papers in the bascment," Husky answered back, and then said, "Give me your card and if I hear of anything else I'll get in touch with you."

Alex handed Sergeant Husky his card and thanked him.

Alex could tell that the Sergeant didn't want to be bothered. At least he confirmed that both Catherines were the same age, size, and hair color. Alex tried to think back to the conversation he had had with Catherine in the barn. He had detected an accent, but he thought it was more northern. Their conversation had been so short and she spoke mostly in a whisper. He had not been around many British people and was not sure how they talked. Alex tried to convince himself that he had done all he could. He felt a bit defeated and thought about looking up John Merit, but if her husband had her declared dead, and remarried, he figured Mr. Merit would not welcome Alex trying to find her. Alex went back to the train station and caught an afternoon train to Houston with a thirty-minute layover, as he had to wait for a connection to Beaumont.

Husky pondered over his discussion with Alex. He hadn't meant to be so short with the man, but Alex was not the only one who came in with sightings of Catherine. John Merit had posted a reward, if anyone had information about her disappearance, and dozens of people gave false reports, hoping to get the $1,000 reward.

It felt good to be back in Beaumont, and Alex went back to the boarding house he had previously stayed in. Dianne had moved one of the boarders out, so that Alex could have his old room back. She was excited to see him again and kissed him. Alex told her he still had business to take care of and left his suitcase. He hadn't eaten since breakfast and he decided to walk across to his favorite eating place. He had just gotten his food when David and Catherine came in. Catherine looked healthier and nicer than when he had last seen her, and she appeared to have gained a little weight. David and Catherine walked back to a table and ordered. Alex could still see Catherine out of the corner of his eye and she was looking at him. Alex finished eating and walked back to their table.

"Good evening," Alex said. Catherine looked down and David stood up to shake his hand. "I wanted to get back with you, Mr. Billings, and see if you have given our offer any consideration?" Alex said.

"Still not interested," David said and sat back down. Alex said goodbye and left.

Consuelo was devastated that she had lost the baby. She did not know what a miscarriage was except that she was no longer pregnant. David had hoped that Consuelo would just forget about it, but she cried off and on for a couple of days. It was hard for Catherine to console her, since she was unable to talk to her, and David continually threatened her if she spoke to anyone. She decided to wait until she was farther along to let Consuelo know she was pregnant. It was hard for Catherine to keep track of the days and she had to guess when the baby might be due. Most of the time, she had no idea what day of the week it was, much less the month. She figured the baby would arrive sometime in the later part of July or maybe the first part of August. She knew it would be difficult being pregnant in the heat of the summer, and the temperature in the morgue often reached one hundred degrees. The fans helped some, but it was still difficult to breathe at times. Catherine was also concerned about what David had said regarding the fact that he wasn't sure he would let her keep the baby. She wondered if he intended to get rid of the baby after it was born. Surely he wouldn't kill his own child. It was an agonizing thought, and she was haunted by it every time she saw David.

It had been over a month since Consuelo had lost her baby and she couldn't help but notice that Catherine had gained weight and had a baby bump.

"Are you with child?" she asked Catherine.

Catherine nodded yes reluctantly. "Mr. David, he did not tell me," Consuelo said, and went to the apartment crying. Catherine felt badly for Consuelo and wondered why David had not told her. Later that evening as they were going to the farm, Catherine asked David why he hadn't told Consuelo that they were going to have a baby.

"It's none of her damn business," he said. Catherine decided it best not to bring it up again.

The days had begun to get longer and the workload had not let up. Catherine was exhausted at the end of the day, and she had to sometimes wait for David for hours. She knew he was out drinking and she knew better than to say anything. Many nights, she would fall asleep in the hot barn beside the wagon. She would sometimes hear him come in through the back and go to Consuelo's apartment, which meant she would be sleeping in the barn all night. Jasper slept in the barn, too, and he would often bring her food that he bought with his own money. She had thought several times about going to the Catholic Church and asking the sisters to give her shelter, but she was afraid that David would just wait for the right opportunity to kill her. The sisters would be no match for him, and she didn't want any of them to get hurt. Catherine also thought of asking Alex for help, but she would never forgive herself if David killed him. She was doomed and she figured she only had a few months to live. If David was going to hurt her baby, then he would have to kill both of them. She could not live this way anymore. She dreamed of Daniel often, and she guessed he was about six months old now. He would probably be sitting up by now and grabbing things. She imagined what he looked like and prayed for him every day. She longed to hold him, and sometimes she would close her eyes and fold her arms like she was holding a baby and hum songs when no one was around. She did not want to feel sorry for herself and tried to keep her spirits up by thinking of John and their happy times together, and sometimes she would think how much fun they would have at the beach when Daniel got a little older. She could still see his piercingly deep brown eyes looking at her while she nursed him, and could still feel his tiny fingers kneading her breast while she fed him. She prayed she and her unborn baby would live long enough to have the same opportunity.

David had not only started drinking heavily, but he had also started gambling. He never was a good gambler and with all the money changing hands every day, the professional gamblers poured in by the dozens. There were gambling houses above every saloon and they offered dice, poker and faro tables. David preferred poker, but he was no match for the professionals. He began losing small amounts of money at first but then got invited to the bigger games. He would often take $100 or more and usually came home when he ran out of cash. Jasper, Consuelo, and Catherine were doing all the work at the business, and David only came in to get money out of the safe. Consuelo didn't like David being out every night, and she made the mistake of saying something to him when he came home late one night. David beat her up so badly, Catherine could hear her screams all the way back in the barn. She did not come out of the apartment the next day and Catherine feared David might have killed her. When David left, Catherine quietly opened the door and saw Consuelo lying in bed. Her face had lacerations and bruises all over it, and she was lying very still. Catherine walked over and put two fingers on her neck to check her pulse. It took her a moment to feel it, and she wasn't sure, so she retrieved her stethoscope and checked her heart. She had a pulse and Catherine was relieved. She knew that David's drinking was escalating his personality disorder and she had no way to stop it. Catherine retrieved some clean gauze and alcohol and she tried to clean Consuelo's wounds. Consuelo moaned from the pain, but Catherine thought that was good. She looked in her mouth, as it was bleeding, and thought she must have bitten her gum during the fight. She washed the remainder of Consuelo's wounds and bound the ones with gauze that needed it. When she finished she quietly left the room.

There was a corpse on the table and she knew she had to work fast, in the event David came back and saw she had not finished. She hoped he would not be back for a while. She heard the front door open and close and she froze. David must have gone to the safe, she thought. A few minutes later David came down the hall and opened the door. She did not look up.

David walked past her and opened the door to the apartment. He saw Consuelo sleeping and that she had bandages on her. He closed the door and came up behind Catherine and twisted her left hand behind her.

"If you ever touch her again, I'll do the same thing to you. Do you understand?" David said with gritted teeth.

Catherine shook her head yes.

"It's a good thing I have somewhere I have to be, so I'll give you your punishment later," David said, and left. Catherine closed her eyes and tried not to dwell on what he had just said.

Jasper showed up to help Catherine dress the body and move it to a coffin. It was the last one of the day and she walked over and looked in on Consuelo. She went in and checked her. One of her eyes was swollen shut and she really needed stitches on her cheek but Catherine knew David would kill her if she sewed it up so she used tape and gauze. She went back out and sat in a chair. Jasper came over and stood in front of her until she looked up.

"Miss Catherine, can I get you some food or something?" he asked.

She hated for Jasper to pay for her food, but she was starving and Consuelo needed something, too, so she shook her head yes. Jasper left.

Alex was at the counter when Jasper came in and ordered some soup and a cheese sandwich to go for Mrs. Catherine and a ham sandwich for him. He stood in a corner while he waited for the order. Alex walked over and asked him how he was and he said fine.

"I heard you order some food for Mrs. Catherine, is she all right?"

"Uh, yes sir, Mr. David don't allow her to leave when he ain't around, so I'm getting her some food."

Alex walked over to the cash register and paid the tab for Jasper. Jasper grinned and said, "Thank ya, sir." Jasper took the food back to the morgue and told Catherine that a nice tall man paid for the food. Catherine put her hands on Jasper's shoulders and then put her finger up to her mouth like she was saying, shh.

Jasper grinned and said, "Oh I ain't gonna tell Mr. David, don't you worry."

Catherine took the soup in to Consuelo and made her sit up. When the soup cooled, she fed her the soup and had her drink some water from a spoon. When she finished she went into David's office to eat her sandwich. The smell in the morgue made it impossible breathe and the air in David's office was cleaner. She ate slowly and occasionally wiped tears from her eyes. She tried to keep her spirits up, but she was worried about the baby more than anything else.

Alex watched through the window of the office and saw Catherine sit at David's desk and take out her sandwich. He saw tears coming from her eyes and he watched her wipe her eyes and then wipe her wet hands on her jacket. She stood up and he saw she was pregnant again and his heart sunk. Alex had not noticed that when she was in the café before because she was sitting behind the table. Catherine turned the light out and left though the door behind her. Alex stood where he was, wishing he could just walk away. Alex took out one of his cards and wrote a note on it, "I know who you are, Catherine Merit, and I can help you."

Alex walked to the rear of the building and saw Jasper open the door. He stopped him and gave him his card and asked him to give it to Mrs. Catherine, and he would wait there for a few minutes for her answer. Jasper went over to where Catherine was resting by the wagon and gave her the card. She turned it over and read it. She was stunned and jump up and ran into the office and wrote a note back. She went back and gave it to Jasper and motioned for him to take it to the man and also put her finger to her mouth.

Jasper said, "No ma'am, I won't say nothing."

Jasper handed Alex the note. It read: "I am not that woman; you have to leave me alone."

Alex's heart sank and he felt like a complete idiot. He shook his head and then left.

Catherine wanted to run to Alex and ask him to help her, but she knew David would kill both of them. Jasper would probably tell David anyway, and she dreaded that he would be suspicious. She needed to sleep so she opened the door to the hearse and crawled in. It was hot, but was more comfortable than the floor of the barn. She fell asleep and woke up an hour later gasping for breath. Jasper came over and asked if she was okay and she shook her head yes. She heard the door to the barn open and David came in.

"What's going on? David asked.

"Mrs. Catherine just had a bad dream, that's all," Jasper answered.

"Find someplace else to sleep tonight," David ordered Jasper.

Catherine stood frozen while David waited for Jasper to leave. He was barely out the door when he heard a slap and then a scream. David grabbed Catherine's hair and pulled her over to the hearse and opened the door.

"Please don't hurt the baby," she pleaded.

"Shut up." David pushed her up in the hearse and then he took off his shoes and pants.

"If you didn't have to work tomorrow, I would beat the living daylights out of you," he slurred. David was drunk and crawled up into the hearse and then fell over and went to sleep. Catherine managed to get out of the hearse and she dressed. She thought about running, and she got as far as the door before she lost her nerve. She willed herself to just leave, but she couldn't move. The fear of the unknown was holding her back. She felt she was being punished for something, but she didn't know what it was. She walked back over to the wagon and sat by the wheel and fell asleep.

It was after midnight when David woke up. He had trouble going back to sleep and he decided to leave and go back to his favorite gambling house. After getting fifty dollars from his safe, he left out the front door and headed down the street. David played poker for a couple of hours and hit a winning streak. He decided it was time to leave, feeling good that he had made back the money he had lost earlier. He stuffed the roll of bills in his pocket and figured he had ended up with a little over $200.00.

There was some commotion coming from an alley and he heard someone asking for help. He figured if someone had been shot or hurt really bad, maybe he could just finish him off, and wait for someone to bring him to the morgue. David was greedy, and when it came to money, he didn't always use good judgment. He walked over to the body lying on the ground and was instantly shot. It was a setup. Two men came over and robbed him and left him for dead. Fortunately, it missed his heart and hit him in the top left shoulder. David was stunned, but managed to get up and make his way back to the morgue.

"Get up," he yelled at Catherine. It was 3:00 a.m. in the morning and Catherine had fallen into a deep sleep. Catherine had no idea what time it was and she was still dazed from her deep sleep. David grabbed her by the arm and pulled her up. It wasn't until he lit the lantern in the embalming room that Catherine noticed blood covering his shirt.

"What happened," she whispered.

"I got shot. I need you to get the bullet out," David said. She walked over to the shelf where the chemicals were kept and she took three bottles off the shelf. She opened the drawer and took out a needle, thread, scissors and gauze and brought them over to the table.

"I'm going to need a scalpel," she said to David. She could see David was in pain and she wondered if this might be her opportunity to finally escape. David went into his office and opened his safe. He took out two surgical knives, each a different size, and closed the safe door, spinning the lock. He went to the bottom drawer of his desk and pulled out a set of leg chains and went back in the embalming room.

"Put it on one of your ankles and the other around the table leg," he said.

Catherine stared at him and didn't move. Just then the door to the apartment opened and Consuelo came out and saw David was hurt. "Do as I say," he yelled at Catherine.

She took the chain and closed it around her left leg and then attached it to the table leg. David grabbed a chair with his good arm and pulled it over to the table. Consuelo watched, afraid to say anything. She watched cautiously.

"Do you want me to use the chloroform?" Catherine asked.

"Hell no," he said. "Consuelo, bring me the whiskey bottle."

The two women watched as he chugalugged a quarter of the bottle.

"You do something stupid and you're as good as dead," David said with gritted teeth.

Catherine carefully cut David's shirt away and began cleaning around David's wound. She motioned to Consuelo to bring the lantern closer so she could see better, and Consuelo complied.

She had not washed her hands, but it was too late, now. She had to be silent. There was no way to ask David to release the chain with Consuelo standing beside her. She cleaned the blood away as best she could. The bleeding wouldn't stop, so she needed to work fast. She was able to determine the size of the hole and realized that even the smallest pair of flat head scissors was too large, so she used the scalpel to open the wound. David gritted his teeth and groaned. He pushed her hand away and picked up the whiskey bottle again. When he put it down, she carefully and meticulously entered the hole and felt the bullet. As soon as she gripped it, she slowly pulled it out, all the while David was screaming. It had crossed Catherine's mind to shove the bullet deeper and cause him enough pain to make him pass out, but she was a doctor and she saved lives, not ended them. She pressed some gauze hard up against his wound and took Consuelo's hand indicating she needed her to hold it in place. Catherine threaded her needed and began closing up the wound. David reached for the bottle again and she stopped and waited. He watched her intently. Jasper had come in the back door and stood watching, not saying anything. He had no idea Catherine knew how to do what she did.

When Catherine finished, Jasper and Consuelo helped David get into bed. Catherine did not know where the key was to the chains and pointed to her chains when Consuelo came out. Consuelo went back into the apartment and asked David about the key and he had already passed out. Consuelo brought her a blanket and a pillow and said she was sorry, but she was too afraid to look in his pockets. Catherine understood. She turned off the lantern and lay on the blanket.

The next morning David woke up and got out of bed. He released Catherine from her chains and told her to get ready for a body that Jasper had to go pick up. He said nothing to Catherine about saving his life.

CHAPTER 19

John and Carla Merit had been married six months, and the tension they had experienced in their marriage the first month only continued to grow. Carla constantly complained about having to live as poor people, and she used sex to get John to be more consensual with the money. John had finally gotten to the point of sleeping in the guest bedroom just to get away from her nagging. After dinner, he would go out on the porch and sit in one of the rocking chairs. Even as hot as the summer was, he thought it better than being in the house with the three women. Occasionally, Carla would come out and sit with him, but she simply couldn't stand the heat, and wouldn't stay more than ten or fifteen minutes. It was usually just to ask for something, anyway.

John had started back swimming on Saturday mornings at the YMCA and one Saturday after he had been swimming he stopped at the Catholic Church to visit with Father Jonathan.

"He is in the orphan's wing," one of the sisters told him and pointed to a door.

John opened the door and walked down a long hallway. He heard children and decided to follow the voices. Father Jonathan was reading to a group of small boys, and when John got closer he saw a small baby in Father Jonathan's arms. John stared for a few minutes and when Father Jonathan looked up, he saw John and smiled. He told John to come in and have a seat and that he was almost through.

When Father Jonathan said, "The end," all the young boys clapped and cheered. The baby smiled and tried to clap his hands, mimicking the young boys. John was fascinated.

"John, this is Daniel," Father Jonathan said.

When John got closer, Daniel put his arms out for John to take him. He almost leaped into John's arms.

John laughed and said, "Hi, little fella," as he took him in his arms. "I wasn't expecting this," John said.

"Daniel never meets a stranger and he just assumes everyone loves him," Father Jonathan said as he started to walk away.

"Wait, where are you going?" John asked.

"I have work to do. You can stay and play a while with Daniel, and when you are through or need to go, just set him on the floor beside the other boys. He can take care of himself," Father Jonathan said.

John sat down in the chair that Father Jonathan had been sitting in. Daniel looked up at John and smiled at him. John smiled back and then reached for a rattler he found on the floor. Daniel took it from him and started shaking it and jabbering to John. John laughed, and then realized he hadn't really laughed in a long time. He looked at Daniel and he was shocked when he realized Daniel looked just like his own baby pictures. John stayed for an hour playing with Daniel. He had gotten down on the floor with him and started rolling a ball at him. When he hit Daniel's foot with the ball, Daniel would break out in laughter. John was laughing, too.

Father Jonathan had walked into an adjoining office and watched the two from a window. He was also amused at the two playing together. John was a natural father, and this was what Father Jonathan had been praying about. He watched a few more minutes and then left to go to his office.

An hour later, John was standing in the doorway of Father Jonathan's office. "That's an amazing young boy you have in the orphanage."

Father Jonathan smiled and looked at him, like, "I told you so," but he didn't say anything.

"He looks a lot like my baby picture," John said, "Even though the picture is a bit fuzzy."

"I kind of thought he had Catherine's nose," Father Jonathan said.

"Do you still have the note that came with him?" John asked. Father Jonathan opened his side drawer on his desk and took it out. John looked at it and there were tears in his eyes.

"It's Catherine's writing," he said. "My mother is dead," were the words that hit John the hardest. "I've been such a fool," John said.

"You can still make things right," Father Jonathan said. "Daniel needs a father and a loving home."

"I can be a good father to him, but I'm not sure I can give him a loving home," John said.

John spent the next hour telling Father Jonathan about his dreadful marriage and the financial problems he had. By the time he was through talking, he looked at his watch and it was after 4:00 p.m.. "Oh God," John said. "Carla will be furious with me for not checking in with her."

"What do you intend to do about your son?" Father Jonathan asked.

John shook his head and said he really didn't know. "I guess I need to speak to Carla and see if she is agreeable with Daniel coming to live with us," John said.

Father Jonathan said, "He is your son, and if she is a Godly woman she will accept him as her own."

John thanked him and left.

He caught the trolley home and worried that his talk with Carla about Daniel would not go well. Carla was furious with John because he was gone so long and didn't call her. She called him selfish and started crying, accusing John of not loving her.

"Will you just shut up and let me talk for once," John said.

Carla was surprised that he was so caustic to her. She stopped crying and looked at him. "Okay, what is it?"

John told her about Daniel and how he had come to Father Jonathan.

"I stopped by the church to see Father Jonathan and he was in the orphanage holding Daniel when I walked in. The boy looks just like me," he told Carla.

"So you think this kid is yours?" Carla asked.

"Yes I do," John said sternly.

"Well I'm not raising someone else's brat. My girls take all my time," Carla said.

"You are a selfish woman and I'm not giving up my son for you," John said and he left.

John caught the trolley and rode several blocks and then transferred to another. When he got off, he walked the two blocks to Amelia's and rang the doorbell. Martha, her companion, answered the door and opened it for John to come in. Amelia could see John was upset and she asked Martha if they could talk in private, so Martha went to her room. John sat down and told her about his unbearable, unhappy marriage, and then he told Amelia about Daniel.

"You have a son?" Amelia asked, not believing what he just said.

John shook his head yes.

"You and Catherine always talked about having a son. That's wonderful," Amelia said joyfully.

"Carla doesn't want me to bring him to her house. She said it would take her time away from her daughters."

"Then let's bring him here. I'm sure Martha wouldn't mind, and if she does we'll find someone else," Amelia said. John hugged her.

"You will love him," John said, and he spent the next hour telling Amelia about Daniel. John stayed the evening and prepared his old room for Daniel. He picked up everything that had been on the floor, that he thought Daniel might try to pick up, and remembered he did not have a baby bed. There was one store he knew of that was open on Sundays, and he called and caught someone before they left for the day. They had one crib in stock and they would hold it for him. Amelia and John sat down with Martha and she said she would be delighted to have Daniel come stay with them. John agreed to give her a small raise. Everything was set and as bad as John hated to leave, he felt he owed it to Carla to tell her what he was doing.

Carla was still up when John got home and he felt better than he had in a long time. He had something to look forward to. He wasn't sure what would happen to his marriage, but that was secondary to him now.

"You left so abruptly, I wasn't sure you were coming back," she said tearfully.

"Look, Carla," John said softly, "I understand you want to spend all the time you can with your daughters, just as I want to spend time with my son. Amelia has agreed to let Daniel live with her, and I will live here and at my old house. I will split my time between the two. Even when I am here, you are doing other things with your girls, so my not being here all the time should not matter to you."

Carla continued to cry and sniffed. "Have I been that terrible to you?" she asked John.

"Look at it from my point of view; I use a small closet in the hall and two small bottom drawers for my clothes. I still have two suitcases I have not unpacked because I have nowhere to put my things. Everything from my study is still in boxes. I feel out of place here," John said and continued. "We barely spend time together, except at supper and a few minutes before bed. I'm sure you won't even miss me." Carla started crying harder. "I'll sleep in the guest room tonight," John said and left.

The next morning John went to confession and mass at St. Mary's Catholic Church. He felt exhilarated, and after mass he told Father Jonathan he would pick up his son at 400 that afternoon, as he had to pick up a crib and things for Daniel. Father Jonathan was delighted and sad at the same time. Delighted that Daniel would have a family, but sad that his daily visits with the boy would now be just periodic home visits. It was God's will, he told himself, and then said a special prayer for John and Daniel.

Father Jonathan changed the birth certificate to read John and Catherine Merit as Daniel's mother and father. Before John picked up Daniel, Father Jonathan suggested that they baptize Daniel the next Sunday at 2:00 p.m. Normally the baptismal would have happened sooner, but Father Jonathan gave it some time so John might come forward as he did. John asked Martha to come with him to get Daniel, and she was delighted. They got instructions from the nurses about the feedings and care of Daniel, and the three left. Father Jonathan planted a kiss on Daniel's forehead and waved goodbye. All the sisters were also sad to see Daniel go, but knew it was the best thing for him.

John had brought some of his clothes back over to Amelia's home, so that if he needed to stay the night he could. He always called Carla and checked in on her, but so far the arrangement was working. Sometimes Carla would call John at the bank and ask if he could have supper that night with her and the girls, and he always tried to be considerate of her. She never asked too many questions about Daniel. Carla always expected John to put up a good front around her friends and he tried to attend the necessary parties she wanted him too. John figured as long as she was all right with the arrangement, he was fine with it too.

Daniel was a joy in everyone's life, and adjusted to his new home without any problems. He had a lot of Catherine's personality and he was a handsome child. Amelia felt Daniel had given her a new life, and John was not the same person. Carla and her girls attended the baptism along with John, Martha and Amelia. Carla's two girls were instantly taken with Daniel and wanted to take him home, but Carla said no. It was a quiet and enchanting moment, except John's only regret was that Catherine was not there to share it with them. He did not want to admit it, but he was still grieving for her.

When Catherine and David went to supper at the café the next night, Alex did not turn and greet them as he always had. It was easier this way, Catherine thought. She and David ate in silence, but David's back was facing Alex and when Catherine would look up, she could see Alex clearly. She tried not to stare at him, but he was very attractive and she wondered again if he were married. She felt sure Alex was probably married and that his wife was probably back home waiting on him. That was most likely where he went over the holidays. He needed to spend time with his family, Catherine thought to herself. Catherine ate her food quietly and was not finished with it when David got up and grabbed her arm to leave. She stumbled and fell. Alex heard the commotion and looked.

"Stupid bitch," David said out loud, "Watch where you are going."

David pulled her up and dragged her out the door. Alex saw she had not finished eating. It's not my problem, he tried to convince himself. Catherine has had several chances to leave, and she keeps choosing to stay with the bully of a husband, Alex was reasoning with himself. He had done all he could.

"Can we take Consuelo some food?" Catherine asked when they got outside.

David kept walking and holding on to her arm. When they got back to the morgue, David took Catherine to the barn and chained her to the wagon wheel. After David left, Jasper came and asked if she was all right. She shook her head yes, and then pointed to Consuelo's apartment and made a gesture like she was eating.

"You want me to get food for Consuelo?" Jasper asked and Catherine shook her head. She put her arms around her baby bump and felt the baby move. She smiled and thought of Daniel, and how she prayed they could one day know each other. She dreaded the thought of not being able to protect the baby from David, and she also knew David would not leave her alone with it, ever. It would be impossible to leave the baby at the church as she had done with Daniel. David had pretty much given it a death sentence and if that happened, he would have to kill her, too.

After Jasper took some food to Consuelo, he took Catherine a small chamber pot.

"When I was on the prison farm with Mr. David, I used to help the plantation owners at the main house. I did all the dirty stuff the proper maids and butlers didn't want to do, like emptying out the chamber pots. I do that for you, too," Jasper said. "I'ss don't mind."

Catherine was surprised, when Jasper said he was at the prison farm with David. She shook her head like she did not understand.

"Oh, I'ss guesses you did not know about the prison farm. You see, there was a big tornado at the plantation house where Mr. David and I worked right when the storm hit Galveston. I went into the storm cellar and Mr. David ran and got under a bridge. I got out of prison because my crime was not that big. I was accused of stealing, but I didn't do that. I heard there was work here in Beaumont and then when I came, I ran into Mr. David. He offered me a job," Jasper explained to Catherine.

Catherine moved her hand to indicate she wanted Jasper to go on.

"Well, that's about all. Like I said, I'll stay in the barn where I can't see you, and you can use that chamber pot when you need too. I'll take care of it," Jasper said and then left.

Catherine's head was swimming with thoughts about where David had stayed in hiding once he left the prison farm. He waited until almost Thanksgiving to get her, once he was free. Had he been in Beaumont all that time getting ready for her? Catherine wondered. She was also curious about how Jasper was hired, and then Manny disappeared. She knew deep down that Jasper's arrival had something to do with Manny's leaving, but she knew there was nothing she could do about it. There was no possible way she could ask David.

The consequences would be too severe and besides, if David did kill Manny and bury him in the cemetery, he most likely would not tell her.

Catherine had to use the bathroom so she moved the small chamber potty around back of the wagon and used it and then put the top on it. The chain was barely long enough. It was nice of Jasper to do that for her, and she wondered why he ever agreed to work with David. Catherine figured she was about six weeks away from having the baby and sleeping in the barn was extremely uncomfortable, especially with her ankle chained to the wheel. She felt the baby kick and she laughed as sweat trickled down her face. She tried to curl into a ball, lying on her side, and she slowly drifted off to sleep.

Her dreams were more vivid now, and they became more randomly unbelievable. She dreamed David had put her and the baby in the same coffin, and buried them in the ground before they were dead. She cried and pleaded with him, as she heard the shovels of dirt hit the top of the coffin. She dreamed that she nursed her newborn, as they slowly lost conciseness and died. She woke up gasping and crying and she wanted to scream. She dreaded going back to sleep, for fear of another dream, but she slowly drifted back to sleep.

David came into the barn and could see Catherine's shadow of a body lying next to the wagon wheel and started to kick at her, but decided he was too tired and he went inside to the apartment. David was on a downward spiral now and he knew his drinking was taking its toll on him. He thought about stopping, but the more he thought about stopping, the more he needed to drink. He liked Beaumont and everything about it. The gambling, the booze, and his business that paid for his weaknesses, supplied him with everything he needed. He was getting tired of Consuelo, and her constant nagging, and figured in the next month or two she needed to go. He had to admit he was attached to her and the sex was great, but she knew too much about him, and he didn't like feeling venerable. Catherine and the baby were a different story. He hadn't made his mind up yet, but he knew he would shortly. He could sell the farm and kill all three of them and leave. No one would be the wiser, he thought to himself. But he wondered if he could kill Catherine. He was still obsessed with her, and she was the only one that really mattered to him.

CHAPTER 20

Sergeant Shaker had just gotten the results back from his investigation of the murdered prostitute several months ago. The chemist at Houston College confirmed that the chemical smell in the pillow that was under the dead girl's head was thought to be chloroform: A medicine-like chemical that made people unconscious. Doctors used it in operating rooms. He also matched the prints to the ones in the other open cases he had on some previous deaths in the red light district. David Brooks was the perfect match. Sergeant Shaker called his brother-in-law, Sergeant Husky, who was with the Galveston Police Department, and asked him if he could have a sketch artist draw a picture of what David Brooks looked like.

Tom Gregory and his wife had been visiting friends in Houston when the terrifying storm hit Galveston and they had survived because of their weekend plans. The house that they lived in had been demolished by the storm, and like so many other people, they were now living with a relative whose house survived the storm.

Detective Husky called Tom Gregory at the Grande Opera House and asked him to stop by his office the next day at 3:00 in the afternoon. When Tom arrived, he was shown into a small room and a few minutes later Husky and another man came in.

"We appreciate your being here and the reason for the request is that we suspect that David Brooks did not die in the tornado last year, as we originally thought, and we need an artist's sketch of what he looks like. This is Paul Allen, and he is an artist who helps us out at the police department. He will ask you questions about Brooks and then draw a sketch from your description," Husky said.

Tom spent the next hour refining the details on the artist's sketch, and when he finished, Husky and Tom felt it was a close likeness. After Tom left, Husky asked Allen to draw another sketch next to it, only this time adding a two inch beard. Husky was amazed at the likeness. He asked the artist to duplicate the pictures onto two other sheets of paper. When he had finished, Husky asked him to write underneath the two drawings the following:

WANTED: DAVID BROOKS

$ 1,000 REWARD

DEAD OR ALIVE

Husky and Shaker had permission from each of their departments to offer a $500.00 reward for David Brooks. Husky put his wanted poster up on the bulletin board in the police department and then mailed one to Shaker. Husky had not only sent an artist's sketch to his brother-in-law at the police department in Houston, but he had the newspaper run off several extra copies that he kept in a file. He took out an envelope and put a stamp on it. He addressed it to the Sheriff's department in Beaumont and wrote a note on a separate piece of paper. He put the poster and the note in the envelope and put it in the outgoing mail. If the man from Beaumont had told him the truth, maybe someone might see the reward and turn Brooks in.

With the influx of people that migrated to Beaumont, the small post office couldn't keep up the with mail deliveries. In the beginning, Beaumont's population of ten thousand people could get by with one postmaster. After Spindletop, another postman was added, but it was impossible to keep up with the magnitude of mail that was going in and out. It was often taking weeks and sometimes months, for a piece of mail to reach its destination. The letter that Sergeant Husky sent to

Beaumont sat in a mail bag for over a month before the bag was ever tended to. After the mail was sorted, the local mail was taken care of first, then it sat another week or two before it was delivered.

By the end of July, the heat was taking its toll on everyone. It was hard for the local sheriff to keep up with fights and brawls that took place every day. It was to the point that they just looked the other way, unless if happened to one of Beaumont's fine upstanding citizens. David's compulsive gambling had constantly gotten him into trouble. He had been warned by everyone that cheating was not tolerated and other gamblers were run out of town for cheating. He had managed to stay out of the street fights, but the serious gamblers had had just about enough of him. They suspected he was cheating, and once they confirmed it, several of the men got together and decided it was payback. They waited for him to get into a Saturday afternoon game and then called his hand. David tried to talk his way out of it, and when he saw they would not listen, he drew his gun and left out the back door. David rolled a barrel in front of the door and then took off on horseback. He thought if he could just get home and use Catherine as a hostage, that they would not shoot him.

The vigilante group hurried out the front and jumped on their horses. They could still see the dust from David's horse as they followed him out of town. David also had a stash of rifles in the barn at his house, and he figured he could outrun the men on his horse, get his rifles and barricade himself in the house with Catherine. Alex was outside talking to one of his men when he heard the commotion. Someone asked a man on horseback where they were going and he yelled, "Billings, we're going to hang him."

Alex left and went immediately to the livery stables to fetch his horse. He knew what a vigilante group of men usually did, and he knew Catherine would be in danger. It took him a couple of minutes to saddle Pilgrim and when he started to leave, he noticed Pilgrim was limping. Pilgrim had thrown a shoe, so he got off and took the saddle off and placed it on another horse that belonged to one of his men.

Alex rode as fast as he could, and figured he was about ten minutes behind the lynch mob.

David was approaching the farm and Catherine was outside hanging clothes on the clothesline when she saw David riding his horse at a really fast pace. Not far behind him was a posse of men. Before she could get into the house, she saw a man throw a rope over David's body and pull him off of his horse. Another man got off his horse and ran after Catherine. When he caught up with her she screamed and he pulled her from the porch.

The man who had lassoed David began pulling him around the barnyard while David struggled to free himself from the rope. Catherine watched in horror. Another rope with a noose was thrown over the large oak tree outside the barn, and then the noose was placed around David's neck.

"You got it all wrong, boys. I wasn't cheating," David said. "You don't need to do this; I'll give you back your money. It's in my pocket, take it."

After getting the money from David's pocket, two men tied David's hands behind him and hoisted him back up on his horse. David was pleading and begging for his life. Another man slapped David's mare and the mare pulled out from under David, leaving him dangling in the air, swinging from side to side. Catherine was horrified when she heard his neck snap as David swung from the tree.

"What about the little lady here?" asked one of the men. "We could have some fun with her," he said.

"Let's get the hell out of here," said another and they all got back on their horses and rode off.

David was still swinging from the tree and Catherine stood motionless watching, not believing what had just happened. Then she ran into the barn and found an old axe and she picked up a shovel. She ran over to where the men had tied the rope around the tree, and she pulled the axe back over her shoulder. She was angry, and began hacking at the rope and missed it on the first two strikes. She hit it again and finally made contact. She heard the thud on the ground when David dropped. She walked over to David's body and pulled the axe back again, wanting to strike him, but stopped herself. Catherine began trembling and fell to her knees, crying. The tears were not for David. Catherine was relieved that her nightmare was over, and she would never be tormented by David again.

Catherine went to the clothesline and grabbed a sheet and walked over and placed it over David's body. She picked up the shovel and walked a few feet from where David's body lay and started digging a grave. She stopped and hit the ground several times with the axe to break up the dirt, and then she fainted.

Alex was just coming over the hill to the farm and watched as he saw Catherine cut David loose from the noose and cover him with a sheet. She had picked up a shovel and started digging the grave and he got there just as she fainted. David stopped at the well and put some fresh water in his canteen and rushed to Catherine's side. He put a few drops of water into Catherine's mouth and she coughed. Alex picked her up and carried her inside and placed her on the bed. She seemed to be incoherent and Alex went into the bathroom and wet a towel to blot her face. Catherine had gotten overheated and he needed to cool her down, so he undressed her down to her slip and began giving her a sponge bath and tried to get her to drink some more water. About thirty minutes later she began to come around and she was surprised when she looked up and saw Alex.

"Did I just have a bad dream? What's happening to me?" she asked.

"You had a slight heat stroke, but you are going to be all right," Alex assured her.

"David?" she said.

"I'm sorry Catherine, he's dead," Alex said.

"Why did you come? Were you with them?" Catherine asked.

"No. I heard them say they were going to hang David, so I ran to the stables to get my horse. I was worried about what they might do to you," Alex said softly.

"I have to go out and bury him, Catherine said. "I need to know he is gone and will never come back for me," she continued.

"No!" Alex insisted. "You stay here and I'll dig the grave. I'll come get you before I cover him with the dirt. You can help me do that." Alex gave Catherine a fresh glass of water to drink and then he turned and left.

Alex took off his shirt and walked into the barn to find some gloves. The ground was hard and he alternated between the axe and the shovel; Alex worked the ground until he had dug out a four foot by seven foot grave, four feet deep. He had stopped a couple of times to get water and it took him over an hour. When he finished, he went over to the well and poured a bucket of water over his head to cool off. He looked back at the house and saw Catherine standing under the porch staring at him. She looked like she was in shock. Alex walked over to her and took her hand. She walked quietly over to David's body and stood there while Alex rolled him in the sheet and dropped him into the ground. Without a word, Catherine began putting small shovels of dirt into the grave, and then she handed Alex the shovel. Alex finished filling the grave with the dirt and when he was through, he looked at Catherine. She stood there staring at the grave and then she said,

"May God have mercy on your soul." She walked a few steps and stopped. "Oh no," she said.

Alex rushed to her side. "The baby, I think it's time," Catherine said.

Alex picked her up and carried her into the house. "I'll go and get the doctor," Alex said, as Catherine moaned again when she had another pain.

"There's no time, please don't leave me," she pleaded with Alex.

"I've never done this before, Catherine. Don't we need to get a doctor?" he asked.

"I am a doctor and I will have to just walk you through it. The baby won't wait," she said. "You have to boil some pots of water on the stove to sterilize the water."

Alex did as she asked. Catherine had put a robe on before she had come out to help with the grave, so she had already taken it off. She had on a camisole top and she removed the rest of the clothes, putting a sheet over herself. Alex came back in and Catherine asked him to bring an armful of towels from the bathroom.

Alex moved quickly. "Catherine, I'm not sure I can do this," Alex pleaded. "What if you pass out?"

Catherine screamed as another pain came. "I won't," she said, breathless. "When the water cools bring it in beside the bed. Do you have a knife?" she asked.

David took out his pocketknife and Catherine pointed at the sterile water.

"Hold my hand," Catherine said and Alex obliged.

A couple of minutes later Catherine squeezed Alex's hand hard and she began pushing.

"I think coming," she blurted out. "You need to lift the sheets and see if you can see the baby's head."

Alex timidly raised the sheet and looked at a small head with brown hair slowly oozing between Catherine's legs.

"Make sure the umbilical cord is not wrapped around his neck. You need to secure his shoulder and head with your hands once he starts coming out," Catherine instructed.

Alex was astonished at the miracle he was witnessing and it was like the baby just slid into his hands.

"Once he is out, you need to cut off the cord about five inches and tie a knot in it," Catherine said. Alex worked quickly.

"Hand him to me," Catherine said. She took her finger and gently cleaned out the baby's mouth and then turned him upside down so the fluid would drain out. A huge cry let out and the relief on Catherine's face was a site to behold. She was grinning from ear to ear and looked at Alex.

"It's a boy," she said. "Would you please soak some towels for me so I can clean him?" Catherine asked.

Once the baby was clean, she wrapped him in another clean towel and handed him to Alex.

"You need to leave the room while I clean myself up," Catherine said.

Alex walked out of the room with the baby and sat at the kitchen table reflecting on the miracle of what just happened. The baby had fallen asleep in Alex's arms while he waited for Catherine. She came into the kitchen in a clean gown. She walked over to Alex and stood behind him, wrapping her arms around both him and the baby and reached around and kissed Alex on the cheek.

"We would have both died if you had not come," she said. "There are no words to tell you how appreciative I am. Thank you is just not enough."

Alex smiled and put his hand up to hers. She came around slowly and sat in the chair beside him, their eyes never leaving each other.

Alex handed the baby to Catherine. "Do you have a name picked out?" Alex asked.

"Adam, after my father," she said. Alex smiled and told her he liked the name.

They heard a wagon pull up outside and Jasper and Consuelo came to the door.

"Is it true?" Consuelo asked. "Did they hang him?" she cried out.

Catherine shook her head yes. "We buried him by the tree."

Consuelo ran out the door to David's grave and threw herself on it. They all stood on the porch and watched as Consuelo cried and wept. After a while Jasper and Alex went out and brought her back into the house. Catherine took her into the bedroom and the two girls talked for a while. The baby cried, and Catherine nursed him. Jasper was sitting at the kitchen table alone when the two girls came back into the kitchen.

"Where's Alex?" Catherine asked Jasper.

"He said his job was done here and he left to go back into town."

Catherine was sad that she did not get to tell him goodbye. The three sat around the kitchen table and Jasper finally told Catherine and Consuelo about Manny. Consuelo cried again. Now she had lost two men she loved. It was getting late and the three agreed they would meet on Monday to discuss what they were going to do with the business. Jasper would pick up Catherine and baby on Monday morning at 8:00.

Catherine stood and watched as the two left in the wagon and tears welled up in her eyes. She had not made a decision for herself since she had said "I do," when she married John. She would soon be twenty years old and she never felt so alone. She wished Alex had not left so abruptly, and she had wanted to explain to him about why she had lied and deceived him. He had been a guardian angel to her, and now he was gone. She went into the barn and found his card under the rock she had hid it under. Catherine wiped off the dirt and saw his name was Alex Cooper. She put the card to her cheek and smiled. When she went outside, the mare that had run away was standing by the barn waiting. Catherine took his rein and led him into the barn. She put the baby, who was wrapped in a blanket, down on some hay, and she removed the saddle and tack from the horse and fed and watered him.

Catherine picked up her baby and started to go back into the house but she stopped halfway there and turned around. She walked back over to where David was buried. She stared at it for a while, and was surprised that she felt absolutely nothing. There was neither hatred nor love. This man had taken almost two years of her life away from her and he had dearly paid for his sins with his own life. She supposed that was punishment enough. She turned and looked at the farmhouse. There were too many horrible memories for her to stay there, but she would give it a little time before she made a decision. Tomorrow she would take the wagon to St. Louis Catholic Church and talk to the sisters. Finding Daniel was now her mission.

CHAPTER 21

Alex tried to get some sleep that night, but every time he woke up his thoughts were on Catherine. It nagged at him that maybe he should have at least told her goodbye. He didn't want her to think he was mad or something. He just felt awkward standing around when Consuelo and Jasper got there. Alex had no idea that Consuelo lived in an apartment at the morgue and David was having sex with both women. At least that was what Jasper had told him when they were along. Alex felt uneasy that Catherine's life was unveiling in front of him and when Jasper began telling Alex how David tortured them, he had just had enough, so he left.

It was 5:00 a.m. when Alex woke again, so he got up and dressed. He went to the livery stable and saddled up Pilgrim. Usually when Alex went riding early in the morning it helped to clear his head. The fresh air away from the oil rigs and sulphur seemed to make him feel better, but he could still hear the pumps several miles out. Alex found himself getting closer to Catherine's farm and the sun was just coming up. He stopped about a hundred yards out and strained to see if he could see any light coming from the house. It was dark. He walked his horse a little closer, and he could hear the faint cry of Adam. Alex waited about five minutes to see if he stopped and he didn't. Alex got off his horse and went to the door. It was unlocked when he turned it.

"Catherine, its Alex, are you all right?" There was no answer.

Alex walked into the bedroom and saw that blood had saturated through the top sheet. Alex rushed over to her and tried to wake her, but she moaned and didn't open her eyes. He found his business card that he had given her several months back clasped in Catherine's hand, and he was touched. Alex ran to the barn and hitched up the wagon to the mare, and brought it to the front of the house. He pulled the sheet up off the bed and wrapped it around Catherine and carried her to the wagon. Alex went back and picked up the basket with Adam in it and put him in between his feet on the bottom below where he sat. Alex tied Pilgrim to the back and then drove the wagon to the hospital. He went to the back where the emergency room was and told a nurse that Catherine had given birth to the baby twenty-four hours earlier, and that she was bleeding really badly. He didn't think the baby had had nourishment for a while. The nurses and a doctor put Catherine on a stretcher and took Adam to the nursery. They told Alex to wait in the waiting room. Alex wondered if he had failed to do anything after Adam was born. Catherine seemed to think everything was okay, but he could kick himself for not staying there. If she died he would never forgive himself.

Two hours passed before the doctors came out and talked to Alex.

"Your wife is lucky you brought her in when you did. She had a busted blood vessel and she could have bled to death. She is stable now, but needs to stay here a day or two to regain her strength. Your son is going to be all right also, and he's eating very well. You can see your wife now," the doctor concluded.

Alex tried to tell the doctor that they were not husband and wife, but the doctor left abruptly. Alex walked into the ward and the nurse pointed to a bed behind a wall of white curtains. He sat in a chair beside Catherine, and for the first time, he finally admitted to himself that he was completely infatuated with her.

A nurse came in a while later and checked Catherine's pulse and heart rate but Catherine did not stir. The nurse smiled at Alex and he smiled back at her.

"The doctor gave her a sedative so she will probably sleep for a couple more hours. You can leave and come back if you want to," the nurse said to Alex.

"Can you tell me what direction the nursery is?" asked Alex.

"Follow me," she said. They walked to an adjoining building and she pointed to Adam's small crib. He was lying on his back and was alert and he looked so small.

"He has had over twelve ounces of milk since he came in. Poor little thing probably hadn't had much to eat," one of the nurses said.

Alex stood and watched him for a while and then left. He stopped at the cafeteria and got two cups of black coffee. He knew one would get cold before he drank it, but he was used to that at the oil rig. Alex went back to Catherine's bed and sat in the chair beside her, drinking his coffee. He knew things were going to be complicated, and he wondered how he was going to tell Catherine that she had been declared dead, and her husband had remarried. He figured that Catherine was still in love with her husband, so he decided he would not let Catherine know how he really felt about her. He would stay and play out the hand as it was dealt, but he had to at least stick around and see if he had a chance.

Catherine began to stir a couple of hours later, and it woke Alex from his nap. When she opened her eyes Alex smiled down at her and took her hand. She looked up at him, confused. "I came by your house early this morning and heard Adam crying. When you didn't come to the door I went in and found you in a pool of blood. I brought you and Adam to the hospital early this morning. You are both going to be fine."

Catherine was groggy and she tried to sit up. Alex helped her, and handed her a glass of water. After she drank, she handed Alex the glass and when he put it down, she put her arms around his neck and hugged him. They clung together like two lovers and Alex closed his eyes and wished it were so. Catherine finally released him and smiled up at him.

"You keep saving my life and I will forever be indebted to you," she said sweetly to Alex. She asked Alex what time it was, and he told her.

"You've been here the whole time?" she asked. "Yes, except for about thirty minutes when I went to check on Adam, and he is doing great," Alex told her.

The nurse brought in a small tray of food for Catherine, and she was told to eat it all. Catherine was not really hungry, but knew she needed nourishment, so she ate.

"Do you mind if I ask why you left so abruptly last night and didn't tell me goodbye?" Catherine asked.

Alex was surprised by her frankness. He blushed a bit and said, "Honestly, Jasper started telling me about the brutality you had suffered, and I felt uncomfortable that it was coming from him. I figured if you wanted me to know about your life with David, you would tell me in time. I didn't think it was his place, so I left. I know I should have told you goodbye, and I apologize about that," Alex said softly. He looked away and Catherine grabbed his hand. Alex looked back at her and started to say something, and stopped.

"Go on," Catherine said.

"Are you Catherine Merit?" Alex asked.

"Yes, I am. I didn't want to tell you because David would not have hesitated to kill you, and I would have never forgiven myself if he had," Catherine confessed.

Alex reached in his back pocket and pulled out his wallet. "You will probably hate me for showing you this but, I feel you need to know something before you go back to Galveston," Alex said and handed Catherine the newspaper clipping.

Catherine took it and looked up at Alex before she opened it. She unfolded the article and read the fine print from the newspaper. Catherine folded it back up and handed it to Alex.

"That does complicate things for me," Catherine said. "I'm not sure he would want me back now anyway, and it is probably best he moved on. I was hoping he was not still grieving for me. There is one more thing," Catherine said and stopped. Alex looked at her with concern, still holding her hand. "Daniel is not dead," she said and she told Alex about the night David had come home and threatened to kill Daniel. "I need to find out from the sisters whether or not Daniel is with Father Jonathan."

"Would you like me to check on that for you?" Alex asked.

"Yes, I don't think the doctors will release me for a couple of days and if Daniel is here, I need to find him," Catherine said.

It was late on Sunday afternoon when Alex walked to the back of the Catholic Church where the sisters stayed in a small convent. He rang the bell and a young woman in a nun's habit came to the door. Alex took off his hat and apologized for disturbing her. He asked her if he could talk to someone about a baby left in a basket last year whose name was Daniel.

Alex was only gone about forty-five minutes when he returned with a nun who identified herself as Sister Angelina. She told Catherine that they had complied with her wishes and notified Father Jonathan about the little boy. She said that a sister from St Mary's Hospital came and took Daniel back to Galveston the next day. Catherine was delighted to know he was safe.

"We received a very nice thank you note from Father Jonathan a couple of months later and he told us the baby was well and healthy and he appreciated our concerns," she finished saying. "I understand you have another baby, and I would hope that you will keep this one," she said curtly, and then left.

Catherine was embarrassed and didn't answer.

"She shouldn't have said that, Catherine. She has no idea the stress you were under. You did the right thing," Alex assured her.

Alex left that evening to go back to his room and catch up on some sleep. He had to work the next day and reassured Catherine he would be back to see her after work. The next evening Catherine was nursing Adam when Alex stopped by. He had picked up some flowers at the florist and brought them to Catherine.

"They are beautiful," Catherine said and thanked him.

The nurse came in and took Adam back to the nursery. Catherine seemed distracted and Alex asked her if she was feeling all right.

"I need to sell the farm and I know you had previously talked with David about it. How much do you think it might sell for?" she asked.

"My company had originally offered David $100,000 but that was seven months ago. Because there have been so many wells come in, the oil has glutted the market and it is not worth as much as it was then. I think the best I could get for you right now would be at $45,000 and that would be selling the land outright with no reserves," Alex said.

"How soon could I sell it?" she asked.

"We could probably close it by the end of next week, and you would have your money then," Alex said.

"There might be one problem," Catherine said. "David and I were never legally married."

"I doubt that will be a problem since David told everyone you were his wife. There should not be anybody who would protest it. Adam is David's son and you are his mother. I'll check with the attorneys, but I don't see that as a problem," Alex assured her. "Do you mind if I ask what your plans are after you sell the farm?" Alex asked.

Catherine thought for a moment and said that she wanted to find Daniel, and that she might stay in Galveston and go back to medical school, if she could make some arrangements for her children.

"What about your husband?" Alex asked.

"That is a question I don't have an answer for," Catherine said and looked at Alex. "I really don't think I would make a good wife for anyone, Alex," she said. "I've lost my sense of ever belonging to anyone. I want to be a good mother and I think that is all I am capable of right now." She could see the hurt in Alex's eyes.

He got up and walked over to the window and looked out. Catherine had not told him anything he did not already know, but it didn't stop the pain he was feeling inwardly.

Alex walked over and kissed Catherine on the forehead and told her he would check on her in the morning. Catherine watched as he walked out the door. She could sense his disappointment, and she wanted to call him back. Alex had saved her life and her baby's life, and the last thing she wanted was to cause him any hurt.

The next morning Alex stopped at the hospital at 10:00 and Catherine was dressed and waiting for the nurse to bring Adam.

"I'm glad you're feeling better," Alex said casually to Catherine. "Good news, my company will be ready to close on the deal for your farm on Friday morning. The money should be in your account by noon."

Catherine thanked him and told him that she was going over to the morgue and split up the business profits with Jasper and Consuelo as soon as the nurse brought Adam to her. "Do you need a ride back home later?" he asked Catherine. "Your mare and wagon are in town at the stables," Alex continued.

"I think I can manage, but thank you anyway," Catherine said.

Alex walked over and picked up her hand and kissed it. Their eyes locked for an instant, and then he turned and left. Catherine wanted to call him back, but she did not want him to see the tears in her eyes.

Alex stopped by the nursery and watched Adam as they put a tiny shirt and clean diaper on him. He smiled when he thought about delivering him and how scared he had been. It would probably be the only childbirth he would every witness again, and he was glad he had that opportunity. He would miss them terribly and he looked down at the floor when he left. He had never felt this way before about anyone in his life, and for the first time he understood what a broken heart felt like. The only woman he had ever loved was married to someone else.

Catherine left the hospital with Adam and walked the six blocks to the morgue. Consuelo and Jasper had cleaned up everything and Catherine was surprised at how nice it looked. She asked them to come into the office and asked Consuelo to open the safe. There was not a lot in it. David had spent most of the cash but there was about fifty dollars and Catherine gave each of them twenty-five. She asked Jasper to contact the other funeral home and see if they would like to buy the hearse. For now she needed the mare and the wagon. Catherine waited while Jasper left and went to Raymond Porter's Funeral Home, and Mr. Porter followed Jasper back to speak to Catherine. They arrived at a price and Mr. Porter went to the bank and brought the money back to her. She told Mr. Porter that Consuelo was very good with the make-up and preparation of the bodies and she recommended that he hire her. She also praised Jasper and asked if he would hire him also. She told Mr. Porter she would give him the two horses, the left over coffins and the chemicals, if he would hire them, and he accepted her offer. Porter gave Catherine $150.00 cash and when Porter left, Catherine gave Jasper and Consuelo another fifty dollars each. The three hugged and Catherine suggested that Consuelo move out of the apartment immediately, because they did not own the buildings the morgue was in. She also told them to take whatever clothes were in the closet. She hugged each of them and wished them well.

Catherine had finished with the morgue business and nursed Adam before she left to go to the bank. The bank was another story. Without some kind of death certificate they could not let Catherine access David's account. As Catherine was leaving the bank she saw Alex at the end of the street and called out to him. He was talking to another man and excused himself.

"I'm so sorry to interrupt you, but the bank won't give me

access to David's account without a death certificate and I don't know what to do," Catherine said.

Alex took her hand and walked down the street to the city attorney's office. After signing an affidavit that they both witnessed David Billings' death, the city attorney prepared a death certificate and gave it to Catherine. She asked Alex to go with her to the bank and he agreed. After showing the bank the death certificate Catherine found out that there was less than seventy-five dollars in David's account and when she accessed the safety deposit box, all she found was the deed to the farm and a couple of gold watches.

Once the accounts were closed, Catherine opened an account in her name and put most of the money in that account. She took the watches and deed and left.

"Would you like to eat something?" Alex asked.

"That would be great," she answered.

Alex took Catherine and the baby to a new restaurant called the Road House that had opened at the end of the street. It was crowded but they finally were seated at a table by the window. Catherine told Alex about selling the hearse and the morgue contents to the other funeral home, and that she thought they were going to hire Consuelo and Jasper. Alex listened intently. Catherine seemed upbeat and he enjoyed listening to her talk. She was actually animated at times and he saw a beautiful side of Catherine he had never seen before. He soaked his mind in her beauty and he didn't want the lunch to be over.

"Honestly, you have let me do all the talking and I have been babbling for an hour; what are your plans?" Catherine asked Alex.

"Guess I'll finish up here, maybe another six months, and then wait for my next orders," Alex answered.

"What about your family?" Catherine asked. Alex didn't answer right away.

"I guess my family is my work. My parents are both deceased and I was an only child. I never stay in any one place long enough to find a wife," he said. "But I do love my job and that's why I do it."

Adam was getting restless and began fussing. "I guess that's my clue that we need to leave," Catherine smiled and said. Alex walked her to the stables and hitched up the wagon for her. "You sure you can handle this and the baby?"

"I'm sure," she said. "I'll stop at the mercantile and get a bassinet and put him in it after I stop at the morgue and nurse him. Thanks again for everything," Catherine said and touched Alex's face with her hand.

He put his hand on hers and moved it to his mouth and gave it a soft kiss. "Good bye Catherine," Alex said and left. She watched as he disappeared out the door. Alex did not look back.

Catherine was tired when she finally got back to the farm, and decided it was too depressing to stay there. She saw Alex's card lying on the kitchen table and she picked it up. She was glad she didn't have a phone or she might have tried to call him. She found David's suitcase in the closet and packed the few things she thought she would need. There wasn't very much. It was mostly baby diapers and clothes for Adam. She had very little there. She put the suitcase in the wagon and went back in the house to get Adam. It was sundown when she got back into town. Catherine stopped at several hotels and had not considered the possibility that all the rooms would be taken. She tried a few boarding houses and there were no rooms. She went to the morgue and there was a sign on the door that said the morgue was closed and it was boarded up. Apparently David had not paid the rent on the building and she was locked out.

CHAPTER 22

Catherine took Alex's card out of her small purse and looked at it. His name and his company's name and phone number were on it, but it was not a Beaumont phone number. She turned it over. Alex had written on the back that he was staying at the Mason Boarding House. She looked up and down the street and finally asked someone if they could tell her where it was. They gave her directions. Catherine got into the wagon and rode down the street to the boarding house and got out. Alex answered the door on the first knock. He was surprised to see Catherine and Adam at the door.

"I'm sorry to bother you, but it was too depressing to stay at the farm. I've packed up what we needed and now I can't find a place to stay."

Alex took her suitcase and told her to come in. "My place is a bit small, but you are welcome to the bed. I have a bedroll and I can sleep on the floor. We can try and find you something more comfortable tomorrow."

"I really don't mean to put you out," she apologized.

"It's not a problem," Alex said. "The maid put on clean sheets this morning and there are clean towels in the bathroom, so make yourself at home," Alex said. "I was getting ready to head out and pick up some dinner to bring back. What would you like?" David asked her.

"Anything, anything is fine," she said.

Alex left and wondered why Catherine kept walking back into his life. He was having a hard enough time trying not to think about her, but she just kept showing up. He reminded himself that she was just barely twenty, and had been married since she was sixteen. She had no idea she was tormenting him. I guess I have become a father figure to her, he thought. He was nine years older than her, Alex reminded himself. He walked to the café and ordered two specials to go.

He was back within thirty-five minutes and Adam was asleep in his bassinet. They sat at the small table in the corner.

"I don't have much to offer you to drink. I'm having a scotch," David said.

"That works for me," Catherine said. Catherine began telling David about her home in England and how they ended up in America. She told him how her mother had gone to work at the Grande Opera House in Galveston and that was where they first met David Brooks. She said David told her he had been responsible for her mother's death. Alex listened intently as she told him of her first abduction, and how she had gotten away. She talked about the Galveston flood and the destruction of the orphanage and how it had taken her so long to get past what David had done to her the first time. He could hardly believe that David had actually had the nerve to kidnap her the second time. Catherine stopped and put her hand on Alex's hand.

"I don't know why I am spilling my guts to you, I'm sorry….I guess it's the scotch." She got up and picked up the leftover food and put it back in the paper bag.

Alex watched her and resisted pulling her to him. Adam was stirring, so Catherine picked him up and changed his diaper. She opened her blouse and lifted Adam to her breast. Alex excused himself to go wash up in the bathroom. He came out and walked over to the closet and took the bedroll out, spreading it on the floor. Catherine watched him as he gracefully navigated around the room. He had taken off his outer shirt and the sleeveless undershirt hugged his muscular physic. Alex felt Catherine staring and he looked at her and smiled. She smiled back at him. Alex opened a drawer and took out a sheet.

"I hope you don't mind, but it's too hot to sleep in my pants." Alex slipped off his pants, holding the sheet around his waist, and then laid down on his bedroll.

After Catherine finished nursing, she put Adam in his bassinet and went to the bathroom to put on her nightgown. She came back in the room and crawled under the covers. They returned goodnights to each other and Catherine turned out the lantern. She had only slept for about an hour when her nightmares began. She saw David putting a noose around her neck. She dreamed that she and the baby were being put in coffins and buried. Catherine was whimpering and crying, begging for her life.

"Shh," Alex said. "You're having a bad dream, Catherine," and he was stroking her hair. Alex was lying beside her now, with only his under shorts on, and Catherine turned and put her arms around him and cried into his muscular chest. He put his arms around her and started kissing her wet tears.

"It's all right Catherine, I'm here and no one is going to hurt you."

Catherine stopped crying and looked up at Alex. There was a dim light coming through the window from an outside street light. She could see the sincerity and concern in Alex's face and she began kissing him. She felt Alex's strong bulge beneath her stomach, and he pulled away.

"I'm sorry," he apologized, "I'm not going to lie and tell you that I'm not attracted to you. I think you know I am."

He knew Catherine had been raped in every imaginable way, and he knew she was fragile. Alex was crazy with desire, but he left the bed and laid back down on his bedroll. Several hours later the light was coming through the open door in the bathroom and Alex saw Catherine sitting up in bed nursing Adam. He got up and asked if he could join them the two of them, and watched as Adam nursed. Later, when Alex woke up, he was lying in bed with Catherine and the baby. It seemed so natural, he thought.

Alex got up and took a shower. He dressed and looked down at Catherine. He had no idea where this was going, and he knew nothing would stop Catherine from leaving on Friday. For now, he was going to savor every moment he could spend with Catherine. He was in love with her. Alex wrote Catherine a short note and told her he had an appointment and to make herself at home. He would check on her at noon.

Catherine pretended to be asleep when Alex left. It surprised her that she was just as attracted to him, as he was her. Catherine really didn't think she would ever have feelings for another man. Alex was different, though. He was gentle and had a sweet disposition. He was also very handsome. This is crazy, she thought. She was leaving Friday to find her son and she couldn't let herself get involved with a man who spent his entire life travelling. She had her own agenda, and she didn't want to be tied down to anyone or anything. She really cared for Alex, but she couldn't let herself get serious about him. She wasn't sure if she was still married to John.

Catherine was dressed and had Adam in the bassinet on the bed when Alex came back.

"I found you a room at the hotel. Are you ready?"

Catherine was relieved but surprised that Alex acted as though he was glad she was leaving. She picked up Adam and followed Alex out the door. She felt hurt, but she didn't say anything.

Alex didn't say anything until he checked her into the hotel. "Call me if you need anything," he said and kissed her on the cheek. She watched him leave and then went up to her room.

Alex tried to be casual when he took Catherine to the hotel. Actually, he almost felt uncomfortable. It was probably better this way. She would be gone on Friday and they both could move on with their lives.

Catherine went shopping for some new clothes for her and the baby and bought a new travel bag for their clothes. She was walking by the city attorney's office when she noticed a poster on the door. It looked like David Brooks, and there was a one thousand dollar reward. She stared at it and wondered how long it had been there. Two ladies walked by and stopped and looked at it.

"Why, that's the undertaker," one of the ladies said.

Catherine stared at them and one of the ladies spit on her. It caught the corner of her sleeve, just missing Adam.

"How could you stay married to that man? Everyone hated him," the other one said.

Catherine turned and walked away and headed back to the hotel. She stayed in the room most of the time with Adam and she rested. Alex did not visit her and she was sorry she had been so cold to him when he came back to get her. He had been more than a friend to her. He had watched over her the whole time they were in Beaumont and she had rejected him from the start. There was a strong bond between them and she missed him terribly, but knew it was best that they didn't see each other again.

It was Thursday afternoon and Catherine was anxious about the closing on Friday. More so, she was anxious about Alex. He had done so much for her and he had sent mixed messages to her. She wondered if he really did find her attractive, or if he were just saying that because he wanted her. She scolded herself for being so blunt about not wanting another man. She couldn't stop thinking about him, and she wanted to see him again before Friday. Catherine sat at the desk in her hotel room and took out a piece of hotel stationery.

The note was simple and to the point:

"Please join me for supper tonight at 6:00 p.m. My room number is 228. Catherine."

She put it in the envelope and licked the seal. Catherine thought the least she could do was have a nice dinner in her hotel room where they could talk in private and she could nurse Adam if she needed too. She walked to the boarding house and left the letter stuck in the crack of the door and door knob where he couldn't miss it. She made arrangements with the hotel concierge for their dinner to arrive at 7:00 p.m. that night.

Alex had not slept well the night before and he had an aching feeling that everything was coming to an end with Catherine. Once she signed the papers, she would probably leave on the next train going to Galveston. He put his hat, gun and holster on and left his room. The sun had not come up yet, and he knew it would be a long day. His company had requested that he walk the Billings farm and make whatever notes he deemed necessary. He stopped and got some coffee at the diner, and he saw a poster that had been nailed to the wall. It was a picture of David Billings, only the name on the poster was David Brooks. David shook his head at the untimely poster and wondered why it took so long.

Alex made his way to the livery stable and saddled Pilgrim. They made their way to the farmhouse and Alex stopped and slowly walked over to the empty hole that had once been David's grave. He shook his head and figured that some vigilante hunter had come back for the body, so he could claim the reward. He kicked some dirt back into the cavity of the hole. He wondered what could make a man like David become a monster. He got what he deserved, thought Alex, and he was relieved for Catherine that her ordeal was over.

The house felt empty when Alex walked inside. He wondered what the walls might have to say, if they could talk. It was a stupid thought. He saw the bloody mattress and remembered how concerned he was that Catherine might have been dead. There wasn't much inside the sparsely furnished house, but the house was not his company's concern. It was what might be underneath it. Alex closed the door and saw the cut rope and noose that he had thrown to the side when he was digging David's grave. He looked at the open grave and couldn't help but kick some more dirt into it again. Had he known everything Billings had done to Catherine, he would have just killed him himself. He hesitated before going into the barn. He picked up a sleeve off Catherine's torn clothing and put it to his nose and smelled it and it penetrated down his spine. He looked up at the pulley and rope dangling from it and the horror of the moment made him angry.

Alex felt the air sucked out of him, and he went outside to breathe. He took out some matches and he really had no idea why, but he threw a lit match into the hay inside the barn, watched it burn for a few minutes, then left. He got on Pilgrim and galloped off a few hundred feet and turned, watching the fire being sucked through the roof. He considered burning the house too, but thought better of it. If his company did drill on the land, the house would make an office for the crew.

It took almost an hour for the barn to burn down and the memories go up in smoke. It was over, and he needed to start a new chapter in his life. Alex never spent much of his own money. The company paid all his expenses, so he just put it all in his savings account. The last time he had checked at the bank he had over $28,000 in cash, along with some company stock he had earned. He would give it all up for Catherine and her children in a heartbeat. Alex knew he probably would never find love again.

Alex was riding the outside perimeters of the property when he saw some men on horseback coming up to him. "We saw the smoke and wondered what happened," one of the men said.

"Not sure, my company is buying the place since Billings died. They don't care about the barn," Alex said.

The men tipped their hats and rode off. Alex took out some of his instruments and measured some distances and then wrote them down on a tablet he kept in his saddle bags. He spent three hours doing this and then rode back to town. Alex often went back to his boarding house to freshen up after surveying the land, but decided to eat some lunch first. When Alex finished he stopped at the attorney's office to see if the paperwork was in order and he saw another poster of David Brooks and tore it off.

Alex thought about buying Catherine a going away present, but thought better of it. She had enough things to worry about and he knew once she arrived in Galveston, he would be a distant memory in her past. Alex did something he usually didn't do. He walked over to the saloon to get a drink. He was tense and he felt the weight of the world on his shoulders. A stiff drink would help dull his conscious thoughts and maybe, if he were lucky, he would forget about Catherine. Alex was invited to play in a small stakes poker game and he figured it would help pass the time. He thought if he could just get through the next two days, he would be fine.

It was 6:30 p.m. when Catherine checked the time and wondered if she should cancel the dinner. Maybe Alex got tied up with his work. Surely he wouldn't just ignore her. Catherine decided to call downstairs and ask them not to bring the food until 8:00 p.m. With that done, she nursed Adam and changed his diaper. Afterwards she walked over to the window and looked out. She saw Alex walking back towards his apartment. He must have worked late, and she hoped he had not eaten, she thought to herself.

Alex almost didn't see the envelope when he opened the door, as it fell on the floor. He picked it up and saw his name on the outside of the hotel stationery where Catherine was staying. Alex opened it and read it, and then looked at his watch. It was 6:45 and he was already forty-five minutes late. He knew he smelled of smoke, so he quickly changed his shirt and took out a clean jacket from his closet. He was at Catherine's door in five minutes.

Alex tried to be casual when Catherine opened the door and reached up and kissed his cheek. "Sorry I'm late, but I worked later than usual and just went back to my room a few minutes ago" Alex said.

Catherine had picked up a bottle of scotch and she poured each of them a drink. "You were reading my mind," Alex said trying to be nice, and the he walked over to take a peep at Adam who was asleep in his bassinet.

"I didn't like the way we left things the other day and I wanted to see you before we finished the transaction on the property," Catherine said.

Alex listened and he sat down in a chair across from Catherine.

"I'm Catholic and I don't think I told you that. We don't believe in divorce, but I don't know how it is if I'm declared dead. There are too many unanswered questions that I have to clear up before I can think about any kind of relationships, and if John are I are still married in the eyes of the church, I would accept that fate. John is a distant memory to me and even if he were not married to someone else, he might not want me back anyway."

Alex reached over and took her hand and kissed it. They looked at each other for a long time and then he said, "Deep down I already knew that, and I've tried to keep my distance. From the beginning, I have been drawn to you and I had this premonition that you were being kept against your will. In the process I have taken quite a fancy to you. I've known from the beginning that you were forbidden fruit, and that even if Billings was out of the picture, you still had other issues to deal with. John, your husband, would be a fool not to take you back and I won't get my hopes up." Alex could see the relief in Catherine's face.

"I want us to stay in touch and I'll write you. I don't expect you to wait on me. This will take some time," Catherine said. "Just knowing you are here gives me great comfort."

There was a knock on the door and the bellman pushed the food cart into the room. Catherine tipped him and then he left. They were both hungry and they sat down to eat.

"I did something today you will think peculiar," Alex said and continued, "My company wanted me to survey the property around your farm and when I went in the barn I lit a match and burned the barn to the ground. I guess I thought by doing that, it might erase some of the memories. It was a stupid thing to do. My company could have used the barn for storage," he laughed.

Catherine laughed too and said, "I wish I had done it myself," and they both laughed.

"Have you seen the posters?" Catherine asked.

"Yes, I have," Alex said. "I wasn't going to tell you this, but I don't want you to hear it from anyone else. They dug up David's body. I assume to collect the reward."

"That doesn't surprise me," Catherine said. "When I saw the poster on the wall of the city attorney's office, two ladies stopped, and one spit on me."

Alex looked concerned, but didn't say anything.

"It's all right, everyone hated him and I knew that. I hated him, too," Catherine said.

"You have nothing to be ashamed of, Catherine," Alex assured her.

She smiled and shook her head, understanding.

Alex changed the subject and began telling Catherine some funny stories and they chatted through their dinner. It was the first time they had really laughed together, and they felt a strong, close bond with each other. Catherine knew in her heart what a loving sensitive man Alex was, and she knew he would be a friend for life.

Adam woke and Catherine nursed him while Alex watched. Alex was possessed by her subtle beauty and he soaked the moment up like a sponge. Catherine asked Alex to hold Adam while she went to the bathroom and he willingly took him. It was almost 11:30 p.m. and Alex knew it was time to leave. He stood up and handed Adam back to Catherine when she came back in. She laid Adam in the bassinet and walked over to Alex. Catherine casually looked at the bed, wanting Alex to have her, but knew in her heart it was the wrong thing to do.

Alex kissed her forehead and said, "I think it's time for me to leave." They stood holding each other for a long time, and then Alex gave her one long kiss, turned, and left out the door.

The closing only took about thirty minutes and then Alex walked her and the baby over to the bank to make the wire transfer. They were through by 11:15 a.m. and went to the hotel to change Adam's diaper one more time and get Catherine's travel bag. They lingered in the room for a few more minutes holding each other and then Alex walked her to the train station.

The departure was difficult for both of them. Alex boarded the train with Catherine and walked her to her compartment in the Pullman car. They hugged again and when the whistle blew Alex gave her a brief kiss and left. He stood outside the train watching as it slowly chugged away and Catherine watched him from the window. He gave her a slight, sad smile and watched the train pull away from the station. Catherine was gone, and his worst fear was that he might never see her again.

CHAPTER 23

Catherine was apprehensive about leaving Alex and Beaumont. In a way she loved Alex, too. She knew she could have stayed and he would have asked no questions, but it would not have been the right thing to do. She had to find her son, Daniel, and she had to make peace with her past.

Alex had called ahead and reserved a room for her at the Tremont, and also a driver and buggy to take her there. Alex was efficient and knew how to get things done, and she liked that about him. She vowed to never lose sight of him. She would write to him as soon as she got to the hotel and thank him again for everything he had done for her.

Adam was fussy part of the trip and he kept her occupied. She heard the whistle and figured they were arriving at the train station in Galveston. It was 4:40 p.m. when she got into the buggy and headed down the strand toward the Tremont. John Merit was sitting at his desk when he looked out the window and saw her. He was stunned by the likeness of the woman in the buggy and he stared as she passed by. No, he thought to himself. The note said my mother is dead.

John assured himself it was not Catherine and besides, she was holding an infant. He noticed on the side of the buggy she was in it said "Tremont Hotel." John quickly put his files away and left.

It was five minutes before he caught the trolley and headed toward the hotel.

John was breathing hard and for a moment he almost couldn't catch his breath. He figured it was from the stress he had been enduring trying to juggle so many things. Carla, his job, finding time for Daniel and now, possibly, Catherine. John was beside himself and his nerves were getting the better of him. John ran into the hotel just as he saw Catherine turn to go up the stairs.

"Catherine!" he yelled.

Everyone turned and looked. Catherine stood motionless for a few moments and then turned and stared at John.

"Is it really you? Where have you been all this time?" he demanded angrily.

It was not the welcome she had expected, and she was shocked by John's angry demeanor. John took her arm and walked through the lobby and over to a quiet corner of the terrace. They sat down at a table and looked at each other.

"I need some answers," he said.

Catherine noticed his pale grey face and he had lost a great deal of weight. She was shocked by his appearance and thought he had aged ten years. "You don't look well," Catherine said and continued, "Are you all right?"

"I'm just fine, Catherine. The fact that you left town without saying as much as goodbye shouldn't have concerned me at all," he said. Catherine's mouth dropped open. "Well, are you going to say something?" John demanded.

"I didn't just leave," she said. "David Brooks kidnapped me and took me to Beaumont. Where is my son, Daniel?" she asked.

"You mean our son," John said. "He's with me and that's where he is staying." Catherine couldn't believe John was the same person she had been married to. He was arrogant and angry, and she pitied him. She hoped she had not been the cause of this change.

"Look, why don't you and your bastard child just go back where you came from," John said and he got up and left.

Catherine couldn't believe what had just happened. She

wondered if she had called first, if he would have acted the same way. She was at a loss of what to do, and decided to go up to her room and see if she could make an appointment with Father Jonathan. Catherine put Adam in his bassinet on the bed in her hotel room and called St. Mary's Catholic Church. Father Jonathan answered on the first ring. Catherine was surprised and didn't say anything at first. Father Jonathan said his name again.

"Father, this is Catherine Merit and I need to see you," she said, almost crying.

"Where are you, Catherine?"

"I'm at the Tremont and I'll be waiting in the lobby," she answered.

"I'll be there in ten minutes." Father Jonathan said.

Catherine changed Adam's diaper and she knew he was hungry, but decided to wait. Catherine was waiting in the lobby when Father Jonathan came in and she got up. "Can we talk on the veranda in private," she said.

Adam was fussing and when she sat down, she placed a blanket over her and the baby and allowed him to nurse. Father Jonathan watched and patiently waited.

"Thank you for coming," she said.

"Does John know you are here?" he asked.

"He does now," Catherine said and told him of their meeting and the way John had treated her. She was almost in tears as she spent the next hour telling him of the abduction and why she sent Daniel away. Father Jonathan listened to the unbelievable tale that Catherine was confessing to him, and the fact that she had gotten pregnant again and the boys were half brothers.

"I don't know what to do, Father," she said. "I don't even know if John is still my husband under the laws of the Catholic Church, and I certainly didn't mean to make him so mad at me. I'm the victim. It was not my choice."

Catherine was trying to dry her tears with the end of the baby blanket and Father Jonathan was sympathetic to her problems.

"John is under a lot of pressure, Catherine, and I will speak to him. You have to understand though, that you have been gone almost two years and John felt he needed to move on with his life. He was apprehensive about taking Daniel at first, but he recognized your handwriting, and when he saw the resemblance, he finally accepted Daniel as his son. He does not want to lose him, either," Father Jonathan said.

"Could you at least tell me if John and I are still married?" she asked.

Father Jonathan looked puzzled and said he would have to look into it.

"I want to see Daniel, if you could arrange that," she said to Father Jonathan.

"I will talk with John after he has had a day or two to digest this, and then I'll get back with you," he said.

Catherine went back up to her room and cried. She had at least hoped that Father Jonathan would be on her side. She was at a loss of what to do. The phone rang and Catherine jumped. Maybe it was John calling her back.

After Alex watched the train disappear down the tracks, he went back over to a bench and sat down; staring in the direction the train had gone. He never dreamed it would be this difficult to watch her leave. He decided he would call her later and just make sure she had made it and then he would be through. He felt he needed to talk to her just one more time.

"How was your trip?" Alex asked Catherine when she answered. Catherine tearfully told Alex of her impromptu meeting with John and how he had treated her. She also told him of her meeting with Father Jonathan, and that she felt everyone was against her.

"It will be all right Catherine," Alex told her in a tender voice. "You knew this would not be easy and it's a lot for John to take in.

Just give him a day or two and he'll come around. I'm sure he will let you see Daniel."

"I'm not so sure," Catherine said. "You didn't see him."

"Do you want me to come?" Alex asked.

"Of course I want you to come, but I don't think that will help the matter, it might make it worse. Oh Alex, I just don't know what I'm going to do," Catherine cried.

"I'll take the midnight train out of here and I'll get my own room. No one will have to know who I am. I'll just be there for you," Alex said. "What's your room number?" Alex asked.

Catherine gave Alex her room number and was relieved that he would be there for support. She hated that she might be leading him on, or giving him false hope, but she had no one else and she needed Alex now.

When Alex hung up, his heart was racing and he hated that he had no will power. If only he could just be with her another day, he thought, just one more day.

Alex went back to his room and packed up a small black bag and left to catch an 11:00 p.m. train to Houston and then change to another going to Galveston. He would be there by 5:00 a.m.. He stopped at his office and called the Tremont to make a reservation. Alex boarded the train and went directly to the dining car. He ordered a scotch and sat at a table by the window. He tried to put himself in John's place, and how he would have reacted under the same circumstances. Your presumed dead wife shows up, unannounced, with another man's baby. Alex thought, that would be a lot to digest. Still, that was not a reason for him to treat her so rudely. Father Jonathan is John's friend and, of course, he would be on John's side. Priest or not, the whole situation is beyond comprehending by anyone. It was an unusual story and he felt badly for Catherine.

Alex had just checked into the hotel and the phone rang as he walked into his room. He picked up on the first ring.

"I checked with the desk and they told me you had checked in.

I haven't slept all night, could you come now," Catherine pleaded.

"I'll be right there," Alex said.

There were on the same floor, so Alex knocked lightly on the door. When Catherine opened it she grabbed Alex's hand and pulled him in quickly, throwing herself into his arms. She was sobbing now, and Alex did his best to console her. If she was up all night, the loss of sleep was enough to escalate her emotional trauma. Alex picked her up and laid her on the bed. She inched over and grabbed him.

"Please don't leave me," she said like a small child.

"I'm here and everything will be all right," Alex said. He had not slept either, and he lay down beside her on top of the covers. Catherine fell asleep with Alex holding her and soon after, Alex fell asleep, too.

CHAPTER 24

John and Carla were supposed to go to a black tie event Friday evening, and Carla was furious that John was late. He didn't say anything to her when she started fussing at him, as he came through the front door. He was finding it hard to catch his breath and when he went to the guest room upstairs, he sat on the bed and tried to rest for a minute.

"I don't feel so good," John said breathlessly to Carla.

"Don't tell me you are trying to get out of going. You know how much this means to me," Carla said.

"Just give me a few minutes," John said and he took another deep breath and blew it out. His head was hurting and he asked Carla to bring him a scotch.

He needed to calm his nerves, he thought. Carla went downstairs and poured some scotch in a glass. When she handed it to John, she asked if he could be ready to leave in thirty minutes, and he shook his head yes. He took two big swallows and felt some of the tension slowly leave his shoulders. He would just have to deal with Catherine through the lawyers; it was more than he wanted to face right now.

John's health had been declining over the last few months. He stopped swimming on Saturday mornings, because it made him tired, and all he felt like doing was sleep. Daniel was a sweet boy, but he was beginning to scoot around on the floor and he liked to play with

John, but he was an active toddler and soon he would be walking. John felt like he was being pulled from every angle, and Carla was constantly finding things for him to do to keep him away from his son.

The party was noisy and John sat on the sofa with a drink. Carla came over and scolded him for being anti-social. He got up and tried to act like he was having a good time and after a couple of hours, he told Carla he was tired and going to walk home. They were only a few blocks from his house and he told Carla to stay. John left and halfway home he had to stop and throw up. It hit him that he had missed a physical a few months back. He did not want to spend any more money on a doctor, and at the time, he was feeling just fine. He decided whatever the cost, he needed to make an appointment and would call the doctor's office on Monday morning. John walked the five blocks to his house and was glad when he got home. He hoped he had not picked up some kind of bug.

John slept in on Saturday morning and Carla woke him at 9:30 a.m. "Weren't you supposed to go to Amelia's and relieve Martha so she could have a day off?" Carla asked.

"Shit," John said and jumped out of bed. He called Amelia and told her he was on the way.

John skipped breakfast and rode the trolley a few blocks and then walked the rest of the way. Martha was not happy that John was cutting into her time off.

"I'll make it up to you," John said.

Daniel was in his highchair when John walked into the kitchen, and he immediately grinned and got excited. John walked over and tousled his hair as he always did and said, "How ya doing little fella?" He kissed Amelia on her cheek and she greeted him back.

John poured himself a cup of coffee and sat down at the kitchen table beside her.

"You don't look well, John," Amelia said. John shook his head and frowned. "What is it, are you all right?" Amelia asked.

"Catherine is not dead," John said, and then told her about the events from the day before. Amelia really loved Catherine and she was surprised that John was so irritated, but did not comment.

"She's not taking Daniel away from us," John said.

Amelia finally spoke, "I understand this is not anything you were expecting, but Daniel is her son, too, and she does have a right to see him."

John did not comment.

"She actually had the nerve to bring her bastard child."

"Did she give you an explanation about why she stayed in hiding so long?" she asked.

"I guess I didn't give her a chance, I was just so surprised when I saw her."

"Perhaps you should take the time to hear her side of the story," Amelia said.

"What difference does it make? I had her declared dead and I am married to Carla. Carla would never give me a divorce. I have really messed up my life. Daniel is the only bright light in my life right now," John said.

Amelia didn't answer him. She rarely talked back and always tried to please John. She was afraid she might say something she would be sorry for.

"Have you told Carla?" Amelia asked.

"Hell no," John said angrily. Amelia winced when John cursed. It was not something he did very often, but lately it happened when Carla's name was brought up. Daniel started fussing because he had been sitting in his high chair for so long. John got up and wet a clean rag to wipe the food from Daniel's face, and take him out of the high chair. John knew that Daniel expected him to get on the floor and play ball with him, as it was their usual routine, so he got Daniel's ball and began rolling it to him. He loved Daniel and his most happy moments were the times he spent with him. He could not let Catherine take Daniel away from him.

Amelia pondered the things Catherine had told John. She knew that Catherine loved John more than anything, and that there had been a reason she stayed away so long. John had said that Catherine was kidnapped by David Brooks. The whole story seemed unbelievable.

Whatever the case, her brother was trapped in a loveless marriage by a money-spending socialite and she felt deeply sorry for him. Since John had Catherine declared dead, she wondered if they were still married now. It was much too complicated for her to figure out. She could only imagine what Carla would say when John told her.

"I'm going to speak to my lawyer on Monday and see what the legal ramifications are. I don't need two wives right now. I can hardly afford the one I have."

"What about the money Catherine's mother left her?" Amelia asked.

"It's almost all gone. I spent a good bit of it on private investigators searching for her. I had no reason to suspect she was ever coming back. When the bills began stacking up, I started using it. There is not much left." John shook his head and looked down at the floor. Amelia rolled her eyes in disbelief.

It was 10:30 a.m. when Alex woke up and heard Adam cooing. He gently moved Catherine's arm from around him and slipped quietly out of bed. He walked over to the baby and looked down at him. He could smell Adam had dirtied his diaper, and Alex smiled. He looked around the room and saw that Catherine had laid the diapers out neatly on a chair close by. Alex went into the bathroom and put a wash rag under some warm water and rung it out. He picked Adam up and laid him on a towel on the floor and took off the diaper.

"Hmm," Alex said, "That's a lot coming from a little fella like you."

He cleaned Adam's bottom and sprinkled some baby powder

on him before putting the diaper on. Adam's gown was also wet, so Alex took it off. He stood up and then reached down and picked up Adam. He looked over at Catherine and she was sitting up smiling at him.

"Good morning," Alex said sweetly and put Adam in her arms to nurse.

Catherine did not try to hide the nursing as she usually did. Alex and Adam were her only family now. She reached for Alex's arm and pulled him to her and she kissed him.

"You are always coming to my rescue," she said sweetly. Alex smiled at her, but didn't comment.

"Would you like me to order breakfast?" Alex asked.

"Sure, just hot tea and scones for me," she said.

Alex called downstairs and ordered the tray to be sent up for her.

"Aren't you going to eat with me?" she asked Alex.

"I think it would look better if I dined alone downstairs. You know a lot of people around here I'm sure, and it wouldn't look good for me to be eating breakfast in your room on Saturday morning. The bellboy might say something to the wrong people."

Catherine had not thought of that, and appreciated the fact that Alex was worried about her reputation. "Would you like for me to check back with you in about an hour?" Alex asked.

"That would be great," she said and smiled at him. Catherine finished nursing Adam and then got up and dressed.

John had played on the floor with Daniel for about an hour, and he got up and picked up the telephone directory. Amelia had been sitting on the sofa watching the two on the floor and she looked at him and wondered what he wanted with the telephone book.

John saw her questioning look and said, "A friend of mine I went to school with is a lawyer. He moved back to Galveston after the storm because he figured most of the other lawyers left. He was the one who did the paperwork when Catherine was declared dead. I'm going to call him at home and talk to him. "Do you mind keeping an eye on Daniel for a few minutes?"

Amelia smiled and grinned at Daniel. She clapped her hands and Daniel began crawling in her direction. John laughed and picked him up and sat him closer to Amelia, and then went into his old study to use the telephone. Amelia heard her brother speaking in a low voice and she couldn't understand anything he said. He talked for about twenty minutes and came back in the room. Amelia looked at him.

"He said everything was legal when we had her declared dead, and since she had abandoned Daniel she had pretty much given up her parental rights. He's going to call her and try to come up with some kind of written agreement for her to have some visitation," John said.

Amelia hated that John was being so harsh with Catherine. If she were kidnapped and unable to get away, it wasn't her fault. Amelia had no idea why Catherine sent Daniel away, but she knew Catherine well enough to know that she did it protect Daniel.

John had just hung up the telephone when it rang. It was Father Jonathan, and John went back to his study to talk. The conversation lasted only fifteen minutes and John hung up.

"Father Jonathan is coming over. He'll be here in about an hour, which will be Daniel's nap time," John told Amelia.

Catherine was pacing the floor when the phone rang. She knew it was probably Alex and she was relieved that it was him. She asked him to come to her room. Alex was there in a matter of minutes and he could tell Catherine was anxious.

"The silence is unbearable. Neither Father Jonathan nor John have tried to reach me," she said.

"Catherine," Alex said as he took her hand calmly, "you have to realize that you have had a long time to think about what your new life would be like with your children. John just found out you are alive, and now he is in a pretty complicated mess and he feels threatened. Give him some time."

"You are right," she said. "I just want to see Daniel. It's been ten months and I have no idea what he looks like."

"Why don't I rent a horse and buggy and you could show me around Galveston?" Alex asked. "I'll be your driver and no one will know any different. We will only be gone a couple of hours and if we stay longer, you can call the front desk and check for messages."

"That sounds great," Catherine said. She gave Alex directions to the stable and told him she would be downstairs in forty-five minutes.

Catherine couldn't stand the confines of the room so she gathered up the things she would need for Adam. The August heat was really warm, so Alex selected a covered surrey to use while they were in Galveston. Catherine was waiting outside and she waved when she saw him coming.

God, she was beautiful, he thought to himself. Alex couldn't believe John had chosen to reject her. As they pulled away Catherine gave him some directions and he followed them.

Catherine and Alex rode through town and out the cemetery road. "Pull up here," she said.

They had stopped at an unmarked grave. Catherine went to her knees and her eyes began to tear up. My mother's tombstone disappeared in the big storm and John promised me he would get it replaced for me. Alex walked over and put his hand on her shoulder and she reached for it. Alex did not say anything. She sat by the grave for a few minutes and then got up. Alex helped her back into the surrey and they rode down to where the orphanage had stood on the beach. The buildings and all the memories were gone now, and she felt numb for a moment. "I used to live here and now it's all gone," Catherine said.

They went back to the hotel and there were no messages so Catherine suggested that they ride over to Minnie Wyman's boarding house where she used to live. When they reached the boarding house Catherine handed Alex the baby and got down, and then took Adam.

She walked up to the front door and knocked. A few minutes later Minnie came to the door. She put her hands up to her mouth and she was obviously surprised. She opened the door and put her arms around Catherine and Adam. Catherine went in and they closed the door. He figured she would be awhile so he tied the horse to a post and walked down the street a ways. There were still vacant lots where houses had been and some construction going on. Alex heard Catherine call his name and he walked back to the house. She waved for him to come, so he went up the stairs, taking them two at a time. "Minnie, this is Alex Cooper, the man I was telling you about."

They exchanged greetings and Minnie brought out some cold lemonade. They visited for over two hours while Minnie filled them in on John's marriage to Carla and the fact that she was spending him into the poor house. She was a barrel of information and Catherine listened to all of it. Minnie told her that John did not accept Daniel at first and that Father Jonathan had looked after the baby the first six months. She said that when John saw him, there was no question the boy was his, and that he had also recognized her writing on the note. She told Catherine that Carla would have nothing to do with the boy, so John was keeping him at Amelia's with a live-in sitter. Catherine was surprised by this.

"That woman he married is nothing like you, Catherine," Minnie said. "She is vindictive and those two daughters she has are spoiled rotten. Amelia and I talk about it all the time," Minnie said. "Will you be staying in Galveston?" Minnie asked her.

"For a while, at least until I can get Daniel back," Catherine said.

"Why don't you move back in here? I still have Professor Gordon, but you know how picky I am. I had a renter for awhile, but I had to ask them to leave a month ago," Minnie said.

The baby still wakes up during the night for a feeding, and I wouldn't want to disturb you," Catherine answered.

"Nonsense," said Minnie. "I sleep like a log and I've missed you. I would love to have you stay as long as you need to."

Catherine looked at Alex and he smiled his approval. "That sounds wonderful. I'll stay another night at the hotel and then Alex can bring me by tomorrow after mass," she said. "He has to go back to Beaumont before Monday. He's been like a father to me," Catherine said, and then regretted what she said. It just came out of nowhere. She looked at Alex, and he pretended not to pay attention, but she knew her remark had to hurt him.

Catherine nursed Adam and then they left. Alex was quiet and waited for Catherine to tell him where to go. "I'm sorry I said what I did. I didn't mean it the way it sounded." Alex ignored her apology and asked her where she wanted to go next.

"I guess back to the hotel."

Alex dropped her off at the hotel and took the surrey back to the livery stables. He decided to walk the twenty or so blocks back to the hotel, even though it was hot. He was used to the Texas heat and at the moment he really didn't care. When Alex got to the Tremont he went into the bar and ordered a scotch. Catherine's words had cut through him like a knife. At least he knew where he stood now. He would see it through till Sunday and then go back to Beaumont.

Catherine had dialed Alex's room several times but he did not pick up. She picked up Adam and went downstairs. She looked around the lobby and on the veranda, but didn't see him. She walked over to the entrance to the bar and saw him sitting at the bar by himself. She bit her lower lip trying to decide what to do. She knew she must have really hurt him, and there was no way to make it right. Did she really think he was a father figure, she asked herself. She decided to act like nothing was wrong and she walked over to him.

"When you finish your drink, would you mind coming to my room?" Catherine asked Alex.

He finished his last swallow and followed Catherine upstairs. Adam was asleep so she put him in his bassinet. She walked over and poured both of them a glass of scotch and sat in the chair.

"That was a stupid remark I made to Minnie and I wanted to apologize," Catherine said.

"Apology accepted," Alex said.

Catherine walked over and took Alex's drink from his hand and led him over to the bed and started kissing him.

"Are you sure you want to do this, Catherine?" Alex asked her.

Catherine answered him back, kissing him and taking his shirt off. Their passion escalated and Alex took the lead, touching Catherine and kissing her breasts, and she responded back encouraging him to please her. Alex had never wanted anything so badly in his life, and even though he felt Catherine was using sex to apologize, he couldn't resist her advances. They explored every inch of each other's body, kissing, moving into different positions and then the ultimately succumbing to the peak of ecstasy. They collapsed into each other's arms. After a while, Catherine got up and put her clothes on and Alex followed her lead.

There was a long silence and Alex said, "Having second thoughts?"

"I'm sorry. I keep leading you on. You deserve better." Catherine said. Alex looked at her and shook his head like he understood.

"You don't have to feel guilty, Catherine. I'm a big boy. I know you have a lot of things on your plate and you don't need to worry about me. It's probably best if I go back to Beaumont now. I'll stay in touch."

Catherine moved quickly and stood in front of the door. Alex stopped and waited.

"I don't feel guilty. You are the best thing that's happened to me since I left Galveston. I don't want to lose you, but I don't feel I have the right to ask you to wait."

"Why don't you let me decide that?" Alex said.

Catherine smiled. "I don't want you to leave. Please stay until tomorrow. Catherine took Alex's hand and walked him over to the table and poured them each a drink.

"I wasn't sure I could ever feel intimate with another man, and I want you to know that when I am with you, I feel human again, like the past never happened. Does that make sense?" she asked.

Alex smiled and took her hand.

"It wasn't that I felt guilty, I was embarrassed. I was afraid that you might think less of me because I desired you, and wanted to be intimate with you. I don't have the same feelings for John that I used to have. He doesn't seem to be the same person. Even if he wanted me back now, I don't think I could be happy with him. I just need some time to sort things out and I don't want to hurt you. You mean so much to me." Catherine took Alex's hand to her lips and kissed it.

"Stay the night with me," she asked.

Alex was spinning his glass around on the table absorbing every word Catherine said. Catherine picked up the bottle and refilled his glass.

Alex smiled and said, "Scotch and a beautiful woman; how can I say no?"

Catherine bit her lip and grinned. They sat at the table talking for another hour and Adam began crying.

Alex walked over and picked him up. Catherine got on the bed and Alex handed him to her. Catherine patted the bed beside her and Alex lay with her while she nursed. It all seemed to be so natural. Like, they were meant to be together. When Catherine finished nursing she looked over and Alex had fallen asleep. She changed Adam and put him in the bassinet. Alex's pocket watch was on the bedside table and Catherine looked at it. It was 8:30 and they had not eaten. Catherine called room service and ordered whatever the special was. At 9:15 the doorbell rand and Catherine opened the door.

Alex woke up and smiled when he saw that Catherine had ordered dinner. "What did you order?" he asked.

"I'm not sure. I told them to send up two specials of the day."
Alex laughed and took the cover off one of the plates. "Roast beef,
and it smells delicious."

Catherine had ordered a bottle of wine and Alex opened it.
After pouring the wine in their glasses, Catherine picked hers up to
make a toast.

"Words could never express how much I care about you.
Could you just give me a few months to figure things out?"

Alex raised his glass and said, "Forever, if I have to."

The evening was like none other than Alex had ever
experienced. He didn't know if it was the wine or the fascination and
excitement of being with this extraordinary woman. She gave herself
to him completely and asked for nothing in return. If he had to wait
forever, he would.

He had heard Catherine get up during the night to nurse Adam
and each time she put Adam back into his basinet, she crawled back
under the covers and cradled herself back under Alex's arms. He
knew he wanted to spend the rest of his life with her and he prayed
she felt the same way. They woke up early before Adam, and
Catherine gave herself to Alex again, sweetly and without remorse,
and their bond would never be broken.

CHAPTER 25

After Alex left, a letter was delivered to Catherine's room. It was from an attorney who asked her to be in his office at 10:00 a.m. on Monday. Alex had left to go to his own room and pack. She had to start making decisions for herself, she told herself, and so she decided not to say anything to Alex. Catherine and Alex checked out of the Tremont Hotel separately and hired a buggy to pick them up and take them to Minnie's house.

Minnie greeted them warmly and Alex took Catherine's things upstairs to her old room. Catherine felt at home there and told Minnie how grateful she was that it was available. She took out some money to pay her and Minnie said, "We'll settle up later. I'm not worried. Supper is at 5:00 p.m.," She said.

Catherine put Adam's bassinet on the floor and fell on the bed. She could almost feel her mother's presence and she longed to talk to her. She looked at Alex and she knew it was time for him to leave. Alex walked over to her and they kissed. Catherine took his hand and held it, not wanting to let go. Stupid girl, she thought, she was in love with this man. They walked downstairs and Alex got Minnie's phone number. He told Catherine he would stay in touch and then he walked outside. He had asked the buggy driving to wait and before Alex pulled himself into the buggy, Catherine threw her arms around him and told him to have a safe trip. After a brief kiss, Alex left. Catherine watched as they rode away and she was saddened by the fact that she had no idea when she would see him again, or if she ever would.

At dinner Catherine listened intently while Minnie and Professor Gordon filled her in on what was happening in Galveston's society and they told her that the Grande Opera House had reopened in the same location. Catherine finally got up the nerve to tell them that John had hired an attorney and she was to meet with him in the morning.

"I was wondering if I should hire my own attorney," Catherine said, more as a statement than a question. They both agreed, and Professor Gordon gave Catherine the name of a friend of his who specialized in these types of matters. Professor Gordon called him and set up a meeting at 8:30 a.m.at the attorney's offices for Catherine.

William Monroe was an older, distinguished man in his early forties and he welcomed Catherine as she entered his offices. Minnie had insisted that Catherine leave Adam with her for the three hours she would be gone, and so she nursed Adam before she left and left a bottle of milk in the icebox in case she ran late. Catherine spent the first hour giving Mr. Monroe all the information regarding her capture, her pregnancy and the birth of her son. She told him that she left Daniel at the convent because she feared David would harm him. The rest of the story unfolded and William Monroe listened intently. "I think our best approach is to attend the meeting and see what they are proposing. We won't give them an answer, and we will tell them we will get back with them.

William Monroe and Catherine Merit arrived at the offices of Attorney Clay Segal at precisely 10:00 o'clock. John Merit was already in his attorney's office. Catherine was surprised that John was there and it made her feel ill at ease. This was the man she had loved with all her heart and soul and he was the father of her child, and now there were sitting on opposite sides of the table in an adversary position. The introductions were made and Monroe and Catherine sat silent, waiting for Clay Segal to begin the meeting. It was awkward and uncomfortable, and Catherine wished that Alex were there holding her hand.

Clay Segal began the meeting. "We understand that Miss Merit is wishing to be reunited with her son, Daniel Merit, and we are prepared to set out some conditions that Mr. Merit has agreed to: Mrs. Merit may have weekly visitations Tuesdays and Thursdays between the hours of 2:00 p.m. to 5:00 p.m. at the home of Amelia Merit. Once the child attains the age of one year old, she may take the boy overnight on Tuesdays and return him back the next day by 9:00 a.m. in the morning. She may have visitations for two hours only on Christmas and Thanksgiving."

Catherine was angry and stood up and said, "I don't want visitation, I want my son."

Monroe stood up and whispered something in Catherine's ear and she sat down. "I apologize for my client's emotional outbreak, please go on."

"That's about it," Mr. Segal said.

William Monroe and Catherine stood and Monroe said, "Mrs. Merit and I will discuss this matter and get back with you. In the meantime Mrs. Merit would like to visit her son tomorrow at Amelia Merit's house from 2:00 p.m. to 5:00 p.m."

They turned and left. John glared at Catherine and their eyes locked on each other. Monroe took Catherine's arm and coaxed her out of the office. They went back to William Monroe's office and he visited with Catherine about the offer.

"I must admit this is a very unusual case and I need to confer with a few people as to how we proceed from here. I knew you wanted to see the child and for now we have to take what they give us until we can file a petition for joint custody.

"What's joint custody?" Catherine asked.

"It's where you share him fifty-fifty," Monroe answered.

"I don't want to share him; I want to be his mother."

"I understand, but you gave up custody three days after he was born. I am afraid you don't stand a chance of getting full custody."

Catherine began crying. "Then tell me this, am I still married to John?"

"Legally, no." Monroe answered.

Catherine sank into her seat.

"It could get very expensive if you want to put up a big fight," Monroe continued.

"My mother left me some money in a trust fund and John is the trustee. Can I get that money?" Catherine asked.

"I'll check and see if he will turn that over to you without going to court. Meanwhile, if you have no money to pay your own legal fees, I'm afraid we will have to accept their offer."

"How much will it cost if we go to court?" Catherine asked.

"It could cost $250 to $500," Monroe told her.

"I have my own money outside of the trust and I will spend it all, if that's what it takes to get my son back." Catherine said.

"Very well then, I will need a $250.00 retainer up front," Monroe said.

Catherine took out her check book and wrote the check.

Catherine called Minnie and asked if she could stop and order a crib for Adam and Minnie told her to take her time. Catherine stopped at the dry goods store and picked out some new clothes for Adam, a crib, and more diapers, and asked them to deliver all of it to her house.

After giving them a check and the address, Catherine was pleased with herself that for the first time in her life she was making her own decisions. Catherine noticed a pretty, bright blue dress in a store window and she went in and bought it. She wanted to look her best when she went to see Daniel the next day.

The dry goods store brought the merchandise to Catherine's boarding house before 2:00 o'clock that afternoon and they set up the crib for her. Catherine was glad to have her own place now, and it felt so good. Thoughts of Alex continued to run in and out of her head and several times she called Adam, Alex. She lay in bed that night thinking of Alex and their weekend together. She knew in her heart that she wanted to grow old with him. He was the sweetest, most understanding man she had ever met, and his love-making was incredible. She prayed that he would wait for her and not give up, and she wondered if he would be willing to give up his traveling. Catherine finally gave in to sleep.

Alex got off the train at 4:00 o'clock on Sunday afternoon. It seemed to take forever once he left Galveston. He still had a piece of Catherine's torn gown in his bag and he took it out when he got back to his room. He lay on the bed looking up at the ceiling and wondered how long it would take for Catherine to sort everything out. It was clear to him now that he deeply loved her, and wanted to spend the rest of his life with her, even quitting his job, if it were necessary. He reflected back over the last few days and Catherine's toast that she made, wanting him to wait for her and he wondered how long that could take. He could understand that Catherine had a lot of insecurities and maybe he had expected too much from her. She owed him nothing. He folded the piece of cloth and laid it on the table beside his bed and fell asleep dreaming of Catherine in his arms.

On Monday when Alex got to work, there was a large package that had arrived on the early morning train waiting for him.

It was from his company in Dallas. They were instructing him to begin negotiations with the farmers and land owners in Hardin County located roughly forty miles northwest of Beaumont. He was to make his headquarters in a small town known as Sour Lake.

Alex took a careful look at the map and breathed a sigh of relief when he saw it was only twenty miles northwest of Beaumont and only seventy-five miles to Houston. He packed up his personal things from his office and put them in his saddlebags. Alex stopped at the livery stables and saddled up Pilgrim. After he collected his things from his room, he stopped in at Dianne's small office to tell her goodbye. She kissed him on the cheek and told him she was sad to see him go.

Catherine thought 2:00 o'clock would never come and she paced up and down. She had dressed in her new blue dress and put Adam in his new little sailor suit. She had called for a carriage to pick them up at 1:30 p.m. and she was outside waiting when they arrived. Catherine rang the doorbell to her old home at 1:55 p.m.. Martha answered the door and invited her in. "He is still napping Mrs. Merit, but he should wake up soon. Please wait in the living room."

Catherine felt uncomfortable, but went in and sat on the sofa she had picked out as part of the furnishings. Amelia came in and hugged her. She looked at Adam and told Catherine he was a beautiful baby. Catherine had brought the bassinet so she would have someplace for Adam to sleep and she put him in it. She sat there for over thirty minutes and finally Martha walked in with a beautiful little boy. Catherine stood up and Daniel reached out his arms to her.

"Oh my, he's so beautiful."

Daniel pulled her hair and Catherine laughed. She sat on the floor and he tried to pull the clip from the side of her hair. Catherine was fascinated with him and could see so many of John's facial expressions on Daniel's face. Martha put a box of toys down on the floor and Daniel reached for one. Catherine had thought about bringing him a toy, but didn't know what he might need so she decided to wait. Daniel immediately took to Catherine and he loved her long hair. They played on the floor together and then Daniel heard Adam cry. He crawled over to the bassinet and pulled himself up. He began jumping up and down and screaming with excitement. Adam started crying and Catherine picked him up. Daniel crawled over to her and crawled in Catherine's lap next to Adam.

"This is your brother," Catherine said.

Amelia stood in the doorway watching. Catherine looked up at her and they both smiled at each other. There was a knock at the door and Catherine said, "Oh it can't be time to go yet."

It was her driver coming back to get her. It was 4:55 p.m.. Catherine kissed Daniel and hugged him. It was hard for her to leave.

She felt like she was leaving part of herself. Catherine picked up Adam and the bassinet and told Amelia good bye, and that she would be back Thursday at 2:00 p.m..

That evening Catherine sat in her room and tried to read. She took Alex's card out of her purse and touched it again. She thought back to the first time she saw him at the dry goods store in Beaumont, and knew there was an instant attraction. She spent the rest of the evening daydreaming about every encounter they had ever had and the more she thought, the more she realized that he was the most remarkable man she had ever met. He was the only person who understood her and was sympathetic and understanding of everything she had been through, and she realized she had been selfish. She looked at the clock and it was 11:00 p.m. She decided to call him the next day.

Catherine waited until 9:00 a.m. to place the person to person call to his office, and she quietly prayed he would be there.

"Not here," answered the man on the other end of the line.

"Ma'am, do you want to leave a message?" asked the operator. "Could you ask him when he might be back?" Catherine asked the operator.

"Not sure, moved out yesterday," the man said, and hung up.

There was a knot in Catherine's stomach and she felt like someone had just stuck a knife in her heart. Moved out yesterday, the words hung in Catherine's mind. Moved out where? She thought. How he could just leave like that and not let her know, she wondered. Then it hit her. She had driven him away with her insecurities and foolish actions. She hated herself for that. Catherine looked at the card again and picked up the phone.

"I need a number in Dallas, Texas, for Glacier Oil Company."

"Would you like me to connect you with that number?" asked the operator.

"Yes, please," she said. A few seconds later a woman's voice said, "Glacier Oil Company."

"Uh, I'm a friend of Alex Cooper and I wondered if you could tell me how I might reach him," Catherine asked.

"Mr. Cooper is travelling, would you like to leave a message?" the lady asked.

"Yes, tell him to call Catherine, and that it's urgent," Catherine said.

"Sure thing," the lady said, and hung up. Catherine put the phone down and cried.

It was noon when Alex and Pilgrim road into the little town of Sour Lake, Texas. Alex wasn't surprised that the sleepy little town only had one hotel. The hotel was practically empty and he got a room for seventy-five cents a night. It wasn't much, but it was better than sleeping on the prairie, which he used to do a lot. He was getting tired of the travelling and he liked South Texas even though the summers could get really hot. He checked at the front desk to find out where he could find a telephone. The clerk told him that there was none, but there was a telegraph office inside the depot. Alex left Pilgrim tied up at the front of the hotel and walked down the street to the depot. He sent a wire to Catherine.

"Boss moved me to Sour Lake, Texas. Granger Hotel, No phones, Alex."

Catherine had been on his mind since he left Beaumont, and he was hoping that his new assignment would keep him busy. He had no idea how long he would be in Hardin County and Galveston was still close to a hundred miles away if he took the route through Baytown.

Alex found a blacksmith just outside of town and made arrangements for Pilgrim. Not having access to a phone made Alex uneasy, and he felt it put more distance between him and Catherine. He had seen a lot of the men he worked with get their hearts broken because they were not able to make frequent calls or visits when they were on the road. Perhaps being inaccessible was a good thing, he thought.

Alex opened up the package from his company again and looked through several maps that would take him from one end of the county to the other. He also noticed that some of it was covered by dense forest know as the Big Thicket, and it was going to take him some time to compile the information that he needed. Most all the trip would be on horseback and would cover over eight hundred ninety-seven square miles. The map showed about three square miles of water not including the creeks and streams that flowed into the Neches River. This was probably going to be a long assignment, and as far as Alex was concerned it would probably be his last. He was getting tired of the shabby hotels, living on the prairie, and peeing behind a tree. Alex decided he would wait until the next day to make his way eighteen miles north to Kountze, Texas, which was the county seat. The September heat was stifling and he preferred making the trip in the early morning. It was a short thirty minute ride and he would be spending most of his day there. Surely, the county seat had a phone, he hoped.

He had left Pilgrim at the blacksmith's barn and walked back into town. It was after 1:00 p.m. and he would be on his way by 6:00 a.m. the next day. He stopped at a small café and ate lunch, then headed back to his room to chart his route.

Catherine was nursing Adam when she heard the doorbell. She jumped out of bed still holding Adam, and disrupted his feeing. Adam began to cry, but she put him in his bassinet and ran downstairs. She answered and a young man handed her a telegram. She went back upstairs to collect some change for a tip for the young man. She ripped open the telegram and read it several times. She was relieved, but concerned that there were no phones and she really wanted to hear his voice. Adam was screaming so she picked him up and began nursing him. When she finished taking care of his needs she decided to take Adam and visit the Rosenberg Library. She had no idea where Sour Lake, Texas, was, and Texas was big.

Catherine breathed a sigh of relief when she located Sour Lake on the map. It meant that Alex was still in the vicinity of Beaumont and Houston, which made her happy. If he didn't come to see her soon, she would go to him, she thought. She missed him terribly and she hated the idea of just sitting around waiting. Catherine checked out the book on Texas and then went to the Science area and picked up several books. If she returned to medical school, she knew she would be studying about different diseases and she found two books, one on disease and another regarding the heart and lungs, so she checked them both out.

Alex checked out of the hotel and after getting some supplies, he saddled Pilgrim and was in Kountze less than an hour later. There was a phone at the depot. It was still really early and Alex hoped Catherine was up. She answered on the third ring.

"How are you doing, Catherine?" Alex asked.

"Better, now that you have called," she said. Catherine filled him in about the attorneys and the Tuesday and Thursday visitations. Alex told her he was glad she finally got to be with Daniel and was sorry John was being so difficult. He explained that he would be in a new town every day and that unless he was in a larger town, the chances of finding a phone were small. Neither wanted to say goodbye and Alex promised he would try to call her every chance he got.

CHAPTER 26

The weeks dragged by for Catherine. She loved her visits with Daniel, but the petition her attorney had filed for full custody would not be heard for another month. She constantly thought about Alex and wondered where he was and why he had not called her. She missed him so much and he was constantly in her thoughts. She had wanted to go back to work at the hospital, but her attorney had told her that John might bring up in court the fact that she was not home to take care of her children. She loved being a mother and spent most of her time with Adam and two afternoons a week with Daniel.

Catherine was growing anxious about Alex. She had studied the area on the map that Alex told her he was covering, but they were mostly small towns and she knew it would be unlikely for Alex to find a telephone.

That evening the phone rang again around 7:00 p.m.. Catherine raced downstairs and answered the phone by the third ring.

Alex apologized and told her he had not been near a place that had a phone in over a week. Catherine was trying not to cry. "I miss you so much, and," Catherine hesitated, "I love you, Alex, and I want you here."

"I'm a little ahead of schedule and if it is all right with you, I could leave Thursday night and spend a few days in Galveston," Alex said.

"Of course, it would be wonderful. You have no idea how

much I've missed you."

Alex could feel Catherine's excitement and he longed to hold her.

"I plan on heading over to Beaumont, and catch the overnight train there. I'll be able to leave Pilgrim at the livery stable. Could you make a reservation at the hotel for me?"

When John told Carla about Catherine's return to the city she was furious.

"You mean you believe her? Don't tell me she couldn't have escaped during the two years she was gone. Who does she think she is?" Carla asked.

John hated Carla's demeaning comments and didn't answer her. She continued griping about how she was not going to let some hussy break up her marriage. "Maybe you could just pay her off and get rid of her?" Carla finished.

"Pay her with what? You spend every extra penny I make," John shouted back.

He didn't think he could stand much more pressure. Now with the added attorney's fees he felt as if the whole world was caving in on him. If he didn't love Daniel so much he would give him to Catherine, but Daniel was the only thing in his life that brought him joy.

John hadn't felt well for several months now, and the pressure was really beginning to take its toll on him. He was certain that his constant nausea and loss of appetite was the result of a nagging wife and Carla's expensive taste. He had made an early morning appointment with his doctor and he was hoping he could also get something to help him sleep.

"The doctor will see you now," the nurse said to John.

"It's been two years since I last saw you," Dr. Wellborn told John.

"I know, new wife, busy job, I just couldn't find the time," John said.

"Looks like you have lost about fifteen pounds," Dr. Wellborn said and continued, "Have you been feeling okay?"

"Not really; I get tired easily and sometimes I throw up for no reason," John answered back. The doctor drew some of John's blood and put it under a microscope in a private room away from the examination room. He looked at it for several minutes and didn't like what he saw. Dr. Wellborn went back to talk to John again.

"I'm not sure what we have here," Dr. Wellborn said, "And I'm going to shoot straight with you. The last time I saw blood that resembled yours; the man was dead in six months. Your blood cells are multiplying and eating up your insides. It's a bad disease and there's not much we can do. There's no cure, I'm afraid," Dr. Wellborn said sympathetically.

John looked at Dr. Wellborn, not believing what he had just heard. "I'm going to die in six months?" John repeated.

"I suspect you have had this for at least six months, maybe even longer. Even if we had caught it early, there is nothing we could do. You need to get your affairs in order. You'll be fine for now. I'll give you the name of something that will help you with the nausea. Come back and see me in two weeks. I want to take another blood sample and see how fast it's spreading."

"I would appreciate your not saying anything to anyone right now, doc," John said and the doctor said, "Of course, I won't."

John left Dr. Wellborn's office in shock. It was barely 10:00 a.m. when he left, but he couldn't go back to his office. He was thirty-two years old and he was dying, and he couldn't quite comprehend that he was that ill. He had to think. John walked several blocks and then had to sit down to rest. He tried to remember back when his symptoms had started. He remembered last Thanksgiving, and that he felt sick after eating, but figured it was the rich food. Whatever, it really didn't matter now. John put his head in his hands and felt helpless. John did not look forward to telling Carla. He knew if he did, it would be all over the neighborhood and she would tell her uncle. John couldn't afford to lose his job right now, so he decided he would do as the doctor ordered and get his affairs in order.

John knew there was one person he could trust to keep the secret, and he decided now was as good a time as any. Minnie Wyman's house was only a few blocks from where John was, so he knocked on the door. Minnie was surprised when she went to the door and John was standing there.

"I need to see Catherine," John said and started up the stairs.

Minnie was surprised, but she did not try to stop him. Catherine heard a knock on her door and assumed it was Minnie, so she opened it right away. She was surprised to see John.

"Come in," she said.

Catherine sat on the sofa and John sat in the chair. It felt strange for them to be here in the same house they had shared for almost a year. Catherine waited for John to say something first.

John stared out of the window a few minutes before he began. "I was wondering if I could talk you into dropping this whole custody matter," he said as he took a deep breath.

Catherine waited to see if he was going to say something else but he didn't. "Why should I do that?" Catherine asked.

"If you drop the suit, you can have full custody in six months," John answered.

Catherine looked confused and asked, "Why in six months?"

John coughed and then tried to breathe. Catherine watched and realized John must not be well.

John looked down at the floor and said, "That's all the time I have left."

Catherine stared. "Are you sure?" she asked.

"Doc says the cells in my blood are multiplying and eating away at my insides and there's no cure," John said. "You're the only one I'm telling. Carla's uncle is my boss and I can't afford to lose my job right now. Too many expenses," John said.

"John, how long have you known?" Catherine asked.

"Just found out, "John said.

"Of course, I'll drop the petition for custody. Will you give me parental rights in your will?" she asked.

"That's not a problem, Carla won't want Daniel and Amelia can't physically take care of him," John said. "I'll let you see him as much as you want; I just want to be able to see him on the weekends and at night. He's been my whole life, and I love him so much," John said.

"There's one more thing," John continued. "The money in your trust is almost all gone. I used almost $1,000 for private detectives and following leads trying to find you. After a year, they assured me you were probably dead. I guess I wanted to believe that. I've used the rest of the money for our house and Amelia's living expenses, and I'm sorry about that. Now you will have nothing. I'll have to leave my life insurance money of $15,000 for Carla to pay the bills we've incurred. I guess I really made a mess of my life. I feel really bad that I acted the way I did, when I first saw you. I'm really glad you're okay." John said. "Do you mind telling me what happened?"

Catherine looked away and dreaded the thought of bringing up her horrible past, but she took a deep breath and said, "Somehow David Brooks escaped from the prison farm and he changed his name to David Billings. He moved to Beaumont and became the undertaker. The reason why I disappeared into thin air was because he had purchased a hearse here in Galveston and was waiting outside the emergency room exit when I came out that night. He used a rag soaked in chloroform and put it over my face. It made me unconscious. He took me to Beaumont and told everyone I was his mail-order bride and that I was a deaf-mute. He forbade me to talk to anyone, and I was pretty much his sex slave. When I got pregnant right away, he put two and two together and figured it was yours. He was going to kill Daniel, so I got away and took him to the sister's convent in Beaumont. I went back because I knew he would come looking for me if I was gone. He would have killed anyone who tried to help me escape. I got pregnant with Adam a few months later."

"Catherine, I'm so sorry, how did you get away?" John asked.

"David was greedy and he was accused of cheating in a poker game. A posse of men chased him to the house we were living in, and they hung him while I watched. Adam was born that evening." Catherine said, as she put her head in her hands and looked down.

"I wish I would have waited for you, Catherine, I've never stopped loving you," John said.

Catherine began crying and John went over and put his arms around her. "We made a beautiful son, didn't we?" John asked and Catherine smiled. "I'm really sorry about the money," John said.

"It's all right," Catherine said. "Since everyone thought I was David's wife I was able to sell the farm. He had previously been offered $100,000 when oil at Spindletop was discovered, but he was greedy and decided to wait it out for more money. Unfortunately, others took the money and they kept finding more wells, glutting the market with oil. A year later, a few weeks ago, I sold it for $45,000 and came here to find Daniel and see if you still wanted me. I had found out you had remarried, but I was hopeful."

John shook his head as if he couldn't believe the whole story but he knew Catherine wouldn't make up something up like that.

"I don't know what's going to happen to Amelia," John said.

"I don't think there are any easy answers, John," Catherine said and continued, "You've had a lot thrown at you today, and you still have time to take care of Amelia. We could sell the house and use the proceeds for Amelia to live in a private facility. I'll make sure she is taken care of."

John hugged Catherine again and left.

Catherine sat on the bed and she couldn't help but cry. She had loved John deeply at one time and the two years away from each other had pulled them in different directions. She felt terrible about his impending fate, and Daniel would also be without a father.

Alex made his way back to Beaumont, Texas by 4:00 p.m. Thursday afternoon, and he left Pilgrim at the livery stable. He had never felt as anxious as he did now, waiting for the train to come. He was early, so he walked up and down the side of the depot, waiting. When the train finally came, he headed for the dining car. He had skipped eating lunch to save time. He felt like the luckiest man in the world, and he could hardly wait to be with Catherine the next morning.

Alex wasn't able to check into his hotel room until later so he left his bag there and stopped in the restaurant to order some coffee and eat a decent breakfast. He had just finished when a bellboy told him there was a call for him on the house phone.

"I've missed you so much and I have a lot to talk to you about. Can you come over now?" Catherine asked.

Alex walked to Minnie's house and Catherine was waiting on the steps. She ran down them and into Alex's arms. She kissed him and she could barely hold back the tears. John's death sentence made Catherine even more aware now, how precious life is, and she didn't want to lose a moment being with Alex.

Alex walked over to Adam's bassinet and commented on how much he had grown. Catherine took his hand and walked him over to the small sofa and sat down beside him. She began telling him about John's visit the day before and she began crying. Alex tried to console her; he knew she had loved John dearly, and that he was the father of her first child.

"It would mean that after his death, I would be free to marry," Catherine said.

"Would you marry me, Catherine?" Alex asked.

"Of course I would," she said. "I really hate it has to be this way. I would rather that we could have worked out our differences about Daniel and he would not die. I hate that for him and for Daniel," Catherine said.

Alex understood what she meant, and he was ecstatic that

Catherine said yes. "Let's not wait. Marry me today," Alex said. "I should be finished up in three more weeks," he told her. "Then I'll be in Dallas a couple more days to finish up, but it's close enough for me to come in on the weekends."

"I would like that, Alex, but..." Catherine stopped.

"I'm going to quit my job Catherine. I don't want to be away from you any longer than I have to be. I can't promise we'll stay in Galveston, but we have plenty of time to decide where we want to live," Alex said. "I do need to finish what I've started and I'll be through in a month."

Catherine grinned and they embraced each other. "Yes, oh yes," she said.

The next morning, they talked for a while longer and waited for the courthouse to open at 9:00 a.m. and then the three of them got on a trolley and rode to the federal offices. After waiting for over an hour the clerk told them one of the judges had ended his trial early and he would see them in his office.

"Well, I see you waited until after the little one was born to make an honest woman of her," he said to Alex. He and Catherine smiled at each other and didn't say anything. They were holding hands and Adam was in Alex's arms. They were staring at each other when the judge interrupted. The judge made a few more comments and Catherine and Alex exchanged their vows. Alex put his arm around Catherine and kissed her, all the while holding Adam between them. They both couldn't have been happier.

Catherine had packed a small bag for her and Adam and they all went back to the hotel.

Alex ordered some champagne and some sandwiches to be sent up to the room. Adam had awakened and Catherine nursed him while they waited for room service.

The bellman placed the cart in their room and opened the champagne bottle. "You must be celebrating something," he said.

"We are," Alex beamed. "We just got married."

The bellman looked at Catherine who was holding Adam and he smiled.

Alex poured each of them a glass of champagne and Catherine put Adam in his bassinet. They sipped their champagne and Catherine picked up a garnish off of one of the plates and put it up to Alex's mouth, all the while staring into his eyes. He opened his mouth and sucked it off her finger. She repeated it again, and Alex grabbed her arm and stood up, pulling her closer to him. He put her finger in his mouth and then took her in his arms.

"You're messing with me, and I like that," Alex said, as he kissed her behind her ear.

He began dancing with her, even though there was no music. Catherine moved to the rhythm of his body and he pulled her closer. Alex reached behind her neck and unbuttoned her dress, moving slowly down her back to each button. He pulled if off her shoulders and it fell to the floor. Alex took a step back and looked at her.

"God, Catherine, you are so beautiful," Alex said in a low voice.

Catherine reached up and slowly unbuttoned Alex's shirt and took it off. She moved her hand down his arm, caressing his muscular body and then she pulled his undershirt over his head. Alex sucked in his breath in anticipation of what she might do next. She put her arms around his neck and began rubbing up against him, all the while looking into his eyes. Alex couldn't wait any longer, so he swept her into his arms and carried her over to the bed. Catherine had already pulled the covers back when she nursed Adam, and Alex laid her on the smooth, crisp, inviting sheets.

Catherine pulled Alex closer to her and unbuttoned his trousers. Alex pulled the clip out of Catherine's hair and it fell loose over her shoulders. He helped her take off his clothes and then Alex finished undressing Catherine. They both wanted the moment to last, so they took their time with each other. Catherine came first and Alex followed and they held each other, not wanting it to be over. Alex kissed Catherine's beautiful breast and told her he was jealous of Adam. Catherine laughed, and she couldn't remember when she had been this happy.

They were absorbed in their love for each other and Catherine had no regrets. She knew Alex was gifted with many qualities, but she had never known a man who gave of himself so completely. He was so easygoing and patient with Adam and didn't mind when they were interrupted for Adam's feeding. He always lay on the bed with her and watched her nurse.

On Saturday morning Alex asked Catherine to get dressed; he wanted to take her shopping. He stopped at a jewelry store and they bought matching wedding rings for each other. Catherine saw a sign that said, "Photographs in one day." She had never had her picture taken except as a young child, so she asked Alex if they could stop and look into it. They were there for about an hour, taking pictures as a family and one of Adam, who was just over two months old. She would have to wait to pick up the pictures on Monday morning. Alex was disappointed that he would not be able to have one to take with him when he left on Sunday. The photographer offered to make just one and he could pick it up at the end of the day. Alex told him that he wanted a picture of the three of them and they agreed to return at 4:30 that afternoon to pick it up.

Catherine had told Minnie about their marriage, so she wouldn't worry when Catherine didn't stay at the house over the weekend, and Minnie was delighted for her. It was time Catherine found some happiness again, she thought. She had had so much tragedy in her young life.

Alex and Catherine spent the rest of the day walking the strand, having lunch and shopping. Alex noticed Catherine looking at some clothing in a small boutique and he took her arm and coaxed her into the shop. More than anything, Catherine wanted some nice lingerie and Alex grinned and approved everything Catherine wanted. He loved buying things for her and he was already anticipating how she would look in them.

It was almost 4:00, so they took the trolley back to the photography shop and they were delighted that the photographer had managed to complete the entire order. When they got back to the hotel, Catherine laid all the pictures out on the bed. Alex selected one of all three of them and was surprised when he saw one of Catherine.

"I didn't know you had your picture taken by yourself. When did you do that?" Alex asked.

"When you offered to take Adam to a dressing room and change his diaper on the bench. I wanted to surprise you." she said.

Alex stared at the picture and felt a tear in his eye. "It's beautiful," he said, as he picked it up and put it with the other picture. He placed the two pictures in a hotel envelope and put it in his inside vest pocket. They both looked over and saw that Adam was asleep and they quickly undressed and crawled into bed. They made love until Adam woke up and demanded their attention. They both looked at each other and said simultaneously, "It's your turn." And they laughed.

Catherine watch as Alex's tall, muscular, naked body got out of bed and carefully picked up their delicate treasure. He smiled at her, as he handed Adam to her, and got back under the covers. "I think I need to talk to him about his timing," Alex teased.

Afterwards, Alex put on a new robe that Catherine had bought him while they were shopping, and ordered room service. Neither of them wanted to leave the room and they spent another memorable night at the Tremont Hotel and had breakfast in the room. Catherine watched as Alex put his things in his travel bag.

"Adam and I are coming with you to the train station," she told Alex.

"I'd like that," Alex said and then thought for a minute. "I really didn't think I would ever feel this way about a woman, much less get married. I love you Catherine." They hugged each other and Catherine told him she loved him, too.

Alex stood holding Catherine outside by the train and waited to board until the last minute. It was hard when he had to pull his hand away from Catherine, as he ran to jump on the train. He turned around to watch the two of them and he could see Catherine was crying. She waved once more, and then left. He found a seat, but stood up again and made his way to the dining car for a drink. It was going to be a long month, he thought, and he took out the envelope with the two pictures. He smiled as he looked at them and knew they would be a comfort to him on his long rides through the countryside. He had never felt such happiness in his life.

CHAPTER 27

Catherine and Adam took the trolley back home and she wondered if God would forgive her for marrying outside the Catholic faith. She had always tried to be a good Catholic, but she figured she had already been excommunicated from the church anyway, when she did not try to stop David from doing the things he did. She truly loved Alex in a different way than John, and she was happy that they were going to spend the rest of their lives together.

Catherine wondered if her marriage to Alex was even legal, since she and John never divorced. It would only be a problem if John objected to it and he was married to someone else. It was all too complicated, and if the lawyers couldn't tell her if she was still legally married, then who could, she wondered. When she got home she picked up the phone in the hall and called John at Amelia's house.

"I wondered if we might visit again. There is something else I feel in my heart I must tell you," Catherine said.

John agreed to come to Catherine's house on Monday during lunch.

Catherine had warmed some soup for John when he arrived and he appreciated her thoughtfulness.

"I gave you somewhat of a short version of my last two years, but I left out something that I felt you needed to know," Catherine continued, "There was a man by the name of Alex Cooper who made an effort to help me, as he had seen the way David treated me in public. He had seen the article about your marriage to Carla and that I had been declared dead. He made the connection and on several occasions had tried to get me to speak to him. I would not, because I was afraid of being killed, or David taking Alex's life. When I told you Adam was born shortly after David died, Alex arrived after the posse left, and helped me bury David. That's when I began having birthing pains and Alex stayed with me and delivered Adam. He helped me sell the farm and..." Catherine stopped.

"You love him, don't' you?" John asked

"Yes, I do," Catherine answered.

"Does he feel that same way about you?" John asked

"Yes, we got married this past weekend," Catherine answered.

"Everything happens for a reason, I suppose," John said.

"Do you think he will be able to love Daniel, too?"

"Yes, he is very kind, and he is older, like you," Catherine replied

"I'd like to meet him when he comes, if you don't mind," John said.

John and Catherine visited through lunch and he told Catherine he was going to wait as long as he could, to tell Carla about his health. He also told Catherine he was meeting with his lawyer to make sure his will was in order. Half the house was already Catherine's, but John wanted to leave his part to Amelia. Catherine said Amelia could have all of it, and that Amelia could use the money any way she chose, once she sold it.

Catherine told John that Alex had substantial funds of his own, having never been married. There was more than enough with her money, too, to educate both children. John felt badly that he really had nothing left in his estate to give to Daniel.

"My whole life ended when I lost you, Catherine." John said. "I'm glad you have found someone, and I hope he makes you happy."

Catherine felt a heaviness in her heart after John left. John was facing death and she was facing a whole new life with all the advantages.

After John left, Catherine nursed Adam, bathed and dressed him, and then left. She had been used to a much faster pace and not accustomed to staying home so much. She felt the walls were closing in. Adam was almost three months now, and he was a hearty eater. She knew she would not be able to carry him very far, and she needed to buy a baby carriage. The general store had several to select from and she decided on one that that was light weight, with a cover over it to protect his face from the sun. She picked up a teething ring and a rattler and hoped it would keep him occupied when he was awake. After she paid for it, she placed him with his blanket in the carriage and his little fingers curled around the handle of the rattle and began shaking it. Catherine laughed, amused at how quick he was to learn new things.

Catherine decided a nice walk would be good for both of them, and she remembered Minnie telling her about an antique shop just off the Strand and 23rd Street that had been acquiring things that had been found after the flood. She stopped when she saw the sign, "Hollister's Antique Shop," and went in.

She was amazed at all of the beautiful antiques and oil paintings. She knew she probably couldn't afford anything, but she loved looking. Adam had just fallen asleep and she carefully walked through the crowded doorway.

"May I help you?" asked an older man with glasses, seated behind a desk. She had not seen him earlier because the shop was so full.

"Hello," she answered cheerfully. "I heard that you might have some things that may have come from homes that were destroyed after the floor, and I just wanted to look."

"Help yourself," he said. "Looking for anything in particular?"

"I'm not sure," she said. "My mother had given me her dressing table set and I was hoping her locket was in one of the jars. Do you have anything like that?" she asked.

"I don't have any complete sets, but I do have some miscellaneous powder jars with lids and a few odds and ends of things. Come with me and I'll show you," he said.

Catherine looked at Adam and wondered how she could move his carriage through the store without knocking something over.

"You can leave the child right there, he'll be fine," he said as though reading her mind.

They didn't go very far until the man opened the glass door to a cabinet and pointed to about twenty dresser jars.

Catherine looked at them and her eye immediately caught a cut glass jar with a sterling lid. "It's similar to that one, but I can't be sure."

Mr. Hollister picked it up and handed it to Catherine. She slowly twisted the sterling top off and she gasped. "This is it, I think, but there is a piece of paper folded up in it. May I take it out?" she asked.

"I bought a whole box of things from one young man who collected these after the flood, and I haven't had a chance to go through them individually, go ahead," he said.

When she picked up the paper, Catherine felt her heart skip a beat.

"What is on the paper?" he asked.

Catherine opened it and read the note. Mr. Hollister looked at her waiting for her to speak.

My dearest Catherine:

> *Not knowing what God has in mind for me and unsure if I will ever see you again; I wanted you to know that my life began when I met you. You have brought me peace and joy that not every man will receive, and I thank you for choosing me to be your husband.*
>
> *You are with me always, in life and in death.*

I love you,
John

"It's a note my husband left me, when he thought he was going to die in the flood." And she started to cry. "I'm sorry; he never told me he left me a note.

How much do you want for the jar?" she asked.

"Nothing," he said, "it belongs to you. I am glad that it has found its rightful owner; that is payment enough."

He wrapped the jar and handed it to Catherine. She reached up and kissed him on the cheek and he looked surprised.

When Catherine made her way back home, she asked Minnie if she could leave the carriage in the parlor and not take it upstairs.

"This is your home now, Catherine, and I want you to feel comfortable acting as if it is," she said.

Catherine kissed her on the cheek and invited Minnie upstairs to look at their pictures. She also told Minnie about the antique shop and finding the dresser jar, but left out the part about the note. It was much too personal, and since John was married to someone else now, she thought it best to keep it to herself. Catherine lay in bed that night and thanked God that two very special men had fallen in love with her. She knew John still loved her and she loved him, too. His death would be difficult, but having Alex would make it more tolerable and she loved Alex equally as much. She cried herself to sleep, sad over the thought of John's disease and his long suffering. She had laid the family picture of her, Adam, and Alex on Alex's pillow, and longed to be with him.

The next afternoon Catherine packed a small bag to take to Amelia's for the afternoon. She was excited to see Daniel, and she felt the weight of the world had been lifted from her shoulders now that she had told John about Alex.

Catherine and Amelia chatted for awhile while Daniel made funny faces at Adam. Despite the nine months difference in age, the boys favored each other and had somehow bonded. Adam was no longer afraid of Daniel and Adam liked him.

Catherine knew John had not mentioned his illness to anyone except her, so she carefully avoided talking about him.

"I'm so glad you and John are in agreement with the visitation," Amelia said.

"I am too," Catherine agreed.

"I'm sure in time you will meet Carla, and I have to warn you, she is quite the socialite. She has a way of making everyone around her feel inferior," Amelia said. "I was surprised when John told me he was going to marry her. I saw right through her from the beginning and I tried to warn John, but he didn't listen," Amelia continued.

Catherine listened intently but didn't say anything. Since she had never met Carla, she didn't really have an opinion. She felt Amelia just needed to talk, so she listened.

Adam was getting tired and sleepy and it was also time for his feeding, so Catherine nursed him before she left. She played with Daniel on the floor once Adam went to sleep and she hated to leave. The two girls hugged and Catherine told her she would be back the next Thursday at 2:00 p.m.

CHAPTER 28

Alex took out the last few maps he had to complete and he carefully calculate his scouting expedition, so he didn't backtrack or waste any unnecessary time. He figured if he stayed on the trail following the map and spent nights sleeping under the moon, he might be able to cut off a couple of days. He stopped and loaded up on supplies and mounted Pilgrim. He patted his vest pocket where he carried the two photographs of the family and Catherine. They were with him always and it made the lonely trip more tolerable.

He made a lot of progress the first couple of weeks, and worked until sundown. He had checked in with Catherine the night before, when he was in Batson, Texas, and told her that he would be out of phone contact for a couple of days and not too worry if she didn't hear from him for a while. Alex was working his way toward the Big Thicket to the northern part of the county and was making a lot of progress. He had hoped to be through by the end of the next week, but didn't tell Catherine, because he didn't want to get her hopes up. Their phone conversations were brief, because it was expensive. Soon they would be a family of four, and even though they had a substantial amount of money, Alex was frugal.

It had been a long day for him and after looking at the map he decided to head over to a flowing creek he had crossed earlier and sleep under the stars. The few small towns he had passed through were mostly way stations where the stagecoaches used to stop before the railroads put them out of business. When he got to the creek he led Pilgrim over to get a drink. Pilgrim began moving around and Alex could see he was uneasy about something. Alex has just turned around and saw two men on horseback, both aiming their rifles at him. The first blast caught the side of his head, and less than a second later he felt a piercing bullet hit his right shoulder. Both blasts knocked him to the ground. Alex's body was lying in the creek, unconscious.

The two men dismounted, walked over to Alex and pulled him out of the water, dropping him on the side of the creek. They rummaged through his pockets, taking his money, wallet, watch and a baby teething ring, which they threw on the ground. One of them removed Alex's wedding ring while the other took off Alex's boots. Alex's guns were still on his saddle along with all of his possessions.

"Let's get the horse and get out of here," one of the bandits said.

The other one took Pilgrim's reins and tried to lead him away. Pilgrim resisted, reared up in the air, pulled away, and ran off. The two men took off after Pilgrim and chased him for about a mile, until they lost him. One of the men had intended to shoot Alex again, but his need to catch the horse was greater than his need to stay and shoot Alex again. Besides, one of the bullets hit his head and the man was sure Alex was dead.

Alex woke up a while later and he tried to get up, but found it difficult. He felt the side of his head and found blood on his hand. He had a horrible ringing in his ear and a pain in his shoulder. He knew he had been shot, but he wasn't sure how bad his head injury was. A quick look around confirmed that whoever shot him wanted his money and supplies. He noticed Pilgrim was gone, too. He closed his eyes and wondered how or if he could make the five-mile walk to the nearest town on bare feet. He managed to tear off the sleeve of his shirt from his bad shoulder and pressed it hard against his wound, trying to stop the bleeding. His head was hurting and he closed his eyes and thought of Catherine. He didn't want to die here, and not now. Tears came to his eyes as he contemplated the fact that he might not make it out alive and it overwhelmed him.

Alex tore off another piece of his shirt and put it in the water. He held the wet piece of shirt up to his head and thought he heard something. He wondered if the drifters were coming back to finish him off. They had taken his gun and rifle and he had no way to defend himself. He heard the sound of a horse and he waited for another gun shot. Out of nowhere, Pilgrim came up to him and nudged him with his nose. Alex was relieved and knew he needed to somehow get up on Pilgrim and get to a doctor.

"Down, Pilgrim, down," Alex coaxed him. Pilgrim began kneeling down and Alex managed to grab the horn of the saddle and pulled himself up. Once he got one leg over Pilgrim's back, he held on to the saddle and ordered Pilgrim to get up. The quick movement made Alex dizzy and he almost passed out. He had lost all sense of direction and he knew he had to move quickly before he passed out.

"Home, Pilgrim, home," was all Alex could say. Pilgrim stayed close to the creek bed. Alex no longer had control of the reins. He was trying to hold on as best he could with one hand, and willed himself to stay on Pilgrim.

In the distance Alex heard the sound of a train whistle. He figured that Pilgrim would probably go to the train station in the nearest town. That was how they always traveled long distances and he knew the train was a second home to Pilgrim.

"Good boy," he whispered to Pilgrim.

When Alex woke up he was in a single bed in a small room. A young woman, who looked of Indian descent, came in and saw he was awake.

"Welcome back," she said.

"Where am I?" Alex asked.

"You're on a small Indian reservation," she answered. My father is the medicine man and the only doctor close by where they found you. You are lucky to be alive. A clerk at the River Depot found you. They didn't have a doctor there, so they brought you here, along with your horse." What is your name?" she asked.

Alex couldn't remember and he didn't say anything.

"Do you remember anything?" she asked.

Alex shook his head, no.

Just then, a man walked into the room. "This is my father, Dr. Windsong, and I'm his daughter, Mary.

"He has no memory," she told her father.

"I'm not surprised," he said as he looked closely at Alex, removing the bandage around his head.

"A bullet grazed the side of your head. It was a through and through and just missed the brain. It might be awhile before you remember anything," he said. "I removed the bullet in your shoulder and in a few weeks, you should start feeling better. We've kept you unconscious for a few days. Mary, here, hasn't left your side and has kept ice packs on the side of your head to keep the swelling down. I thought I lost you at one time, but you are a fighter. I didn't think you would make it."

Mary lifted Alex's head and offered him some water. He looked at Mary when he noticed he had no clothes on, and saw a blanket covering him.

"We removed your clothes so you would be more comfortable. Mary bathed you and took care of your other needs. She's my nurse, so you don't need to be embarrassed. You're not the first man she has seen naked," Mary blushed.

Alex drifted in and out of sleep for several more days, and each time he woke up, Mary was beside him, giving him water and feeding him broth and herbed tea. He began sitting up and Mary assisted him when he tried to stand. She helped him put on a robe and take a few steps. It was a long, slow process and all Alex could think about when he was awake was the ringing in his ears, his aching head, and sore shoulder. There was little conversation.

Ten days had passed since Catherine had spoken to Alex and she became increasingly concerned as each day passed. She put a call into the Dallas office. Alex had told Charlotte that he and Catherine had gotten married and she congratulated her when she answered the phone.

"I haven't heard from him either," she said. "I'm sure he is fine. That part of Texas lacks in telephone service, but I'll call a couple of the towns he's been in and see if I can track him down."

Charlotte didn't call Catherine until the next day and she was sick with worry.

"I've made a dozen calls and I've been told several conflicting stories, Catherine, and I'm not sure what to believe," she told Catherine. "Alex's boss is having one of his men from Beaumont go to Hardin County and find out the truth."

"What are they saying?" she asked.

"I hate to say anything, because you know how stories get exaggerated," she said.

"You have to tell me what they are saying," Catherine pleaded.

"Someone in Batson, Texas, told someone at the county seat in Kountze that a man was robbed and shot in Northeast Hardin County. That was all they said. I'm sorry, Catherine, Glacier Oil Company looks after their employees and we'll get to the bottom of it," she promised Catherine, and told her she would call her if she heard anything else.

Catherine put the phone down, and started crying. What if Alex was killed? She couldn't bear to think of it. The phone rang again and she grabbed it on the first ring.

"Are you all right, Catherine?" John asked. He could hear her sniff on the other end and she cleared her throat.

"Alex is missing and they think he may have been shot," she said. "Oh John, I don't think I could bear losing him, too," she cried.

"I'm at Amelia's right now and I want to come over. Would

that be all right?" he asked.

John was at Catherine's door twenty minutes later. She told him about Alex's last call and that she had not heard anything from him in two weeks. She relayed the rest of the story and John patiently listened while Catherine told him what she knew.

"It may not be as bad as it sounds, Catherine, maybe he's in a hospital somewhere and there isn't a phone," John tried to reassure her.

"If he were still alive, he would find some way to get a message to me. I know him," she said.

John knew she had a point and before he could say anything else, Catherine asked, "I'm sorry John, you called me. What did you want to talk to me about?" She looked at him for the first time; she noticed how frail and sickly he looked. "How are you feeling?"

John took a deep breath and told her his condition had not improved. He was going to the doctor the next week and he would know more then. He had called to tell her that if she wanted to see Daniel more than twice a week it was all right with him, just to let Amelia know. He reaffirmed that Amelia stilled loved her very much.

Catherine got up and walked over to her dressing table and picked up her powder jar. She twisted the top off, while John watched.

"You never told me you left a note."

John walked over and sat down beside Catherine on the bed and looked at it.

"I meant every word of it," he said.

They embraced each other. "I'm here for you, Catherine, if you need me. I know you love Alex and I wish the best for you. We can't change the past and I hope Alex is all right," John said.

John found it hard to leave and more than anything he would have loved to take Catherine in his arms and make love to her. He knew, for him, it would have physically been impossible. He had been impotent for months and he knew Carla was pleased about that. He also knew that Catherine would not have permitted it, but he could still dream about their incredible love-making. It seemed to get him through the long miserable nights he slept alone.

Mary never left Alex's side. She was the one who had undressed him. She had cut away his vest and before she did, she felt something in the pocket. She took out the envelope and found two pictures. She put them back in the envelope and hid the envelope in one of her father's medical books in his office. Mary was twenty-two and had never married. There were not too many Indian men on the reservation who were close to her age and she turned down several offers from some of the older men who had lost their wives. There was one young brave she had grown up with. His name was Grey Wolf, and they used to swim together in the creek. She knew Grey Wolf wanted to marry her, but he was like a brother to her. The reservation was small and tolerated by the locals because her father was the only doctor in the vicinity. Her father was a full-blooded Indian and was orphaned when his mother and father were killed by some thieves. He was walking alone by the road when a stagecoach stopped to pick him up. One of the men inside the coach was a doctor, and his wife was with him. They took him as their son and raised him. They called him Tobias, Toby for short. Toby was five years old and kept saying, "No. Windsong." That was how he became known as Toby Windsong Alexander. Toby learned all he could about medicine from his new stepfather and after his parents died, Toby found his way back to the reservation and married Mary's mother.

Once Alex felt better, Mary would take him on walks around the reservation. When she saw a man on horseback from a distance, she walked Alex back to the house and told him he needed to rest.

"Good morning, madam. My name is Clarence Henry, and I work with an oil company. I'm trying to track down a man who works for us named Alex Cooper. I was told that he may have been brought here to see the medicine man because he had been shot. Do you know anything?" he asked.

Mary looked up at the man on the horse and shook her head, no. "I'm afraid not. My dad is the local medicine man and I'm his nurse. Nope, I can't help you," she said.

Clarence tipped his hat and thanked her. As he was leaving, he noticed some horses in a corral behind the house. One horse walked over and put his head over the fence. Pilgrim had gotten his name because he had a distinct white mark on his forehead in the shape of a "P." Clarence had never seen another horse like that, and he rode over to take a closer look. Mary saw him turn back and ride towards the horses.

When she got there, Clarence asked. "That's an unusual mark on your horse's forehead. How long have you had him?" he asked.

"Had him since he was born," she said.

Clarence had a questioning look on his face, but didn't say anything. He turned his horse around and started walking around the fence. Pilgrim followed and slobbered. Clarence stopped and put his hand over the fence. Pilgrim came up and nuzzled him. Mary walked over and asked Clarence to leave.

"Begging your pardon, but that horse belongs to Alex Cooper. Do you want to tell me where he is?" Mary looked back towards the house and Alex was standing in the doorway. Clarence saw him and went over to him.

"Good God, man, we all thought you were dead," Clarence said as he walked up to him.

Alex took a step back and gave Clarence a puzzled look.

"It's Clarence Henry…we've worked together for Glacier Oil Company for years. Alex, are you all right. Don't you know me?" he asked. The two men had been friends for the past ten years and worked together off and on, moving from place to place. They were good friends.

Mary had caught up with them and grabbed Clarence arm.

"Leave him alone. Can't you see he's hurt?" Clarence had noticed Alex had his arm in a sling and a bandage on his head, but he was standing on his own.

"He has no memory of who he is, or where he came from. He was shot in the head," Mary said. Clarence already had a dislike for Mary because she had lied to him and he wasn't going to let her intimidate him.

Dr. Windsong came out and introduced himself. He invited Clarence in and told him what had happened to Alex. Mary and Alex sat silent, but he noticed Mary had sat very close to Alex on the sofa and was holding his hand.

Alex finally spoke. "So you are saying that my name is Alex Cooper and that I was a scout for an oil company?" he asked like he couldn't believe it.

"Yes, and I'm here to take you back to Beaumont so you can go home to your wife and kid," Clarence said and continued, "Don't you remember anything?"

Alex shook his head, no.

Clarence turned to the doctor, "Would he be all right if he rode back to Beaumont with me on his horse? We can take him to Houston where he can be treated by some real doctors."

Mary stood up and angrily said, "Dr. Windsong is a real doctor. Alex, if that is his name, would have died if he had not come here."

The doctor told Mary to go outside. She stood looking at her father. "Go. The men will sort this out, now go."

She turned to Alex and he saw the hurt in her eyes. He had grown very fond of her. She had nursed him back to health and he owed her and her father a great indebtedness.

"I'm not sure he is ready to get on a horse right now. It could cause a blood clot. Perhaps in a few weeks, I'll know more about his progress then. Why don't you check back in a couple of weeks?" he asked.

Clarence looked at Alex, hoping Alex would agree to come with him.

"I need to listen to the doctor," Alex said. "He's kept me alive so far," Alex stopped and thought for a minute. "You said I was married. What is her name?"

"Catherine, Catherine Cooper, and you have a son named Adam," Clarence said and left.

After Clarence left, Mary went and got the photographs she had taken from Alex's vest pocket and showed them to him. He stared at the two pictures for a long time. "She is very beautiful," she said as she looked at Alex.

"She's not as beautiful as you are," Alex said.

Mary leaned over and they kissed. After dinner that night, Mary quietly slipped into Alex's room and they slept together. Mary had made up her mind that she would do everything she could to keep Alex, and she did not care what the consequences were. She wanted him all to herself. She knew Alex was attached to her. She had been his lifeline and he had become dependent on her and she was in love with him.

CHAPTER 29

Clarence had called Charlotte at the main office and made his report to her. Charlotte gave Clarence Catherine's phone number and asked that he call her directly. He would be the one who would be meeting her in Beaumont and taking her to get Alex.

It was 6:00 p.m. when Catherine got the call. She listened intently as Clarence told her about Alex's condition. He made no mention of Mary and the fact that she and her father were trying to keep Alex there intentionally. He would give her that part of the news when she arrived in Beaumont the next afternoon. He did tell her that Alex had a head wound and he had lost some of his memory. Clarence would be at the train station in Beaumont when the train arrived at 3:00. They would leave the next morning to go to the reservation outside of Kountze, Texas. It was a little over an hour by horse and buggy.

Catherine hung up the phone and tried to digest everything Clarence had told her. She was relieved and thanked God Alex was still alive. She tried to remember about head trauma from her biology books but she had been out of school for almost two years. Clarence had mentioned that there were some good doctors in Houston and that's where they should take Alex after they picked him up.

Catherine called Amelia's house but John had already left. She did not want to call him at Carla's, so she asked Amelia to call and have him call her.

Catherine answered on the first ring. "They've found Alex," she said, and relayed her conversation with Clarence.

"I'm so glad, Catherine. Have a safe trip and I hope he'll be all right. You take care." When John hung up the phone, he saw Carla glaring at him.

"You still love that little whore, don't you?" Carla yelled at him.

John walked over and grabbed Carla's hand. "Yes, I do, and don't you ever call her a whore again."

Carla started crying hysterically and accused John of being selfish and cruel to her. "I don't know why you treat me this way."

"Cut the drama, Carla," John shouted at her. "You're not half the woman she is. Don't worry, I'm not going anywhere. I'll be dead in less than six months, anyway, and you can play the grieving widow." John was relieved that he had finally told her.

Carla looked dumbfounded.

"You haven't even noticed that I've lost almost twenty pounds and I spend hours on the pot throwing up," John stopped when he saw the hurt on her face.

"You're dying?" she asked.

"You'll get over it. I'm leaving everything to you, except the house that Catherine and I own together, and that will go to Amelia. The life insurance, the cash, my company stock, will all be yours, and I won't be around to tell you how to spend it," John said.

He was hyperventilating and he had to sit down to catch his breath. Carla left the room. When John finally got his composure, he poured himself a full glass of scotch and went out on the front porch.

Carla poured herself a glass of scotch and joined him on the porch. John was staring away and did not turn to look at her.

They sat silent for a while and then John finally spoke.

"I'd appreciate your not telling Walter what I told you. I need to keep the job so I can pay the bills. If he thinks I'm too sick to work, he might ask me to leave. I plan to work until I'm too sick. I'm getting my affairs in order. You'll be all right for a while, but in time, you might want to consider selling the house. The equity should sustain you for a couple of years. I know you enjoy your place in society, Carla, but there are more important things than trying to act like a rich socialite. I'm sorry I'm not the man you thought I was."

John took several drinks and waited for Carla to begin her dramatics.

Carla tried to think of something to say, but she couldn't. She knew John was right. She was trying to live a dream, showing off to her friends, making them jealous, and she had succeeded, all at the expense of her marriage. She didn't blame John for hating her. Carla got up and went back in the house.

Catherine found it hard to sleep. Adam was only waking up once during the night for a feeding and she lay there, waiting to hear him stir. Alex was her life. What if he didn't know her? What if he didn't want to leave? No, she thought. If he couldn't make decisions for himself, she would make them for him. He was there for her through all of her horrible and pitiful existence when she was with David and he had hardly left her side. She would not let him go, no matter what.

Catherine had managed to sleep off and on during the train ride. Adam was fussy and only slept for an hour or two at a time. She was in a private room in the Pullman car and she asked the porter to get her a double scotch. She had never drunk alone, but she needed something to steady her nerves and she needed something now. She would be in Beaumont in two hours. It had been almost eight weeks since they had gotten married, five weeks since she had last seen Alex. Catherine sat up abruptly and looked at the scotch and pushed it away. She started counting backward and tried to remember her last period. She had not had a period since Adam was born. That was nine weeks ago. Adam would be three months in a couple of days. She had been so concerned about Alex she had not paid attention to her body. She smiled at the fact that Alex would be ecstatic. He had mentioned that he hoped they could have a couple of kids together. He was fine having a large family and she was, too. She rubbed her stomach and picked up Adam.

"I think you might have a baby brother or sister in the not too distant future," she said out loud to Adam. For some reason, Catherine felt a peace come over her.

It was October 6, 1902, and a soft fall breeze greeted Catherine and Adam when they got off the train. Clarence introduced himself and took her bag. He walked them over to the hotel where he had a reserved room waiting and told Catherine he would pick them up at 9:00 in the morning. He would meet them in the lobby. Clarence decided to wait and tell Catherine in the morning about the difficulty he had when he first found Alex. No need to worry her unnecessarily, he thought. She'll figure it all out when she gets there, and he wasn't looking forward to the confrontation.

Dr. Windsong saw Mary in the hall as she was leaving Alex's room.

"We need to talk," he told Mary. She followed him into the kitchen. "You are sleeping with another woman's husband. Nothing good can come from that. Only heartache for someone," he said.

"Alex loves me. He will not leave me," she said. "If she comes for him, he will agree to stay a month. If his senses do not come back in one month, he will come back to me," she said. "He told me that his life did not begin until he met me. I am the one he loves, not her," she said. "You had told me he may never remember his past."

"Yes, I did say that. But I also said God has ways of tricking the mind. The brain is a strong organ, and man does not understand how it works. Maybe his memory will return and you need to prepare yourself for that, too."

Alex and Mary were down by the horses when they saw a covered wagon coming onto the property. They saw a man and a woman holding a baby.

Alex told Mary he wanted her to wait at the barn, but she

followed a few steps behind him as they walked up to the house.

Clarence and Catherine had just gotten down from the wagon when they approached them.

"Alex!" Catherine said and walked over to give him a kiss. Alex did not respond. Mary walked up beside Alex and he put his arm around her. Catherine stepped back. Clarence had tried to warn her on the way over and she saw a slight smile on Mary's face. Mary and Alex looked at each and Catherine's mouth dropped open. Her heart began racing and she didn't know what to say. Dr. Windsong came out and introductions were made. They were invited to come inside. Alex's bandages were gone and he looked perfectly well.

Catherine spoke first. "Alex, I am so glad you are looking so well. It looks like you have been well taken care of. I've come to take you home."

"My home is here," Alex said. "I'm sorry Catherine, but I have no memory of a previous life with you, and I don't want to leave here. I like it here," he said.

Catherine was not expecting Alex to be so adamant.

"I was hoping to take you to a hospital and have your injuries checked out," she said.

"My injuries have healed and I feel fine," Alex said.

"Do you remember anything before the accident?" Catherine asked.

"No, I'm sorry, I don't," he said.

"A bullet pierced Alex's head just above his left ear. The bullet went all the way through and I think it may have fractured a part of his skull. There are many nerves in his head and he may never regain his memory," Dr. Windsong said.

Catherine listened in agony.

"We knew this day would come, and we have been talking about it. Alex will go with you, but unless his memory returns soon, he is will come back to the reservation in one month," Dr. Windsong said.

Clarence looked at Catherine and waited for her to say something. Adam had awakened and was pulling at Catherine's hair. She excused herself and went out to the wagon.

She was sitting up on the seat nursing Adam and had draped a blanket over them.

"What do you want to do?" Clarence asked when he came outside.

"Tell Alex that we are ready to leave and that I'm waiting for him," she answered.

Alex and Mary walked outside and walked towards the horses.

Clarence got up on the wagon with Catherine.

He has gone to saddle Pilgrim. I suggested that we leave Pilgrim at the livery stables in Beaumont where we can look after him. You and Alex can take the train to Houston from there."

Catherine watched out of the corner of her eye as Alex saddled Pilgrim. Mary put her arms around him and they kissed before Alex mounted Pilgrim. Catherine bit her lower lip willing herself not to cry.

Alex rode Pilgrim a good ten to fifteen feet behind the wagon as they headed back to Beaumont. She looked back numerous times to make sure he hadn't changed his mind and turned around. Clarence didn't have much to say on their trip back to Beaumont. Catherine was hoping that something might register with Alex when they got back to Beaumont, but nothing did. She gave Clarence directions to where she and David had lived. Surely something there would bring back a hint of his past. When they rode up to the old farm, Alex rode up and asked why they had stopped.

"Does this place bring back any memories?" she asked.

"I'm afraid not, where are we?" Alex asked.

Catherine didn't answer, but got down off the wagon. Alex got down and followed Catherine into the house.

"Is this where we lived?" he asked.

Catherine was fighting back tears and she took Alex's hand and walked him into the bedroom. "This is where you helped me deliver Adam."

Alex stood there and didn't say anything. Does the name David Billings mean anything to you?" she asked.

"I'm sorry Catherine, His name means nothing."

Catherine walked back outside and got up on the wagon.

"What happened to the barn?" Alex asked.

Catherine looked away in silence.

Clarence stopped at the train station and took Pilgrim from Alex.

"Pilgrim will be at the livery stables, when you get ready for him. He's used to the stables here, since he lived there for almost two years.

Catherine walked over to the ticket window and bought two tickets and was relieved there was still a private room in the Pullman car. Catherine asked the porter to bring a double scotch to their room once the train left.

Adam was still asleep and Alex asked Catherine how old he was.

"Almost three months. He's beginning to be a handful," she tried to laugh.

After the train pulled away from the station the porter knocked on the door and handed Catherine the scotch. She set it down and told Alex it was for him.

"Did I like to drink this?" he asked.

Catherine smiled and said, "You used to like it."

"It does have a soothing taste," he said. Alex had only drunk a few sips when he put his head back and fell asleep.

Catherine watched him sleep and cried in silence. She put her hand out to touch him, but pulled it back and wiped the tears from her face. One month, she thought, how will she ever get Alex to fall in love with her, again? She knew that unless something snapped his memory back, she would lose him. She was glad that the train only made a fifteen-minute stop in Houston and continued on to Galveston.

Alex never woke up and she wondered if his injury made him sleepy. She would take him to the hospital on Monday and get him checked out.

It was 11:00 p.m. when they finally got back to Minnie's Boarding House. She had told Alex about the house they lived in and shared with Minnie. She asked him to be quiet and just as they got in the door; Adam woke up and began crying. It had been a long day for everyone and Catherine was looking forward to getting some rest. She hoped Adam did not wake Minnie up and she hurried upstairs with Alex trailing behind her.

"Your robe is hanging inside the water closet over there," and she pointed. "You can use it first. I need to nurse Adam. Alex came out five minutes later and asked if there was an extra blanket. "There's one in that closet on the top," and she pointed to it.

Alex opened the door and took the blanket out. "If you don't mind, I'll just sleep on the floor over by the window. I'll try not to disturb you."

"There's an extra pillow on the bed and you are welcome to it," she answered back.

Catherine watched as Alex put the blanket and pillow on the floor. He turned his back to her and took off the robe, laying it on a chair. He said, "Good night, Catherine."

"Good night, I love you," Catherine answered.

Adam fell asleep while he was nursing and Catherine got up, put him in his bed, walked over and turned the light out. Alex had left the light on in the bathroom and she walked over and pulled one of her new nightgowns out of the wardrobe. Maybe he would notice it on her when they got up in the morning, she hoped.

Adam woke Catherine up at 7:00 the next morning. After changing him, she sat up against her pillow and pulled the small string holding her gown up, off her shoulder. She watched Alex sleeping. He must have gotten warm during the night because the blanket was on the floor beside him and he was sleeping without anything on. He had lost weight, but his beautiful, naked body exposed the curvatures of his muscles. He was facing away from her and she longed to go to him and wrap her body around his. He began to stir and she looked away. Alex grabbed the blanket when he realized he was fully exposed.

"Sorry about that," he said. "Guess I must have gotten warm."

"Your clothes are on the left side of the wardrobe and you can pick something out," Catherine said.

Alex walked over to the wardrobe with the blanket wrapped around him, and took a shirt and a pair of trousers out of the wardrobe. He stared at Catherine and Adam for a minute and then said, "You look just like your picture." He turned and went into the bathroom.

Catherine quickly dressed and was brushing her hair when Alex came out.

"I thought we would go to the hospital this morning and make sure your wounds are healing properly," she said.

"Whatever you want, Catherine. I don't think it will help me to remember my past, and I don't want you to get your hopes up. Believe me; I have really tried to remember. After Clarence left the first time, and he told me who I was, and that I was married and had a son, I spent the whole day trying to go back in my mind, but I just couldn't recover anything. It's just one big blank. I'm sorry about Mary. I know that has to hurt you, but you have to understand, that she was with me the whole time. She bathed me and fed me and took care of me. She was all I had. You weren't there."

"I do understand, Alex," and she told him about the day they hung David and that he had come to her rescue and helped her delivered Adam.

"You took care of me when I needed help, you delivered my son and you were all I had. You had left and came back the next morning. I was unconscious because of the bleeding and you took Adam and me to the hospital and stayed with me there for two days while I healed. I would have died, if you hadn't saved us. I understand more than anyone else could." And she started crying.

Alex left and went downstairs. Catherine heard the door slam as he went outside. He was waiting on the front steps when she came out and handed him a cup of coffee.

He took it from her and took a sip and said, "Thank you. You are a lovely young woman, Catherine, and I can see why I fell in love with you, but I don't feel that way now. I want to be honest with you. I don't remember any of that stuff you told me upstairs."

They went back in and had a quick breakfast in silence.

Alex was in Dr. Copeland's office for over an hour and the nurse called Catherine into his office.

"Alex's wounds have healed nicely and I must admit that it's a miracle that he lived at all. The brain has a way of rebuilding itself over time, but it could take years for Alex to regain all of his memory, if at all. I gave him a few tests with numbers and his math skills are still intact. So are his reflexes. Like I said, he is a walking miracle."

Catherine asked Alex if he would watch Adam while she asked Dr. Copeland about something regarding her own health. She went into Dr. Copeland's examination room and told him she thought she was pregnant. She undressed quickly and got up on the table. Dr. Copeland confirmed her suspicions.

"It is unusual that you got pregnant so soon after your last child, but it does happen," he said.

"I don't want to tell Alex just yet, if you don't mind. Do you think there is much hope that he will ever remember me?" she asked.

"I'm sorry, Catherine, I don't have an answer to that."

Alex looked up and asked if she was all right and she answered, yes. Alex had not lost his good manners and sweet disposition. Other than his memory, he was the same Alex she had fallen in love with. He was warm, gentle, caring and honest.

Their next stop was the bank.

"You had told me to open a joint account for us before you left and you need to sign some papers. I've already transferred all the funds from Beaumont," Catherine said. Alex had no idea what she was talking about but he signed the papers anyway. After they left, Catherine told him that he had a substantial amount of money in Dallas and he could decide what to do with that later.

"What's a substantial amount of money?" he asked.

"With the stock and your savings, you told me it was close to thirty thousand dollars," she answered.

"That's a lot of money. And the money in our joint account, where did that come from? Alex asked.

"Your company bought the farm we stopped at in Beaumont. You were at the closing," she answered.

Alex sighed and shook his head in disbelief.

They stopped and had lunch and then went home. She put Adam in his crib and she told Alex she needed to go downstairs and make some phone calls.

Catherine called John at the bank and told him about Alex's condition and memory loss. He was sympathetic. She asked him about his health and he told her that he had finally told Carla. He said she was nicer to him now.

"The doctor has confirmed that the prognosis is not good and he gave me some more medicine for nausea and something to help me sleep at night.

He seemed in good spirits, though, and when she hung up she said, "I love you, John."

He was silent for a moment, and said, "I love you, too, Catherine." The phone went silent.

Catherine walked out the front door and to the back of the house. She sat in the old swing that she and John had repaired after the flood. She used to sit there when she was fifteen and they had first come to America. She thought back on the hopes and dreams she and her mother had then. It seemed so long ago.

Alex went downstairs to find Catherine and noticed the front door was partially opened and he went out. He walked around the side of the house, saw her sitting in the swing, and walked over to her.

"May I join you?" he asked. She smiled and moved over.

"Catherine, I think my staying here will only cause you heartache. My memory isn't going to come back in a month. It may never come back. The longer I stay, the harder it will be on you. You can have all the money, I don't want it."

"When are you going to leave?" she asked.

"First thing in the morning, if you say it's all right," he answered.

Catherine started crying and he put his arms around her.

"I'm truly sorry about this. I really am," Alex apologized.

"I know it must be hard for you, too. Harder, I'm sure. I can't expect you to stay, feeling the way you do, but I want you to be happy and if it is Mary that you love, that will never change," she said.

Catherine heard Adam crying and she got up and went to him.

Alex didn't sleep that night. He waited until he was sure Catherine was asleep and he got dressed in the dark. He had written a note to her earlier when she was taking a bath and he put it on her dressing table. He quietly closed the door and left.

Dear Catherine,

I don't like goodbyes and I did not want it to be difficult for you, so, I thought it best if I left now. I borrowed $10 to buy a ticket to Beaumont and I have to pay for Pilgrim's care. I know I should have asked you first, but, again, I wanted to leave you in peace. I've decided to stay in Beaumont and start there. If I can figure out the last two years, I think I would be able to make a better decision. It would not be fair to Mary either, if I went back to her, and I am sorry she has made things more complicated. I can't ask you to wait, but I want you know that I won't rest *until I find out the truth.*

Alex

Alex tried to sleep on the train, but there were so many issues he had to deal with. He knew the easy way out would be to go back and be with Mary. Their life would be simple and isolated from the real world. But Alex felt in his heart, that easy and simple was not the route he wanted, or needed, to take. He owed it to himself to find what kind of person he had been. He already felt drawn to Catherine and he needed to explore that more in depth. He knew that being thirty years old, if she was the one that he had chosen, there was reason, and he had to find that out for himself. He owed her that.

When Catherine woke up the next morning, she saw the sun peering through the window and it was like a spotlight shining on Alex's empty pallet. He had carefully folded the blanket and put it over the pillow. He was gone. She rolled over and looked around the room just to be sure. The clothes he had neatly folded and placed on a chair within arm's reach of his pallet confirmed what she already knew. He left while she was asleep. Her eyes moved up to her dressing table and a small white envelope stood next to her powder jar. Interesting, she thought. John's goodbye letter was still in her powder jar and Alex's goodbye letter was next to it. She felt betrayed, empty, alone and she wondered if she was being paid back for the sins of her past.

Three-month-old Adam was still asleep in his crib, so she crept over to her dressing table. She unscrewed the top of her dresser jar and took out John's note and she opened the envelope. She took out Alex's letter, which was folded in half. She didn't need to read it, because he had already told her the night before that he would be leaving in the morning. The note would be sweet and tender because that was who Alex was, but she knew she couldn't bear to read his parting words. She put the two letters together and put them back in the envelope. She opened the side drawer and took out her bible. She couldn't remember the last time she had opened it, and it had been over two years since she had set foot in church. She opened it up and the Book of Hosea was staring her in the face. She knew what it was about. She and her mother often talked about it; sin, redemption, and salvation. She read it again, placed the envelope with the two letters inside, and put it back in the drawer. She closed her eyes and thanked God for speaking to her about the last four years she had suffered hardship. Life was not about happy endings. It was about new beginnings.

"God gives us sin in order to understand Redemption."

CPSIA information can be obtained at www.ICGtesting.com
Printed in the USA
LVOW07s1609170815

450458LV00001B/15/P